THE heart break pill

THE heartbreak pill

{a novel}

Anjanette Delgado

ATRIA BOOKS
New York London Toronto Sydney

ATRIA BOOKS
A Division of Simon & Schuster, Inc.
1230 Avenue of the Americas
New York, NY 10020

First Atria Books trade paperback edition April 2008

Designed by Jaime Putorti

Manufactured in the United States of America

10 9 8 7 5 4 3 2 1

Library of Congress Cataloging-in-Publication Data

Delgado, Anjanette.
The heartbreak pill : a novel / by Anjanette Delgado.—
1st Atria Books trade pbk. ed.
p. cm.
1. Hispanic Americans—Fiction. 2. Miami (Fla.)—Fiction.
I. Title.

PS3604.E4438H43 2007
813'.6—dc22

2007011814

ISBN-13: 978-0-7432-9753-0
ISBN-10: 0-7432-9753-9

For Vanessa and Veronica . . . from here to Planet X

For my mother, Lucy, who always believes

And for Daniel, resuscitator of words and hopes

THE heart break pill

{one}

Alex doesn't love you? Just flip off the love switch and presto: you don't love him either. Charlie needs his space? Pull a small lever and he'll be on a reverse-less rocket ship en route to the stratosphere where he can have all the space he wants.

Imagine what your life would be like if you had a switch, an interrupter of sorts, located somewhere in an unobtrusive part of your body, let's say on your calf, like a tattoo. See yourself pressing this lever, pin, or button and being able to control the most uncontrollable part of your body: your heart.

You wouldn't suffer over what isn't good for you. You wouldn't cry for what cannot be. You'd just live. You'd be happy.

And while we're imagining, just think of the effect this "love switch" would have on the rest of humanity.

Hundreds of suicides and even more homicides would be

avoided. Salacious newspaper accounts of the latest crime of passion would become urban legend. And should our relationships ever become abusive, inconvenient, or, worse, devoid of magic, we'd all be capable of just letting go. We'd have time to pursue happiness and the energy to enjoy life.

And when the person who meant everything to you told you he didn't love you anymore and sent you to Hell without a quiver, you'd be able to smile, wish him luck, and say "all's well that ends well," or even "everything happens for a reason."

"A million dollars," I said, staring back at them steadily in spite of my nerves.

Martin's mouth dropped open like a tire jack while the Lilliputian gnome at his side almost choked on his own tongue.

But let's leave them in shock for a moment while I bring you up to date. *Freeze frame,* as they say in the movies.

My name is Erika Luna, I live in Miami, and the man I've just frozen was my husband, Martin. I'm talking about the tall guy in his late—but interesting—thirties, salt and pepper hair, wide back, and "owner of the world" attitude.

The mustached pigmy at his side was Attorney Chavez, the lawyer he'd hired to divorce me.

And there we all were in February, the month of love-induced chocolate and flower purchases, sitting in that white, flavorless office full of leather seats and framed diplomas, about to "negotiate" the end of seven years of marriage, against my will.

When he'd recuperated, Attorney Chavez, whose basic function in life is to be my husband's human speech articulation system, looked at me condescendingly.

"I'm sorry . . . so sorry . . . I apologize . . . you're asking for a million dollars becaaaaause . . . Okay, never mind. I'm going to have to apologize . . . again . . . for my lack of understanding, but . . . I don't get it, and I have to tell you that even if you were able to prove it, infidelity is not a punishable offense in the state of Florida. You can make things difficult, play baseball, as they say here, and that's your choice, as long as you know it's my job to make sure that when all is said and done, you're the one paying a million dollars . . . in legal fees."

I was about to ask Martin if he paid Chavez to speak in clichés, and if so, to demand that his lawyer threaten me with the correct ones, as I've never played baseball in my life and was still pretty sure he meant hardball.

But before I could open my mouth, my own lawyer, who'd spent hours convincing me that the best way to make a man desist from divorce is to scare him with the possibility of losing a substantial amount of money, stopped her flirting for an instant, stepped away from the oval-shaped conference table, and, with the resolute air of one who charges two hundred and fifty dollars an hour, walked over to the door and opened it before answering for me:

"You'll have to excuse me if I don't allow you to intimidate my client in my own office. It's been a pleasure, gentlemen," she said with a seductive smile.

"Please, forgive me, if I've offended you," said Chavez getting up from his chair and slithering over to where Attorney Lopez stood. "I hope, you know . . . it certainly wasn't my intention to offend such a beautiful woman," he continued, arching his neck a hundred and twenty degrees to impress her with all of his five feet, two inches of sensuality.

"Apology accepted, but when I finish digging in every last

corner of your client's life, what a judge will award this woman will come quite close to that amount. You can choose not to believe me, leave through those doors right now, and find I'm right . . . in court," she countered, charmingly, of course.

It was Martin who jumped like the corner spring on a new mattress as soon as the word "court" was mentioned.

"There's a name for what you're doing, Erika. Extortion. Extortion!" he emphasized as if I were retarded.

"And what you've done? What's that called? Let me see . . . Oh, I know! In-fi-de-li-ty! Chea-ting, *Pe-gar-los-cuer-nos, po-ner los-ta-rros*—"

"Of course . . . here comes the victim. Look, if I had a million dollars, I'd seriously consider using them to hire a hit man," he spit out, exasperated. "What do you want? The house? There. It's yours," he added, throwing a heavy handful of keys on the table. "What else? My car? Here's the damn car," he said, taking another set of keys, this time from his suit jacket, and throwing them on the table with the others, creating a shrill metallic clang that sounded like a bunch of screaming baby birds being forced to fly before knowing how.

"Just like that? Overnight?" I asked as I searched for balance while standing on that rope connecting "I still love you" to "I wish I'd never set eyes on you."

"Erika, we've been at this for a month now. It's not 'overnight.' "

Of course, to him a month wasn't overnight compared to seven years of marriage and another one dating. The fact that we made love three times the night before I found out there were three people in my marriage didn't qualify for ironic in his eyes. That when this happened we were in the middle of extending our living room to eliminate our family room so we could use the extra space to remodel the terrace didn't seem to him reason enough that I should be surprised to be in this mass-divorce-factory of an office only a month later.

I looked into his face, at his black eyes now surrounded by tiny blue lines—brought on, I suspected, by the desire to choke me pulsing through the veins of his temples. I looked at the ends of his salt and pepper hair standing up gladiator style. I looked and, for a second, remembered the simplest things about our life together: nights watching TV while eating ice cream in bed, laughing like idiots at some joke on *Everybody Loves Raymond.*

I remembered how he'd always kiss my nose and say, "It doesn't matter. We'll just go out to eat," whenever I burned, smoked, or undercooked whatever grand culinary production I had insisted on making.

That was the Martin I knew, and the one I continued to look for in his stare, in his stance. I walked into the field of his anger, stubbornly looking for a gesture or a signal, something from the happy life I thought I'd had with him, anything that would allow me to understand and forgive him.

Nothing.

I took the keys and extended them to him without taking my eyes from his.

"Who are you?" I asked finally.

But he just evaded me. Taking the keys, he glanced at his Rolex Submariner, and with that simple gesture he assumed the pose of a man busy with a thousand things more important than I.

"Look, Erika, I'm not a psychologist. If you want to make a

career out of this, go right ahead. Frankly, I won't continue to blah, blah, blah. . . ."

I couldn't tell you what he said after that.

During the weeks before that moment, I had put a lot of time and effort into fighting back my rage, telling myself you don't throw away a marriage you've been happy in for over seven years at the first problem. I'd spent entire nights overpowering my own desire to run him and his lover over with my Jetta, several times, like that Colombian dentist did in Texas. And each night, I'd end up praying, talking myself calm, and telling myself that if I could get myself to forgive, everything would be all right.

But the days passed, and Martin never showed up at the house in the middle of a rainstorm, repentant. Nor did he call at dawn just because he missed me. He never asked for my forgiveness, and it was clear he had no intention of doing so.

How did I feel? Like Mano de Piedra Durán must have felt when Sugar Ray Leonard landed the punch that would make him say *"No más."* My head repeated, what did he say? What? A career out of this gigantic piece of *mierda* he was dumping on my lap?

I understood, then what people mean when they say their head "fogged up." How could I not when I had enough fog in mine to prevent a whole airline from landing in the widest and clearest of landing strips?

"Mira, *desgraaaaaaaaciado,"* I said taking off one of the Marc Jacobs platform wedge shoes I'd scored on eBay and throwing it at him. "You listen to me, you senile cockroach vomit," (shoe reaching opposite wall with a thud) "damn the time of day you were born," (cat-sized paperweight picked up and thrown), "damn the time of day I met you" (cat-sized paperweight landing on Martin's foot), "and damn—"

"Erika, stop this right now!" screamed Martin, using his briefcase as a shield and jumping on one foot while trying to rescue the papers he'd laid on the table. "The consummate scientist . . . quite the professional for some things, but in the end, like the Puerto Rican country girl you are . . . you mess up . . . you either mess up when you get there, or you mess up as you're leaving, but you mess up."

"Country girl your mother, you fermented piece of cow dung," I screamed. "You just wait, because when I'm finished with you, you'll have to be a full-time pimp to that piece of wartime drum pleather you're sleeping with, in fact—"

"Erika, I won't stand for . . ."

But he stood for it. And he continued to stand for it until much after lawyer Chavez threatened to call the police. I kept flinging insults and curses at him even when my own lawyer threatened to fire me as a client if I didn't sit down and stop screaming.

I didn't care. A Ph.D. in chemistry and all Martin had to do was look at me as if I were a plate of leftover food to turn me into a screaming maniac.

And scream I did, right up until both men ran out, a cloud of disordered divorce papers on their arms. I screamed and screamed until I lost my voice and my lawyer had the brilliant idea of threatening to call my father.

Then I walked out onto the street and into the first café I saw, heading straight for the bathroom, not thinking, feeling, or seeing anything. Not the washbasin's porcelain border as I bent over it to throw up. Not the cold water I splashed on my face.

Not even the hum of the wall-mounted hand dryer someone had left on. I sensed nothing other than the "he's gone . . . it's over . . . he's gone . . . it's over" playing in my head.

In the mirror, my coffee-colored hair, long and always too curly, looked as if I'd been coiffed by Diana Ross's hairstylist in her heyday. My lips, normally quite plump, were so swollen they resembled a puddle of reddish-purple blood with a stab wound in the middle. And my eyes, usually almond-shaped, had acquired a watery, shapeless form and were speckled with several very obvious red cracks, clearly visible through my tortoiseshell eyeglasses.

"I'm sorry," I told the woman in the mirror. She was crying an airless, difficult cry, like a premature baby who senses that the slightest sniffle could kill him.

When I managed to calm down, I realized Martin was right. I was a woman of science, a researcher. A woman of arguments, facts, and reason. How could I allow heartbreak—so common it would be a cliché if it weren't happening to me—turn me into a raving lunatic?

I walked out, sat at the counter, and ordered coffee from a waitress so engrossed in conversation with her colleague that she barely noticed me.

"And then I told him, 'Look here, *mijito* . . . What are you thinking? That I'm a twenty-four-hour fast-food sex window available at your convenience? No, *baby.* You're wrong. *Te equivocaste.*' "

"Very mistaken," nodded the other waitress. "Better lonely *que mal acompañada,*" she added as she spread butter on six Cuban toasts, a resigned expression on her face.

Had my best friend Lola been there, she'd have said I was attracting the very thing I was suffering from. You know, the radiations of negative thought and all that hooey.

But there must have been some truth to her theory because in the forty-five minutes it took me to drink four Cuban coffees and two bottled waters, I saw . . .

1. A young guy begging his girlfriend for another chance using a cell phone that lost his call five times during the ten minutes he was waiting for a breaded-steak dinner.
2. A depressed-looking pregnant woman pretending not to notice her husband turning around one hundred and eighty degrees to stare at the ample behind of a woman ordering a *pan con lechón* sandwich and a malted milkshake.
3. At least five people walking past the cafeteria's entrance with the automated sprint of being fed up with life, and the same empty stare that had made me cry when I'd seen it staring back at me in the restroom mirror just minutes before.

Too many samples of the bad substance, as they say in my line of work. Or maybe it wasn't that I was attracting that which I was going through. Perhaps this was just the way things were—a world full of malfunctioning, broken hearts ambling around—and I had never noticed because I'd been too occupied living in my yuppie love bubble, located right in the middle of a house that was always being painted, extended, decorated, or improved.

Hours later, I was still driving aimlessly around Miami,

thinking about how desperately the world needed an interrupter for bad love as I alternated between good and bad neighborhoods, busy and empty areas.

It was a revolting piece of truth, but you don't automatically stop loving someone just because he breaks your heart. You keep loving and carrying around the clunker of a heart your son-of-a-bitch ex-husband broke in two so carelessly and without so much as an ounce of anesthesia.

It must have been close to midnight by the time I drove home and parked, staying in the car, fantasizing in exquisite detail how I'd get the vengeance my half-asleep brain wanted.

I promised myself that I would come up with a plan so ingenious, so diabolical, it would no doubt make me the absolute leader of humiliated wives and broken hearts the world over. Ha! I'd show Martin. Years would pass before the liars, cheaters, and players of the world stopped whispering my name in pool halls, remembering with fear the only other occasion in which an obscure member of their club—one John Bobbitt—had dragged them all toward disaster.

Comforted by this thought, I went up to my bedroom, threw myself on the bed with my shoes still on, and was asleep before my thought-heavy head plummeted onto the pillow.

Despair is the most effective of sleeping aids, and that night I dreamed that dozens of little men, their small brains hanging between their legs, tried in vain to erase my name from some huge international directory of forgotten wives.

{two}

I hadn't quite dragged myself out of bed the next morning when the phone rang. It was my lawyer, calling to fire me as a client. I don't blame her. But to flirt with Attorney Chavez, I could have brought my friend Lola, who'd have done it for free.

I'd lost most of my sanity, and it wasn't stubbornness that kept me from running after it, but rather a deformed survival instinct. You know, better angry and strong than sad and pathetic.

I took a quick shower and drove the ten blocks to the Lincoln Road Café for a *cortadito,* a swig of Cuban coffee served in a thimble-sized plastic cup, strong as an ox and with enough sugar to shock a horse.

My cell phone said I had ten missed calls and a small rectangular envelope on the top left corner of the screen announced several messages.

Biiiiiip.

"This is Metro PCS: hel-looo, hel-looo, hel-looo, permission to speak freely, calling with—"

Yeah, right. Perfect "choose a new calling plan moment."

Biiiiiiip.

"Erika, this is your father. I suppose you remember you have a father. If you have a free minute, which seems unlikely these days, call me. I'm at home and have an urgent question to ask you."

Since I know all about my father's urgencies, I continued listening to my messages.

Biiiiiiip.

"Hey woman, it's Lola. Where are you? Pilates is about to begin and I'm dying to know how it went, so call—"

Lola is my best friend, but I wasn't in the mood to answer questions or listen to advice. I wasn't in the mood for anything, really.

Biiiiiiip.

"Erika, the Cuban is looking for you and says to stop by his office when you make it in."

The voice belonged to Naty, my assistant, and the Cuban she was referring to is Reynaldo Santiesteban, my boss. I am the head of research for NuevoMed Pharmaceutical Corporation, a small but innovative company with one mega-successful product.

I'm sure you've seen the commercials where the wife is waiting for her husband, so worried she's pulling out her hair, unable to quell her tension headache, several bottles of ineffective pills at her side. Then the husband arrives all happy and affectionate and it's obvious he's been drinking. The wife then clips him a good one right on the nose, just as the announcer says, "Win by knockout against migraine. Ask your doctor if

Varitex is right for you. Side effects include vomiting, nausea, headache, muscular aches, indigestion, birth defects . . ." and a litany of others we're forced to mention even if they're only possible in point zero zero zero one percent of women who've reached the age of eighty before 1950, and happen to be pregnant with triplets.

It's very much a family company, founded in 1967 by a couple of Cuban scientists, now retired, who arrived in Miami after the revolution. It's so small that Varitex is its only product, despite pressure from the board of directors that was instituted in 2001 after the company went public.

My work there consists of researching the viability of spinoffs such as Varitex Day, a version that would alleviate pain without causing drowsiness; Varitex ExtraStrength, which would alleviate with such force that it'd be more like dying than sleeping; and Vanilla-flavored Varitex, designed for teenagers with so much stress in their lives that the blood flowing to their brains agglutinates in the blood vessels and causes a migraine.

And since much of my research happens with patients already taking Varitex, I'm also expected to provide the Sales, Marketing and Public Relations Department with useful data regarding patient perception of the medication.

It's all very interesting and, believe me, I love my job, but that afternoon I was incapable of being coherent, professional, or creative. My boss would have to understand.

Biiiiiip.

"Erika Anastasia Luna Morales . . . This is your father. Again. The same father who didn't suffer through demon-induced pains to give birth to you but still remembers your mother's screams when she

did. I really don't know why one has children, if they're not even going to answer when one calls them."

The coffee arrived and with the first sip I remembered I was a grown woman who'd been sustaining herself for years. *Coño.*

"It's me, Papi."

"*¡Ay bendito sea Dios, hija!* What's going on that I know nothing of you or your husband since Three Kings' Day? I was about to send the rescue over to your house."

Eight years ago, my father decided to reveal his homosexuality to the world and moved to South Miami with Benjamin, the love of his life. The problem is, if he was overprotective and dramatic before, then he's been the ultimate in theatricality and sarcasm ever since.

"What happened?" I said, ignoring his theatrics.

"Nothing. Can't I call to ask how you're doing?"

"Of course, Papi, but since you said it was urgent."

"So you're getting divorced . . ."

I began to chant in my head: "I'm an adult. Papi neither orders me nor influences me. I'm an adult. I'm an adult. *Carajo.*"

"Are you going to give me an answer or are you going to wait until I grow a few more white hairs?" he asked.

"I didn't want to worry you."

"So, in order not to worry me, I have to find out from Martin's mother, whose tongue is so long she can wrap herself in it, that my daughter is getting divorced. You don't understand how ashamed I am that María Isabel knows more about your life than I."

Shame is crying to your father over a man who's left you for another woman, in a public place, through a cell phone . . .

"What did he do to you?" he said in a murderous tone when he realized I was crying.

"It doesn't matter, Papi."

Okay, I admit it. I still had a rather minuscule piece of hope that we'd get back together, and I thought the less people knew about what had happened, the better I'd be able to erase it from my consciousness when Martin came back repentant. All of this would just turn out to be a bad movie that extended beyond the usual two hours.

"It doesn't matter? It doesn't matter, but you're getting divorced from one day to the next? And why're you crying over Martin, who's nothing more than the very bottom leftover of a pot of pressed-worm jelly. You know what? I'm going over there right now."

"Papi, please don't go anywhere. Let me solve my own problems."

"What did he do to you? The fact that I'm a gay man doesn't mean I don't remember what I learned in the more than fifty years I lived heterosexually."

"Maybe it was I who did something to him," I said trying to throw him off. Papi had never liked Martin and I didn't want to hear his "What did I tell you? Huh? What did I tell you?"

"What did that gigantic piece of cow dung in a field of sick cows do to you?"

(It is a fact: If I have any talent for insults, it's fully inherited.)

I decided I couldn't cover a cheating husband with one hand.

"He found someone else."

"The bastard, *hijo de su buena madre . . .*"

"I thought you still remembered what you'd learned in more than fifty years of living heterosexually."

"Look, Erika, in twenty-eight years of marriage, I was never—and I mean *never*—unfaithful to your mother. Not with women and not with men, do you understand?"

"I know, Papi," I responded, listening to him breathe impotently, knowing he was probably blasting Mami for dying and leaving him to deal with the serious problem of a grown-up daughter with no husband to take care of her.

"Well," he said, as if preparing to launch a full-blast rescue operation. "No need for tears. It takes a village, right? *Más 'alante' vive gente* and you are a good woman, solid and well-raised, so . . . that's it . . . onward and forward . . . you're certainly well-prepared for life . . . and you can always come live with us. But you know, maybe we just have to relax . . . I have a feeling, when we least expect it, *mi'ja,* Martin will come to his senses and put a stop to this nonsense."

I interrupted the litany with which he tried to console himself more than me.

"Okay, Papi. I'll call you later, okay? *Bendición?"*

"Dios me la bendiga."

Would you believe that of all the things my father said to me that afternoon, only one managed to penetrate my brain as I sat in that colorful little café, with my hair in a bun and my still-tear-stained face? Only one.

"When we least expect it, *mi'ja,* Martin will come to his senses and put a stop to this nonsense."

{three}

But he didn't, come to his senses, that is. Nor did he put a stop to the nonsense. And the worst of it was that I was angrier and sadder about his unrepentance, his not moving heaven and earth for my forgiveness, than I was about the infidelity itself.

Yes, I know it's ridiculous. There I was: a modern, educated, professional Latina, living, reading, watching television, and working in the United States in the twenty-first century, all the while carrying a fifties woman inside, complete with a trunk full of silly, vintage, chauvinistic, not to mention pigheaded, thoughts and beliefs about love and relationships, without the slightest idea of where they'd come from.

Well, not from my parents, I can tell you that.

Gilberto and Carmen Luna always seemed effortlessly equal to me, the perfect partners, the best of friends and, maybe, that's exactly what they were.

Many times I've wondered whether Mami knew Papi was gay. I think she did. I think deep in that secret place where all is truth she always knew and accepted it because she loved him in the only way she knew how: with a profoundly committed, almost patriotic, passion.

And the passion went both ways. It was just their way of doing things: from deciding the appropriate age to enroll their little girl in school, to picking the colors of the flowers they'd use to surround the garden's vegetable patch.

They were both teachers and crazy in love with their seemingly nontranscendent work at the same Rio Grande middle school I attended. Mami taught Spanish, Papi music, and both lived to support each other's worlds with such fanatical fervor to the other's goal that I often felt left out, and was probably the only twelve-year-old in the world who thought having a job with lots of problems to solve and talk about would be a cool thing to have when I grew up.

Take my mother, for instance: always the zealous protector of the space in which my father could create his boleros.

"Gil," she'd say. "He might be the principal/parent/music headmaster, but he has no right to speak to you like that. You are an artist! You need time to create, you need the authority to grade, you need the flexibility to adapt the curriculum. Are you sure you don't want me to have a delicate . . . discreet . . . word with him?"

To which Papi would invariably say no, something she, in turn, would invariably "forget" in order to give whomever it was a piece of her Puerto Rican mind, because she hadn't been able "to help herself."

Meanwhile, my father hates obscenity. Always has, always

will. He's the kind of person who can insult you to Saturn and back without muttering a single curse. Yet for years he walked around with a little notebook and a pencil stub in the front pocket of his guayabera, ready to write the first truly original vile word he heard, so he could offer it to my mother as one would a rose.

My mother, you see, was a collector of "bad" words, thought a word was a terrible thing to waste and was always searching for new examples of what she called "the circumstantial terms of the new world." She dreamed of writing a great big book about these frowned-upon words and how they'd come about, releasing them from their prison of perception.

As I had often tried to explain to Martin's mother, so proud of having descended from "one of the noblest Chilean families of the last century," my cursing was not about my coming from a "low social extract." My parents, though poor, could not have held more education inside their brains. My mother had been pursuing a degree in the particular etymology of the Caribbean when she died and *it* was the reason I'd always been encouraged to say *carajo, coño,* and any other word that flowed forth spontaneously, as long as it appropriately expressed a feeling or idea. As a child, if I came home from school with a new bad word, my mother wouldn't wash my mouth out with soap. Instead, she'd offer me a piece of pumpkin flan and run to get her notes so she could proceed to ask about the context of the sentence in which I'd first heard the word, the emotional demeanor of the person who said it, and any other detail about the ethnic origin of the classmate who'd taught me the word. Those were my parents. That's how I remember them.

In those days, when life was simple, my favorite pastime was listening to grown-up conversations. I was twelve going on twenty, yet never imagined I'd one day live in Miami. I also never imagined that cancer would take my mother from me or that my stepmother's name would be Benjamin.

All three of us usually got home around three-thirty in the afternoon, and it became our routine that I'd sit on the balcony floor to do my homework, Mami on the balcony's sole wooden rocker to correct exams, and Papi (who never had anything to correct because his students heard from him on the spot when they played badly) would leave the door open so he could interrupt us with his singing while he cooked.

At around four-thirty my mother's friends would arrive and the "afternoon gossip session," as Papi called it, would begin.

I'd keep very quiet and still so they'd forget my presence as they talked, and that's when things got interesting. It's how my preadolescent mind found out that when Feliciana, the baker, was tired and wanted her husband to leave her alone, she'd insert her pinky finger into his asshole and manipulate it during sex to make him come quickly, satisfied, exhausted. It's also how I discovered the tragicomical extremes of denial a woman can reach when half-eaten alive by jealousy and the fear of abandonment.

Ana Julia, the noisiest of my mother's friends, once caught her husband cavorting with a neighbor. "You don't understand how that good man cried. *¡Que barbaridad!* When he realized his slip could cost him me, the love of his life, the mother of his children, the only woman who'd been capable of straightening him out once and for all, well, I can't even tell you. He almost commits suicide." I think it still hurts where my mother smacked me on the head for venturing to contribute that he couldn't have been all that straightened out if he was having sex with a neighbor.

Back then I thought Ana Julia was an idiot to forgive her cheating husband. But even she had better luck than I. Martin never gave me the option of forgiving him. Two seconds after I demanded a divorce in a fit of rage, he said to me:

"Erika, this is not about whether you can forgive me. It's about my forgiving myself. It's about my deciding what to do with this relationship that has come into my life . . . unexpectedly. But I don't want you to worry. I'm just about finished packing (when had he started?) and will be out of your way soon."

What happened? I thought that morning, crying like an idiot under the spray of the shower's massage head (my new pastime). And when the hell did it happen? Imagine going through life knowing you can't trust your own judgment. That everything happened under your upturned Latina nose and that the person with whom you shared your days until yesterday is too busy with his new life to remember your middle name.

Didn't I read enough magazines? Wasn't I understanding and loving to disgust? What sex manual did I forget to read? What vital organ was I missing that made me so easy to leave behind?

It had been a week since my Oscar-worthy lunatic performance at my lawyer's office without a peep from Martin, and I was beside myself. A regular Ana Julia. So much so that I decided to try the ritual assigned as homework by the instructor of the self-esteem seminar I'd attended a few nights ago at Lola's dogged insistence. What the hell? *¿Qué carajo, no?*

According to Maria, the professor, an effective way to soar

beyond our humanity during troubled times is to put ourselves in contact with our bodies. She suggests using a big round mirror and spending some time looking at the source of the universe . . . reuniting with our "primary function," with our femininity.

Now I ask, do you have the slightest idea how incredibly ugly a vagina can be, viewed objectively and in plain daylight? Plus, I'm not on board with the whole "primary function" thing, but I kept looking.

Sitting on the toilet seat, still wet after my shower and with a mirror between my wide-open legs, I couldn't help but think that my depressed state of mind had more severe causes than the lack of contact with my vagina. Still, I looked. "This is all your fault," I told her out loud at last. She contracted is if she'd heard me and looked so pitiful I left her in peace.

Since there's nothing more pathetic than vaginal self-pity, I'd gotten up from the toilet with the intention of shaking off the nonsense, and making myself presentable enough to go into the office, when I was surprised into thought by my own reflection in the medicine cabinet's mirror. It was as if by ignoring myself for weeks, I had become invisible. I didn't recognize the person I was seeing, and after several seconds of confusion, I decided to make an effort to describe myself using the tangible terms I'd use to describe the condition of a lab mouse.

- Erika has skin the color of milk and coffee, with a little more milk than coffee.
- In the whitish puddle of her face, a light sprinkling of cinnamon-colored freckles.
- Erika's hair is espresso coffee-colored, long and curly.

- Her eyes are dark, like wells.
- Her lips are the quintessential bemba colorá, as Celia would say, deep brick red and pillowy.
- Erika has a longish face and wears thick, square-shaped, tortoise shell glasses.

I closed the bathroom door to look at my body in the full-length mirror I hang behind it.

- Erika hasn't given birth. Nevertheless, she has a bit of a pancita and a sprinkle of cellulite.
- Erika's breasts are on the small side.
- Hips: wide.
- Upper legs . . . abundant . . . abundantly . . . fat.

In other words, if before I was "not bad, but not spectacular," as I'd once been told by a spiteful lover. Now my body—too thin since the word "divorce" started hounding me—looked like a wire hanger sculpture in which only the hips stood out, always too wide and now even more so in contrast with the rest of me.

My backup, wake-up alarm clock went off. I was mega-late so I stopped taking inventory and got dressed quickly, taking my keys and flying down the stairs. But I hadn't even opened the front door when I noticed someone had slipped an envelope under it. They must've knocked while I'd been showering.

It was a letter from Martin's lawyer, notifying me that the negotiation period had ended. In response to my intransigent attitude, his client saw no reason to "waste more time talking." He was attaching the "fair" breakdown of the marital assets Martin had submitted, preceded only by a scant account of a

Texas divorce case in which "malicious tactics" to delay a divorce had ended in jail time for the malicious party. He finished by asking me to submit my own list of assets for comparison, double-spaced, if possible, and wanted me to feel free to call him with any questions, hoping to help Martin and I put this sad chapter of our lives behind us.

What? Who the hell did "Tattoo" think he was to decide that my marriage had been a "sad chapter"? As you can imagine, there went my good work intentions and the next thing I knew I was standing in front of the fabulous offices of "Quintero, Silva y Echegoyén: Publicists for a New Millennium."

In the midst of last week's screaming, I'd told Martin I knew exactly who he was cheating on me with. I'd lied. The truth was I had no idea. Only the painful intuition that it was someone he worked with or had business with in (where else?) his own office. But that morning, goaded by the desire to scare him into calling off his legal dog, I figured, why not find out every nasty detail once and for all? Maybe it would do me good.

I parked and walked resolutely to where the phone-answering Lolita sat filing her nails. Milagros had worked for my husband for a little over twelve months, had seen me maybe a half dozen times, and had always managed to infuse her face with some form of contempt, often punctuated by the slightest smirk. Unless Martin was present, in which case she just proceeded to allow her drool for him to run rampant through her always too tightly clad body while ignoring me to the point of rudeness.

"Good afternoon, Milagros."

She answered my greeting with silence and the empty stare of those God has punished with the most complete ignorance of their own lack of brain matter.

"I said good afternoon, Milagros, or do we no longer greet people in this office?"

"Good afternoon," she responded, resigned. "Mr. Echegoyén isn't in today."

"Have I asked you for Mr. Echegoyén? Wouldn't it be easier to wait until people told you what they need your help with?" (Before attempting mental gymnastics? I finished the sentence mentally.)

"Look, ma'am, you're no longer . . . associated with this office, so I'm, like, totally not going to get into it with you, okay?"

"Of course you're not. To do that, you'd need a brain."

"Erika!" boomed a voice behind me.

"Fernando!" I responded with the same hypocritical euphoria.

"What brings you here? Have you been offered coffee yet?"

"No, thanks. You know . . . the diet . . . the possibility of cyanide," I said with my best Jack Nicholson in *One Flew Over the Cuckoo's Nest* smile. "And since when are partners treated so formally in this office?" I added, a little jab meant to annoy him, but which immediately made him crispier than a KFC drumstick.

Fernando was the typical "Latino boys' club" president. Forty-something, with a distinguished hairline (thanks to hair plugs), always impeccably dressed in an Italian suit and tie and, once in a while, a Dominican cigar between his lips. His only distinctive trait was the deep basso radio announcer's voice with which he attacked the ears of anyone he managed to surprise.

With Martin, he'd always assumed the role of mentor in business manners, accomplice in matters of women. At the beginning of our relationship, Martin had confessed to me that his partner was not happy about his not following in his footsteps by having a dutiful wife at home and a rotating "first lady," chosen among the more easily substitutable clerks, temps, and assistants. How proud I'd been of my marriage then. How stupid I'd been to think my husband's scruples had something to do with character. Or that his sharing the information with me meant he loved me and not that it was just the general male custom of behaving at the beginning, just so no one could later say they hadn't really tried. It's true. They hate, hate, hate being the "bad ones."

"Forgive me. I don't understand. What do you mean 'partner'?" he said in a way that made it clear to me he knew exactly what I was talking about.

It occurred to me that if they were taking the whole million-dollar thing so seriously, maybe they actually had a million dollars to lose. Maybe, just maybe, my half-cooked threat was the weapon I'd been fantasizing about in my Lorena Bobbitt dreams . . . the one thing I could use to shock Martin out of his "What am I going to do about this new love?" complacency, to hurt him as badly as he had me, striking where it would itch the most, setting his universe on fire; a universe made up of his company, his money, and what other people thought of him. Yes, I know, I know. It's not something I'm proud of, but honestly, it's exactly how I felt, and my evil twin was not wasting any time taking advantage of the momentum.

"What I mean is, well, I imagine you've been appraised of the divorce terms I demand. And since I don't think you have a million of anything just laying around, I've decided to claim my stake in the agency. You know, as part of the settlement. Not that I'm expecting a free ride. In fact, we should set up a meeting to negotiate my participation in terms of just labor, as well as the redistribution of profits. And while we're at it, it would be good to know which of these will be my office. None of those dirty cubicles your employees use as road motels. I mean, that's just nonnegotiable."

I'd barely said three words when I saw his smile run away, chased by the exasperated gesture that replaced it.

"Erika, divorces are difficult and toxic—"

"Which is why I'll be grateful to you for keeping your sermons to yourself," I interrupted him. "You didn't think it was toxic when Martin carried on with another woman in this very office, but I know you'll change your mind when your profit is reduced in equal proportion to his bad judgment."

"Erika, you're an educated woman, a professional," he said not denying the whole "carrying on" accusation. "Don't do things you'll want to take back later. Right now, it's your hurt pride talking, and rightly so . . ."

Right there, at that second, I decided the leader of the forty thieves, as I liked to call my husband's partner, was cooking something. Fernando did nothing without getting something back, and there had to be a good reason for his patience, not to mention his obsequiousness.

"It's my brain talking, Fernando, and don't think I blame you for any of this. I understand you couldn't really say much about the visiting hours kept by Martin's whore, when yours prances around the place with the excuse of being a secretary. So please quit the nonsense and start clearing an office for me. And don't worry, I probably won't use it much," I said, wanting to take my farce to its very reckless end. Let someone else be the uncomfortable one for once.

But when he heard the word "whore," Fernando's face twitched into an involuntary backward glance, and the possibility that Martin and she were there, hearing through some half-open conference room door, instantly deflated my spirit. Maybe they'd been there all along. Laughing at me. Too amused to interrupt.

Meanwhile, Lolita just glared at me with a preoccupied expression, chewing gum like a compulsive goat, three inches of tar-colored roots making their way through her long peroxide blond hair and I remembered her premature, "Mr. Echegoyén's not in today."

"I'd better go, Fernando," I said, cowardly, realizing I was not ready to face the nymph, super-model of perfection for whom, I imagined, Martin had left me, much less to hear him defend her, taking her side, as I imagined he would.

"Best thing you can do . . ." said Milagros.

I stopped and turned to look at Fernando.

"Oh, and, Fernando? Before I forget . . . if you really want to do something for me, and really, no rush . . . but I'm thinking . . . maybe you could help Milagros with her medical plan. I mean, she is the receptionist after all and the one brain neuron is just not enough. She needs that one to breathe, you know," I said, gesturing toward Lolita, the goat, before walking out with three times the attitude of the emperor before finding out he was naked in public, and not in a good way.

Of course, I hadn't so much as turned the corner before I began shaking violently, almost as if my body were unsure of which vital organ was to blame for my predicament and wanted to expel them all in the biological equivalent of a political coup.

That's lunacy for you. You'd think people who are insane are immune to suffering, but if that were the case, there'd be more lunatics than drug addicts or alcoholics.

After all, madness is cheaper . . . and a lot more potent.

{four}

"So let me get this straight, you want to support having an entire population of healthy mice, while people continue to die of cancer, leukemia, and even diabetes. . . . Well, I'm sorry you feel that way, but, again, this is not the customer service department. I have no idea who transferred you, ma'am, but you have yourself a great afternoon just the same. . . . No, you have a good one, well, same to you. . . . No, no . . . thank *you*. Thank *you* very much, you hear?"

It never fails. The more you try to relax and do your job without killing anyone, the higher the probability that someone with nothing better to do than mess with those who are busy will plop right onto your lap.

I needed to focus. While my crap-tolerance levels continued at historic lows, my work refused to be pushed aside any longer, divorce or no divorce, and so . . .

GOALS FOR TODAY:

1. Questionnaire for hospital patients re: migraine perceptions for use in daytime nondrowsy Varitex.
2. Read at least two professional journals.

"Should I throw these out?" Naty had asked for the second time that day, glaring at me reproachfully, dozens of journals and newspapers overflowing out of her arms.

"Oh, no . . . I'll get to them. It's just . . . been hectic."

"You sure? Because I can throw them out so they won't be lying around everywhere," she scolded, even though she knew exactly what was hindering my activity on that particular day: I hadn't so much as stepped into my office that morning when she'd taken my arm and pulled me aside.

"Martin was here."

"What do you mean here? Doing what?"

"With two of his partners," she said, making a letter *V* with her fingers. "I said hi and asked if he was looking for you and he answered 'Not at all' with a huge attitude. *Ay chiquita,* I'm so sorry. If you need anything . . . and not because you're my boss . . . but you know you can count on me."

"I know, Naty," I said. "But I wonder what they were doing here."

"Meeting. In Public Relations. I hear they made a crappy, half-assed presentation to be the agency of record, going on and on about 'organic growth.' Now who do you think told them that that is all your beloved boss talks about?"

(What Naty didn't know about the goings-on of that office, was just not worth knowing.)

"You know how things are in this place, Erika," she continued. "Every day it's something else. The other day I was in the cafeteria heating up my Lean Cuisine because God knows I'm getting fat as a cow and he's doing nothing about it, and I was waiting for the microwave so I leaned on the photocopier, and guess what was sticking out? A signed finance release to give the witch's department a bigger budget and more people, so there you go. . . . I bet that's where this whole meeting thing must have come from," she answered her own question before I had a chance to say anything.

The witch was Lizandra Salinas-Montes. An ultra-thin, big-nosed bitch with hair so freakishly blond it screamed "trailer trash!" as she floated through NuevoMed's hallways tugging her bony, rattling ass behind her, as if she were science's gift to the male species.

"Y ella que se cree que está buena. You know she thinks she's aaall that," said Naty echoing my thoughts.

I just nodded, returned to my office, and closed the door, not wanting Naty's pity—or anyone else's.

And it's not as if I didn't know exactly what Martin had done: he'd officially declared war on me.

For years, I'd suggested to Martin that he go after the NuevoMed Pharmaceutical account, pointing out that though small, the drug company's P.R. needs could make for a nice little cash cow. He'd ignored me.

Now he'd purposely stepped into my territory, making sure Naty saw him, to let everyone know that we were no longer, to pay me back for my little skit in his office the other day.

That's how people end up killing each other during a divorce. One little thing leads to another and by the time you realize it, you're on trial for killing the man or woman you've loved most in your life. And I'd started the day with such good intentions, too. Damn him.

After my little scene with Fernando, I had spent the long weekend at home doing a lot of thinking, trying to shake it all off to the tune of an obscene amount of coconut chocolate chip cookies and a Cartoon Network Flintstones marathon. After all, I was not the first woman to go through a divorce. And men have been cheating on women since the Ice Age and vice versa. I was young and had a great job and people who truly loved me. It wasn't the end of the world. So why was I acting like it was? Why was I not able to get over this? Why not echo Lola with a *"Neeeeeext!"*?

At some point I thought I heard Martin's key. My heart leaped up and out of my chest before realizing it was a false alarm, and for the hundredth time in half as many days I wished for an interrupter for the pain I felt, unable to understand why it was necessary to feel like shit when all I wanted was to be strong enough to move on with my life and have enough pride and dignity to stop pining for a man who'd just stopped loving me.

It seemed that ever since my Humpty Dumpty of a heart had fallen off the wall and turned into a spackled eggshell wall treatment straight out of a Martha Stewart magazine, I was incapable of a logical, methodical, or scientific decision, much less an intelligent one.

After two days of walking around the house with what looked like a "dreadlocks in progress" hairstyle and hyperstinky pajamas, I woke up from among the dead (because it was Monday and I had no choice) and decided to reinhabit my skin.

I dressed for work in a navy blue silk A-line skirt and fitted sweater with a flattering low neckline, knee-high leather boots, and the smallest diamond studs, a gift from Martin. I completed the look with what my stepmom, Benji, would have classified as a category-five, hurricane-force blowout and was off to work.

But now that I was here, I didn't have my head with me. I paced the office wanting to call him to ask why he'd been there that morning, and while I was at it, I'd also ask why he didn't go back to his wife like a sensible man. Enough, I said to myself. Enough of acting as if Martin possessed the last male sexual organ on earth, I continued to berate myself, never giving a thought to the fact that it had been less than two months since my life had changed so drastically. Never mind that. I wanted to be well, sane, and happy again, immediately.

Given my mood, I decided to distract myself with the triumphs of others and begun to flip through the skyscraper of newspapers and scientific journals on my desk. From *American Scientist* to *Pharmacological Reviews* and from the *Journal of Experimental Medicine* to *Brain and Animal Behaviour,* which for a chemist is what *Star* and *US Weekly* is to anybody else.

After a half-dozen magazines, I came to *Brain,* one of my favorites. In it, there was an interview with my idol, the Czech anthropologist Helena Fish, who had a new book out called *Love Is Just a Drug.* She talked about using a functional magnetic resonance imaging machine (a sophisticated sort of X-ray machine) to study the human brain, and stated simply that it's precisely in the brain, specifically in a little-known region called the caudate nucleus, and not in the heart, where emotions reside, and that from this area one could cure or control quite a few diseases, heartbreak included.

"Using this machine, I found that love is also in the brain. But not in the same area as the feelings of excitement and affection, but closer to essential biological impulses such as eating, drinking, or the desire for a drug, which would explain the desperation we feel when it goes missing and the reason many people stalk, become obsessed, consider the possibility of homicide and even suicide."

I couldn't believe it. Helena Fish had found the love switch. It was my own brain. But how to reach my command center?

"The good news is we've identified the chemical neurotransmitters that can regulate our feelings. We know it's possible to control, exacerbate, and maybe even eliminate painful love feelings, and we're very close to figuring out just how to do this."

My heart (or my brain?) began to beat quickly and I had to overcome a feeling of dizziness in order to continue. I couldn't believe what I was reading. If it were so simple and so logical, then why do we spend our existence so limited by breakups and the absence of love?

The journalist finished the interview by asking Dr. Fish, a bit condescendingly, if she wasn't advocating and maybe even announcing the possibility of a pill against "so-called" heartbreak.

To which, by the male interviewer's own account, the elderly doctor just laughed coquettishly before expressing her personal opinion that it would be much more practical and useful to use the results she shared in her book to help the human race cure severe mental diseases such as schizophrenia and paranoia. "It would be wiser to use our findings to understand how to control one's feelings and to learn how to manage one's brain, before focusing on a chemical solution to love."

What . . . what was that? So, something capable of zapping your will to live is not as important to science as curing schizophrenia, which affects relatively few people in comparison to the millions who suffer from broken hearts?

And what was that about "learning to control their brains"? How many people know they need to quit smoking and are incapable of breaking free? How many try to eat better and less, and fail in spite of knowing exactly what it is they need to eat to lose weight? Why the hell not create a pill against bad love?

I read for hours, saving everything I could find on the topic. I read until much after Santiesteban popped his head into my doorway to ask how it was going with the Varitex questionnaire and to ask that I help Lizandra and her team of lizards (my own description) wherever possible before wishing me a good night.

I read until much after everyone had left and the only lights besides the ones in my office were the ones near the security guard who sits at the lobby entrance.

A bit after ten, eyes exhausted, I reached for the last issue of *Animal Behaviour*. There was nothing in it about Helena Fish, the cranial system, or the chemical substances that make it possible for human beings to fall in love, but I found this:

"Heartbreak is rife among orangutans in the rainforests of Borneo and Sumatra. The male orangutan only mates for a few days and when he moves on to the next female, the one left behind literally loses her head. Her vision blurs, her ability to gesture disappears, her sense of smell deadens.

"Instead of lounging in her tree, languorously calling him every so often with flirtatious little screams, she'll venture to the ground and lie on dirt that remembers her lover's warmth; rubbing her bones in it like a crazed jungle robot; short-circuited brain in electrochemical shock."

I realized I was trembling as I read, unaware of even the floor beneath my feet. I thought of the human brain, the size of a mango but still three times the size of an orangutan's, and therefore more capable of making mental prisons, creating a society that is always pushing us to look for the missing half, to blindly say "yes" to love, while keeping every other area of our lives in perfect balance, never a piece out of place.

"The first night *he's* gone is the worst for the female rainforest orangutan. The uncertainty slowly turns into sorrow as she realizes he's not just delayed somewhere where she can reach him by screaming intermittently, as usual.

"He's gone, and that first night, lying on his dust, unending sweat will seep through her pores through the night, and well into dawn, like an internal rain of loss."

I got home that night invaded by a strange mix of adrenaline and exhaustion; my mind/brain a vortex of pain-numbing possibilities, while my heart brain, unaware of anything but its own rosarylike wailing, just let itself drop on the side of the bed that still kept the smell of my orangutan, and began to sweat.

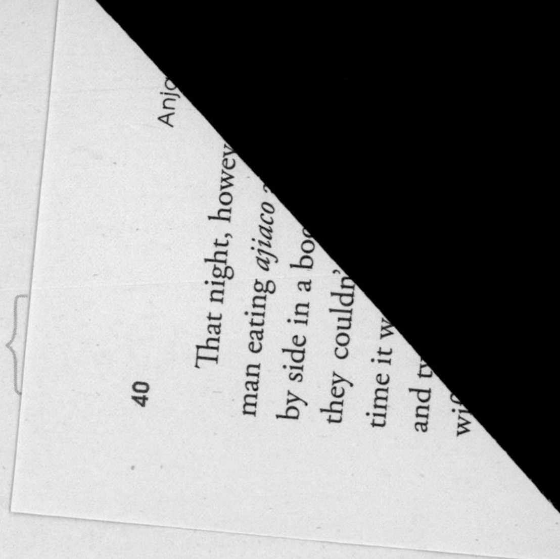

I’ll have the grilled pork chops, please, with uh, no, scratch that. I’ll have the House Churrasco with *moros*-style rice and beans and some fried sweet plantains . . . no, no, make them fried green plantains, and could you give me a little cup with some garlic *mojito* for them?”

“Let me see if they’ll still make ’em for you, sweetie. We’re just about closing,” the waitress replied with an apologetic face.

I’d been leaving work around midnight for a little over a week. I would wait until everyone left the building before turning into Dr. Jekyll with a little bit of Hyde, reading, making notes, and frequently accessing NuevoMed’s vast internal archive of brain images in all its stages and colors.

When hunger and exhaustion kicked my ass, only then would I stumble into La Carreta on Bird Road, a family-style restaurant where you can usually get hot, cheap, fast, Cuban food.

er, at that late hour, there was only an old t mule pace, a pair of sweethearts seated side th, looking tragically into each other's eyes as if t stand not to touch during the short amount of ould take for the *ropa vieja* they'd surely share to come, wo young guys wearing thick, gold chains, jeans, and white e beaters eating huge mountains of rice, black beans, fried plantains, and what looked like stewed oxtails from my vantage point next to the cash register. I realized I'd be as lonely eating there as at home, so . . .

"You know, it's okay," I answered the waitress. "I'll take it to go and please add a chocolate milkshake and a coconut flan."

"Looks like someone's hungry tonight," she answered with the tired smile of someone who'd been on her feet for twelve hours.

And I was. For the first time in weeks, I was actually feeling hunger . . . and eating . . . and keeping my food down, even as my brain felt full of science, bursting with an idea that seemed so much bigger than I.

When I remember those days, I see myself tottering between "What am I thinking? This is so silly" and "I need to know and needing to know makes me feel alive." In other words, I needed to know. And I needed to need to know even more. If curing heartbreak were possible, then all of this happening in the name of science was worthwhile. Not that I thought I could create a heartbreak pill by just setting my heart . . . or my brain . . . to it. I knew creating a new drug and getting it approved by the Food and Drug Administration can easily take eight to twelve years and hundreds of millions of dollars. But if I could just know with a degree of certainty that what I'd spent weeks suspecting—that this shit-eating state could not be good for a human being, which meant that the body had to have a natural, agile, organic mechanism to heal itself from it—then there'd be a point. A point to me. A point to life. Like I said, I needed to know.

I remember just thinking about it and feeling energized as I fantasized that I volunteered to be part of Dr. Fish's research team. I imagined myself in the midst of some exotic jungle, dressed in safari clothes, interviewing the native women of some obscure tribe about their problems of the heart, mixing enzymes and hormones till dawn in a seaside tiki hut, studying a huge leafy tree overpopulated with birds . . .

"Card won't go through, *mima,* and they've already started frying your *tostones.*"

"What do you mean it doesn't go through? Has to be a mistake . . . There's money in that account."

She ran it through another three times. Nothing.

"The code I'm getting is insufficient funds. You're going to have to call your bank tomorrow . . . or if you have another card . . ."

And just like that I again reverted to the wicked witch of the west.

First thing I did when I got home was to turn on the computer and jump on the Internet.

Yep. There it was. Martin had emptied out every single bank account. It's true that I'd been ignoring his lawyer's calls for two weeks now, that I hadn't made the slightest effort to secure representation, and that I had not submitted a response to Tom Thumb's "fair inventory of assets," but even so, I can't explain to you the feeling of impotence (and the craving to puncture tires) that overtook me. I wanted to smash the computer against the floor. I felt such heat that I started stripping all over the house . . . leaving my skirt on the sofa, my blouse on the dining room floor, shoes in the hallway, my bra in the sink, and my panties God knows where.

As I fried myself an egg in the buff, I tried to think, to see my enemy clearly. Because that's what Martin had become. He was now my enemy and I had to get that through my thick head. A man who loves you, or who loved you, doesn't leave you penniless without so much as a warning. Plus, even though it's true he made more money than I, the money in those accounts belonged to both of us.

In chemistry, when you need a starting place to identify the components of a substance, you make lists of all the names and descriptive terms by which these might be identified to avoid surprise variables once you've begun the process of mixing, separating, or coagulating the final jumble.

 UNKNOWN ELEMENT: MARTIN ECHEGOYÉN

Possible names and/or descriptive terms:

- Son of a bitch
- Son of a repentant bitch (of having given birth to him, not of being a bitch)
- Microscopic lice
- Thirdhand asshole
- *Cojudo* (courtesy of Peru)
- Piece of old cow dung
- *Sabandija* ("insect" just didn't do him justice)

- *Come-Pinga* (courtesy of Cuba, meaning one who eats penises, in general terms)
- Impotent bugger
- Stinking hole-inhabiting mice
- *Boludo* (courtesy of Argentina)
- Veteran whore-mattress
- Cystic pimple
- Mental midget
- Emotional midget
- Genital midget
- Homeless dog vomit
- Subhuman phenomenon
- Ex-husband

Believe me, I, too, wanted to be evolved, civilized, elegant, and classy, but as Benji's fond of saying, *"No es fácil, caballeros,"* which means "It's not easy, gentlemen."

One day I'd wake up so tired of whining, feeling almost positive and thinking "What does it matter? I'm still young and have my whole life ahead of me. God will sort things out in the end." But other times, the smallest thing would be enough to send me flying back into the devil's arms—a photo, a credit-less credit card, a song. That night, I turned on the radio full blast and Shakira sang . . .

Si te vas, si te vas, y me cambias
    If you go, if you go, and exchange me
por esa bruja pedazo de cuero
    for that witch, piece of hide . . .

Perfect. I was already feeling the presence of my own spite's malignant glare observing from the corners of the room.

Why, Martin? I thought for the one thousand five hundredth time since all this had begun, as I looked at the fried egg I hadn't been able to eat as it mummified before my eyes. How could you change so much? When? Why didn't you warn me you were running out of whatever it was that kept us together?

Even the way I found out was silly. I'd woken with Martin's arms around me, as usual. He'd been trying to wake me with tiny, mischievous kisses in weird places like my shoulder, my left eye, or the tip of my nose, something he often did to make me laugh, just so he could later claim it as proof of his ability to make me respond to his kisses even while asleep.

"Mmmm . . . Hey! All right, all right, I'm awake . . . What time is it, Papi?"

"Time to cook me some French-style eggs with smoked ham; cream of corn seasoned with a bit of coconut milk, a few raisins and cinnamon, southern-style; home-fried potatoes; oven-baked buns with homemade jelly; and fresh-squeezed orange juice," he'd finished triumphantly, betraying the fact he'd rehearsed it this time.

It was a familiar joke in which the only thing that varied was the menu, Martin playing at coming up with a more complicated one every time. I hate cooking and the results are inedible, probably because I spend my day looking through the window in my office at the nontoxic remains of the unsuccessful chemical waste that the cleaning people dump outside.

I started hitting him with my pillow in order to erase the smug smile from his face, when he got up suddenly; hurriedly, as if he'd remembered something.

"Where're you going?"

"Just remembered . . . something . . . I need to fix on the terrace. Keep sleeping, it's still early."

I nodded happily and got under the covers again, sneaking a last look at his dark, sunburned back and even turning my head to the side a little to look at the cute wedge of his buttocks trapping his cotton pajama pants. I remember feeling lucky that my husband could still turn me on in such a way, after almost eight years of marriage, then closing my eyes, ready to go back to sleep. That's when I felt it: an intense chill running through the left side of my head, as if I had a sixth sense that allowed me to say "I see dead people."

Martin . . . fixing something? It was a signal that told me: Get up! Get up, get up, get up! If it weren't for my intuition I might still be ignorant . . . and married.

I got out of bed quietly, wrapped a robe around me, and went downstairs. I poked my head through the door that connects the kitchen and the garage, then walked over to the family room, peering through the French doors onto the terrace, even peeked into his study, but no Martin. Then I heard him. The voice was coming from the wall, or rather through the studio window. I leaned against the wall that held it and, through it, saw Martin leaning against the fence bordering the left side of the house, the one with the most foliage, talking on his cell phone. He was smiling nervously, his eyes lost on some distant place of no consequence, the flirtatious expression on his unshaven face playing with the excited smile peeking out from the mouth I'd always found so sexy, and I just thought one thing: my husband is talking to another woman. How did I know? Don't you know the difference when your husband is talking to his buddies and when he's talking to a woman?

For weeks I'd been telling myself I was imagining things. Not because I thought there was something really wrong, but because I wondered if those down times other married people had often warned me about might not be upon me. Let me explain: Martin had not been late to dinner a single day, I hadn't found anything out of the ordinary among his clothes and he hadn't switched colognes. On the contrary, he was more affectionate than ever. But there was something strange; a kind of satisfied absence, as if even when with me, he could go to a secret room to which I was not invited, the existence of which had to be denied at any cost, or risk death by firing squad.

"What's going on?"

"Nothing."

"I can see that by the little smile on your face. Care to share the joke?"

"Nothing."

Actually, the correct answer would have been "No joke," but it was as if the word "nothing" was the secret password.

Just the week before that, as we watched our favorite TV show, *Myth Hunters* on Discovery, I'd asked if all was good with him. Was there anything about our marriage, about our life as a couple, that he would change if he could?

"Nope. Nothing. No."

"Sure, hon?"

"Nothing. Everything's good."

"Okay, then . . . what do you see in your future?" I'd said then, playfully sitting astride him.

"You," he'd said taking his eyes off the TV. "I know I want to spend the rest of my life with you and that I love you . . . more than anything."

"More than you love your mother or as you love an ultra-cold beer," I'd said jokingly, faking suspicion.

"More than anyone or anything," he'd answered seriously, almost solemnly.

I'd leaned my head on his chest then, trusting. Now I looked at him for another second, speaking quickly, stretching languorously, eyes closed. Then, with my stomach trembling like a race-track on a Sunday afternoon, I scurried to the kitchen, took the keys to his Lexus, and slipped into the garage still in my night-gown.

Seated on the passenger's seat, my hand hesitated a few precious seconds before opening the glove-compartment. When I opened it, I only found receipts and parking stubs, among other unimportant papers. I sat there in heated debate with myself, as one side of me said, "You're not going to find anything . . . because there's nothing to find!" But the other side egged me on, "Come on, really look. Under the seats." To which the other one taunted, "Shut up, Stupid! You're making a fool of yourself playing the private detective," and so on and so forth. But since I've never known how to ignore a challenge, I looked . . . And I found. There were pictures of a group of people having dinner; Martin among them. In addition to him, there were two women and three men in the photo, all dressed in business attire.

I looked at the women; all vaguely familiar, I wondered which was she. I also found a copy of Manuel Puig's *Kiss of the Spider Woman* (Martin only reads industry magazines, newspapers, and curiosity compilations) and a CVS pharmacy receipt in which, among other things, there was a pair of pantyhose (emergency replacement?) for $3.99. You won't catch me dead wearing one of those things. I consider them the most uncomfortable of inventions and declared myself on strike against them years ago.

I looked at the receipt. It showed the time: 2:50 p.m.—in other words, right after lunch. A respiratory implosion came out of my throat.

When I finally raised my head, Martin was leaning against the kitchen door with a serious yet serene expression on his face, and not a trace of the mirth I'd witnessed earlier.

"What're you doing?"

"I think it's obvious what I'm doing."

"What I asked you was . . . what are you doing searching through things that aren't yours?" he said in a much harsher tone than I'd expected.

But I was feeling quite harsh myself and didn't care.

"Who is she?"

"So this is what I can expect you to do in your old age?" he asked sarcastically.

"How would I know? I'm six years younger than you," I retorted, angry that he'd try to play the professor of civility at that moment. "The better question is what are *you* doing in your old age?"

"Look, Erika, if it makes you happy, search all you want, but do it quickly because I'm showering and then I need to head out," he said turning his back on me.

"Martin?"

"What?" he responded, half-turning toward me.

"You have nothing to hide, right?"

"Of course not, you dope."

"And if you could prove it beyond all doubt, you would."

"Of course!" he said, as if summoning all his patience to talk to a misguided youth.

I got close to him.

"Then give me the cell phone in your hand. Let me see the number of the person you were talking to just a minute ago."

Truth is so fast sometimes. You can glimpse it in a second. Sometimes it's just a gesture . . . his feet, stepping back almost involuntarily. His hands, flying to his waist. At the center of his pupils a little Martin screaming "No!" and running away like a mouse in a cat motel. But his mind, which couldn't see all I did, thought the battle wasn't lost.

"That's enough of this nonsense," he shouted at me.

And he left. I stayed there knowing it was over, that nothing would ever be the same because I wouldn't have a second of peace, and that my brain was already contaminated with the imagined details.

But that's just what drives me crazy: while part of me was furious, the other half was already sifting through the rubble of my psyche for some way to leave everything as it was, to convince myself that I'd just fallen prey to the illusions of my overactive brain.

Back to the present, I sank my head between my knees, wondering if Hillary went through this when the president cheated on her. I'm sure she too wanted to be a *Sex and the City* girl, drown her disappointment in shoes and parties, have faith as if she'd been born with it. I imagined the battle against Martin ahead of me, not knowing how I'd defend myself from the person to whom, until yesterday, as they say, I had given myself. And if I managed to, how in hell would I ever trust myself enough to love again?

I put on a robe and walked out onto the sod to get some fresh air. We had bought the cave three years ago. That's what we called our Spanish-style house facing the golf course between the Jewish side of "Millionaire's Row" and the South Beach of the magazine jet set. It had two stories, four bedrooms, three baths, and a pool.

It was the middle of the night and Alton Road was quiet, with the exception of an occasional car on its way to the clubbing side of Miami Beach. In front of me, the empty golf course. Behind me, my home; one more in a line of beautiful, sleeping houses. Except my house wasn't sleeping. It was dead. The windows had no pupils and the main door looked like an enormous hole through which you could walk straight into Hell. Even the whimsical little Mexican bench flanking the entrance looked sad, like a pathetic, waiting seat.

I thought of our first apartment, where we ate on a small card table, and decided that those had been the happiest days of my adult life. I remembered the glee with which we moved into this house, "christening" every room, because all, with the exception of our room, were just as empty, and it was just as comfortable to make love in the dining room as in the living room. I went up to our bedroom and stood in front of the armoire that had housed his clothes. I knew he'd taken everything, but hadn't dared to look.

"That's enough of your bullshit," I told myself out loud. I had to wake up, and so when my feet started hurting from standing in front of the armoire, I opened it. Actually seeing it empty was like falling down an elevator shaft. Pulling out the drawers and verifying what I already knew, as if the elevator fell on me as soon I got to the bottom. I glanced at the mirror and my expression was the same as Wile E. Coyote's when he figures out that the Road Runner has played him again and he has seconds before falling without hope down into the canyon.

You don't have a husband anymore, Erika, I said to myself. "Right this minute you have no money. Pretty soon you won't have this house, and if you continue with your head wrapped in bubble-shit, any day now you'll be out of a job. Okay, already. Enough."

It was my face. But the voice belonged to a woman much older and a lot wiser.

I nodded, as if agreeing that it really was enough already. I'd be stronger than all of it and, after, I'd be even more so. I showered and put on fresh pajamas. I combed my hair into a ponytail, and took the notebook in which I had made the list of Martin's names, ripped out the page and on a fresh one wrote:

PRIORITIES:

1. A lawyer
2. A new place to live
3. A pill against heartbreak

And then it dawned on me.

{six}

First things first, and that was to know what I knew.

1. Love is in the brain, specifically in the caudate nucleus.
2. It's a biological impulse like eating, drinking, sleeping, and having sex.
3. Our body produces several chemicals that act as neurotransmitters, telling us we're in love or that we're not, that we're suffering over our loved one or that it's all the same to us. Others operate like amphetamines, generating adrenaline, giving us the sensation of floating among clouds.

I thought these were the ones I should concentrate on. My plan was to find the chemical or chemicals that signal lack of love and amorous desperation, then counter them with a combination of elements producing the opposite effect. The next step was to study my options and, for the moment, I had exactly eight:

1. Phenylethylamine: A naturally occurring substance in the brain, better known as PEA. It's the neurotransmitter that sends the telegram to our brain announcing we're in love. It can also be found in animals and plants. Chocolate, for example, has large quantities.
2. Dopamine: It's the neurotransmitter that controls motivation and the desire to meet goals. (He: "I'm going to sleep with her tonight or my name is no longer Mauricio." Her: "This one is proposing before Christmas or my name is no longer Rita.")
3. Norepinephrine: Controls euphoria and the loss of sleep and appetite. It's the one that tells you the person you love is not around.
4. Serotonin: This one is the answer to the question What do love, heroin, and an obsessive compulsive disorder have in common?
5. Oxytocin: It's the cuddling chemical, the hormone that makes us calmer and more sensitive to other people's feelings.
6. Vasopressin: It's been dubbed the monogamy chemical, making us want to dance with the one who "brung" us—and no one else.
7. Testosterone: No explanation needed.
8. Endorphins: The happiness hormones, similar to morphine and opium, they calm and comfort with a sense of intimacy, security, and shared experiences.

Now I saw it clearly. We go through life like crack addicts, sabotaged by our own brains. There was no doubt in mine: love was an illness and it could be cured.

"Isn't it amazing?" I said to Lola. "Here I am, searching like a madwoman for a way to safely interrupt love, while my husband, who's by no means a scientist, has had no trouble interrupting, or rather ripping me out . . . of his reality. You'd think—"

"*Tía, por Dios.* Do we have to do the pragmatic negativism thing?"

To Lola, anything that negates the all-powerful quality of positive thinking to resolve all of life's problems, whether a callous on your big toe or an incurable disease, is "pragmatic negativism." But she's my best friend and I couldn't continue to keep her in the dark. So, Friday after work, I'd driven to her house on Velarde Avenue in Coral Gables and parked in front of her jungle, made up of so many trees and tropical plants that they formed a thick tropical fence around her house.

As I walked the little stone path that leads to the house's balcony, I smelled the small acerola, guava, and tamarind trees and remembered how I'd once thought I'd seen an angel, old and fragile and beautiful, on one of them. Of course, this happened at Christmas, walking to the car with Martin after a party, so I'll concede Lola's champagne could have generated my celestial vision.

Her balcony seems to be made of orchids, so many, so white, all hanging from plywood and wire baskets. The flowers were a gift from an ex-lover who sent them as a bid for forgiveness—with great success because, even though she never agreed to see him again, the orchids continue to thrive despite the heat and are more beautiful with each passing day.

A huge, blackwood rocker, carved with African motifs, and an oil lamp rest in a corner that looks so inviting that many days I just sit there enjoying myself before even pressing the doorbell.

But this afternoon I didn't have to. I found Lola on the balcony reciting a segment of the new play she's trying to open, *Love in the Times of Bush,* about a pregnant woman who's trying to convince her husband to desert the army during a medical pass from Iraq.

"Who is he, my love, to decide that another child deserves his father and not my son? Why have you given him that power and refuse to renege your ignorance?" shouted Lola amid the orchids, grabbing her chest with one hand while holding a script with the other, a minuscule pencil comfortably stationed behind her left ear.

Lola heads a nonprofit theater organization and spends two or three afternoons a week rewriting scripts in her pajamas, reciting entire pages of them before deciding where they might need tightening or making notes to use during the casting process.

She's a tall, big-boned Spaniard with a beautifully imposing voice, walnut-colored eyes, and insurance-worthy cheekbones, identical to her mother's, a renowned Shakespearian actress. From her father, a theater critic for Madrid's daily *ABC,* she inherited the lethal sword of a tongue she tries to tame with positive thinking and meditation. From both she inherited an obsession with justice and an affinity for the theater that, added to the metaphysical fever that has gotten into her, can drive just about anyone crazy.

"Seriously, *Tía.* Before you go in search of Frankenstein-worthy remedies, think for a moment if maybe, just maybe, it's possible Martin is not . . . is just not your ideal soul mate," she told me a bit later, after we'd sat down to talk and I'd told her in broad strokes about my recently begun quest against heartbreak.

"This is not just about that," I said, not wanting her to convince me that the only thing to break through my stupor was just a foolish child's dream.

She was quiet for a few seconds before answering.

"Erika, I know how hard this is for you. But I think it would actually help you to think, really think, if the Martin you're mourning really exists, or if he ever did?"

"What are you trying to say?" I said.

"Well, Erika," she said uncomfortably. "You've always been the creator of magical men. Remember Adrian? He was a drug addict . . . with a huge superiority complex, but according to you he was a 'misunderstood scientist at heart, rebeling against society.' "

"I've told you a million times he was trying to prove the medicinal effects of marijuana . . ."

"All right, okay. What about Hector? The 'sensitive artist, overcoming the spiritual poverty of his environment?' Did he ever pay you the five hundred dollars you loaned him?"

"He needed it more than I."

"And Martin, Erika. You can't seriously tell me you didn't know which leg that chair was limping from."

But the truth was I didn't. Really. I always thought my husband was a man who'd enjoyed his womanizing days, like most, until he fell in love with me. If not, then why would he have married me? Who forced him?

Even after going over every sordid detail of the last two months with Lola, I still couldn't see the thing that was unlike the others sticking its tongue out at me, as I usually could when analyzing a substance in the laboratory.

"Not one signal? Ever?"

I shook my head like an idiot.

"*Hostia,* Erika. At parties, you never noticed how he'd toss a sideways glance at every piece of ass that crossed his path."

By the skeptical expression on my friend's face, it was obvious that Martin's ways were known to all, his infidelity anticipated by everyone but me. There had probably been dozens. I had just happened to catch him, giving him the perfect excuse to reconsider his life as a married man. But in my defense, my blindness was based on the circumstantial theory I call "good man/bad man": all men have a good man and a bad man inside. The best guy in the world with woman number one can be the world's biggest loser with woman number two, while the biggest worm can become a model husband . . . if he falls in love.

In other words, there are inherently monogamous species, such as the California mouse, and there are others for which it is physiologically impossible, such as the Iberian brown bear. Then there are circumstantial monogamists, like the housefly, which has been taught monogamy in laboratory studies for generations. Or the male vole, which will refuse to have sex with any female other than the last one he mated with before being injected with the chemical hormone vasopressin. That was my problem: I had thought I was married to a housefly, when in reality Martin was nothing but a fucking Iberian brown bear.

"Aaaaaargggghhhh, *coño,* I'm so, so, so . . . stupid," I said pressing my temples.

"You're not stupid," said Lola. "He was just the right man for that phase of your life. Successful, intelligent, always the center of attention, and, to be fair, very attentive and affectionate with you . . . although . . . a bit domineering, elitist . . . even paternal sometimes, and, well, we've already established, a cheater to boot."

"Please, don't hold back for my sake," I said trying to make a joke of it.

"You know what you need? A good Reiki session," said Lola, looking at my face and realizing she'd gone a little too far, too soon. "A little aromatherapy . . . and these," she said getting up from the sofa and walking over to a bookshelf by the kitchen from where she took several tattered volumes. "Here," she said like a doctor handing out a prescription. "And here, and here . . . aaaand . . . here. I promise they'll help you."

"You know I don't read self-help, Lola," I said as soon as I glimpsed the titles.

"Didn't you say love is in the brain? Well, these will go directly to your brain. I mean, keep searching for your prescription medication if you like, but don't be surprised if you're holding in your hands the most organic solution of all. Okay? Okay, then. You in the mood for some orange tea?" she asked without a pause as she headed toward the kitchen.

"*The Art of Living* by Erich Fromm?" I read out loud.

"Oh, that one's great. A classic, really," hollered Lola from the kitchen.

I flipped through the thin, pink little book, opening a random page to read: *"This desire for an interpersonal fusion is the strongest impulse in man. His most fundamental passion . . . The inability to reach it means madness, destruction—Without love, mankind could not exist for a single day."*

Well, that was just great. I'd been given the apocalypses of love to read. I thought, "Yeah, this will help." There were about a dozen books with titles like *What Smart Women Know, How to Fall Out of Love,* and *Women Who Love Too Much.* This was Lola's heartbreak toolkit. Her own medicinal potion, her love encyclopedia, surely perfected through her many tormented theater romances before being "enlightened" by the New Age metaphysical movement.

"At least give it a try," she said, reading my mind as she set a cup of steaming tea before me. "Do I accuse you of being crazy when you tell me there can be such a thing as a pill against bad love? With that attitude, I wouldn't have an invitation to dinner and dancing tonight, courtesy of my new electrically inclined friend."

I encouraged her to tell me all about it, looking for any other fiction but mine, as I settled into my favorite armchair, made of black leather so old it felt like velvet.

"Well, this morning I meditated, and I was really clicking along and it felt really fantastic . . . I even went to sea with my higher self . . . at her invitation, and I just felt such great communication," said Lola dreamily, with her habitual gesture of smoothing her short hair with the backside of both hands.

"Why did your higher self want you to go to sea?" I was truly curious to know.

"Ay, hija, yo que sé . . . she invites, you go and that's that."

"So she's a dictator," I said to bother her.

"The points is," she tried to ignore me, "that after an experience like that, one's body wants to commune."

"Commune with whom?"

"With oneself, if necessary, and stop interrupting," she retorted, annoyed. "So here I am, completely naked, caressing my body mindfully as I imagined my higher self would . . ."

"You are talking about masturbation now, right?"

"When did you become rude? Listen, the point is I'm there, happen to look toward the window, and what do you think I see?"

"No idea," I said so she wouldn't accuse me of being rude again.

"A man. From the power company, no less. *Joder,* you'd think they could warn you when they're going to mess with a meter that happens to be next to a bedroom window?"

"So what happened?"

"Well, my aura was just shot for hours. I mean, why would that happen right at that moment?"

"I don't know, maybe the guy's 'higher self' ordered him to look through the window and he didn't question it."

But the truth is her aura was definitely shot, because when I later told her what had happened at my lawyer's, and later in Martin's office with Fernando, she lit enough aromatherapy candles to start a small forest fire before clanging the hell out of her Tibetan bells within inches of my eardrums to "clear my space."

"My God, do you see the negativity? You need to meditate," she sentenced. "Resentment only holds back your spiritual growth, dragging negative karma with it."

"Lola, please, I'm really not up for analysis."

"This, too, shall pass, Erika. Have you ever known of anyone who died from being single? You, more than anyone, could try to see this positively. After all, you went from college life to married life without so much as a pause. Think about it. Your mother dies and, a few months later, you have to leave your father for the first time in your life to go to college in a strange city. Then you graduate and just as you prepare to come home, Gilberto decides to come out. This is your chance to finally be comfortably independent."

"Lola, please, I love the fact that my father's happy, and that he falls in love, and that he doesn't look at gender when he does. Believe it or not, in his own way, Benji is more like my mother than anyone I've ever met."

"I'm sure he is, but we're still talking about major change and upheaval. And in the midst of all this, there's Martin with his pretty words and his extravagant trips and his promises of happily ever after. All I'm saying is, wouldn't it be a good thing to live now what you didn't live then? Go out; be bad for a while; do crazy, young things; take risks . . . Erika, being single is not the end of life. Just the end of the only life you know."

I noticed it immediately. That thought, "single," scared me as much as losing Martin. Me, the mirror-image of today's modern, emancipated Latina.

"Let her have him if that's their destiny," Lola continued to preach. "I mean, who would've told me that an electrical engineer would turn out to be as artistically sensitive as Carlos? You just never know with people . . ."

"Who the devil is Carlos?" I asked, confused.

"You know I don't like you mentioning that 'entity' inside the house and leaving bad vibrations here. Carlos is the light-filled soul who interrupted my meditation this morning."

"I thought he messed up your aura?"

"But that's the challenge!" she said hugging me. "We

just have to transform negative experiences into positive ones."

"And if the transformation includes a bit of much-needed sex, even better, huh?" I said, thinking of myself and my new sexless lifestyle.

"Hey," jumped Lola, misunderstanding me. "It's one thing to be liberal and naturally flirty. It's quite another to be promiscuous and sleep with the first guy who looks in your window."

"I didn't mean you, Lola. I was talking about myself, which is all I seem to be able to do these days," I said, suddenly exhausted. "*Cojones*, who understands you?"

"By the way, I've been meaning to tell you, you should really try to control the cursing. *Coño* and even *carajo* is one thing, but since this whole divorce thing began, you sound like a truck driver studying to become a merchant marine. Not that it bothers me, but who's going to think you're a woman of science on the brink of monumental discoveries if you spout vulgarity after vulgarity in front of anyone."

That's when I grabbed my purse, the books she'd loaned me, and got up and walked quickly toward the door to avoid getting into another existential debate with her.

"Ciao," I said.

"What do you mean, ciao? You just got here . . . What about your tea?"

I slammed the door and left her in mid-sentence, losing myself among the tomatoes and the *ají dulce* plants to avoid another debate with her. Since she'd become "evolved," you couldn't say "shit" in front of Lola without a sermon.

I can imagine asylums full of evolved lunatics who, one day, become tired of repressing their anger. I see them tearing off their clothes while screaming obscenities, sticking their tongues out at strangers through the metal bars. Who are the crazy institutionalized? Surely people who were taught to smile as they let people jump in front of them at the supermarket line so as not to seem crass or uneducated.

As I opened my car door, I noticed a pair of purple houseflies mating on the window. I observed them for an instant before swatting them apart with all my might.

"Why don't you go fuck, mate, *chingar, templar, coger,* cohort, or 'just do it' to the very ends of Hell."

Then I got in my car . . . and headed there, too.

{seven}

A week later, I faced another weekend alone. Lola was out with her new love. Papi was in Key West helping Benjamin scare a tenant who thought he'd live rent-free in the cottage Benjamin had inherited from his first "husband," and Martin still wanted a divorce.

I sat in bed surrounded by Lola's books, some scientific magazines, and my spiral notebook. A good scientist always expresses the purpose of her investigation in clear and honest terms, and knows there's nothing worse than to look for the wrong thing.

 FROM THE DESK OF ERIKA LUNA

External goal: To create a pharmacological solution to the chemical imbalance caused in the brain by heartbreak.

Internal goal: To do something with my life. To feel a complete human being within myself.

You can miss other people. Suffering a bit is normal. But walking around like a zombie two months later? I needed to break free from the pathetically weakening effects of love. I mean, who the hell *was* I? What else did I want in life that didn't have a name and resided outside of myself? Only science, and even that I had treated as "just my job." I didn't own it: the ideas I'd investigated until then belonged to others. How did I expect Martin to be engaged in "us" when I had nothing to contribute to that "us"? Where was that inner world, that mystery that every heroine of universal literature possesses? I worked, I slept, I ate. I loved my father and Martin, and life was eating with the former on Sundays and sleeping nights in the cocoon of the latter's body. Erika in a nutshell.

I closed my eyes, taking the first book I touched from among the ones scattered on my bed and opened it randomly. It was called *Shadow Dancing in the Marriage Zone* by Michael Ventura and read, *"We are all, every one of us, full of horror. If you are getting married to make yours go away, you will only succeed in marrying your horror to someone else's horror; your two horrors will have the marriage, you will bleed and call that love."*

Another one was called, *In the Meantime: Finding Yourself and the Love You Want,* by Iyanla Vanzant. It assured that *"We attempt to create this union with others before first creating it within ourselves. This is absolutely impossible. You cannot get love from the outside until you are love on the inside."*

Oh, for the love of Madame Curie! I hadn't brought horrors into my marriage and it wasn't so easy to have "love on the inside" when the person you love, respect, even admire, throws you away like a steaming *malanga.* I didn't need another book to tell me the obvious or what was too late to fix. I needed a solution.

I decided to put aside my internal goal and try instead to advance my external one: the heartbreak pill.

First, my theory:

If romantic feelings are in the brain (a proven fact) and are regulated by chemical substances produced by the human body (also proven), then to regulate romantic feelings, all I had to do was administer the very same chemical substances to the brain in larger or smaller amounts, depending on the result I wanted to achieve.

Good. I had already determined that there were eight substances possibly responsible for heartbreak. But which one held the key to control?

I began drawing a human brain. It looked like a snow crystal ball filled with water. But besides snow, mine also held dozens of minuscule, colored cables, intertwining in a complicated skein of perfect, precise, patterns.

These patterns actually exist. They're made of chemical circuits or neurotransmitters and there are many in the crystal snow globe that is the mind, hence the problem: How to avoid the possibility that any remedy would result in a general effect? I didn't want someone to take the pill and stop loving everyone and everything. Just whoever made him suffer, a kind of selective immunity aid. I had to find the substance that regulated the brain's balance, the one capable of turning the snowstorm of heartbreak into a crystal ball where snowflakes fell softly, like on a Christmas card.

The phone rang and I was getting up to answer it when I

saw myself in the bedroom mirror and stopped, frozen in time . . . because I looked actually . . . really . . . really . . . beautiful, and so unlike the woman in that cafeteria restroom a few lifetimes ago. My curls were behaving, falling like water over my shoulders, my eyeglasses barely hiding the shining excitement of search in my eyes. And me, laptop on lap, floating amid books, magazines, and notebooks, as if the bed were a canoe in a river of words without hurry. In the middle of all this, my face recognizing itself again, looking almost happy.

"*Negrita,* please call me, I need to talk to you. Please . . . let's not end it like this."

It was him on my answering machine, using the tone he used when he wanted to make up after a small fight, and my heart jumped out the window after him in two seconds flat. Of course, the message had a couple of unnecessary words. It said "let's not end it like this" instead of "let's not end it."

But it was him, and I spent a long time agonizing about whether or not I should call him back. No. Not tonight, I decided. I'd seem desperate. Maybe this was my chance to do things right. Let him stew so he'd think twice before doing something like this again.

I ignored the voice inside me that said "*Si serás pendeja.* One single voice mail and you're already forgiving him? Fine, I've already ordered you a nice shelving unit in which to store your *cuernos.*"

A knock on the front door interrupted the self-pity party. It was accompanied by familiar voices, and I reluctantly put aside my improvised lab and went to open it, heart still teetering on a ledge from Martin's call.

"Please! They were obviously fake, Gilberto. When have you seen real breasts looking like igloos?"

"Looked real to me."

"Sure, it's not like it's hard to slip you a soft one . . ."

"You speaking for yourself? All I'm saying is, if they aren't real, they sure look it, that's all."

"Just to be clear: that doesn't make me jealous. *Ni me va ni me viene, ¿eh?* Just in case."

"All right, all right. Let's just drop it. We're here."

"I wonder how she's doing . . ."

"Splendidly, I'm sure. Got it from her mother: strong and stubborn. Do you have the *ajiaco?*"

"Right here, lots of meat, corn, and pumpkin. Go ahead. Knock again."

I stayed behind the door, waiting for them to stop bickering, hopefully in this lifetime.

Tún tu cu tún tún . . . tún tún.

"Chico, a little more stamina, no?" said Benji.

"You going to tell me how to knock now?"

I opened the door before the bickering turned full-scale.

"It had no strength and no rhythm. I may not be a music teacher, but I do have clean ears, okay?" said Benji before turning to me. "How are you, honey? Look at you. You're thin as spaghetti."

"I'm fine, Benji. *Bendición,* Papi," I greeted them with a kiss. "I thought you guys were in the Keys."

"Changed our minds," said Papi not looking at me.

"Yeah, too hot to drive so far," said Benji.

"You should've called me. I'd have made you something to eat."

"Not to worry. We've bought a little bit of everything," said Papi.

"Yeah, Eri, don't worry. Just talk to your dad and I'll take care of everything," said Benji as he carried some plastic Publix bags into the kitchen before I could stop him.

Papi was already there, passing judgment on everything, starting with my fridge.

"And the food in this house?"

"Don't start, Gilberto. Leave her alone."

"Haven't had time to shop for groceries . . ."

"So what are you eating? Actually, why aren't you eating?"

"Why else? Her idiot husband. . . ."

"I seem to remember that idiot's still your boss," retorted Papi.

Benji worked as a payroll aide at Martin's agency. He's gifted with numbers and they loved him for it.

"You guys want some coffee? Actually, I'm out of coffee . . . Wine? Beer?"

"Beer? Hear that, Gil . . . there's no food, but there's beer," said Benji, raising his salt and pepper eyebrows at Papi conspiratorially.

As I'd already guessed, these two were on rescue patrol.

The unlikeliest of couples, I think my father found that feeling of "us against the world" in Benji, that unconditional love he thought he'd lost forever when my mother died.

They met when my dad was fifty-three years old, almost five years after her death. One day, Papi told me he'd met someone almost as special as Mami, someone with a huge heart he knew I'd like very much and with whom he was planning to move in with if I agreed. The next day he introduced me to Benji.

"So . . . you're gay?" I'd asked later, a bit perplexed.

"Looks like it, *mi'ja* . . . Life's strange, huh?"

And to this day.

My father continues to be a true bohemian joker, an eternal optimist who lives for his music and believes with all his heart that everything always works out for the best. And if it doesn't, it won't be the end of the world, because, as he's fond of saying, *"Más alante vive gente,"* which means, "There are other people living a little farther down the road."

He's sweet and super paternal, but when he's angry, worried, or nervous, he turns into this hysterical entity one wants to run away from. He has hair the color of dark chocolate, like me, big watery eyes, and he parts his hair on the side like a network TV anchor.

Meanwhile, Benji is his perfect opposite. He's fifty-seven, three years Papi's junior, and he's handsome in the style of male models you usually see in tie, liquor, and briefcase ads. He's slender, although he sports a slight paunch he tries to hide with overly large cotton shirts, which end up giving him a bit of a pregnant air, not that I'd dare tell him. He has salt and pepper hair, tan skin, green eyes, and an expression of perennial, mother hen worry on his face. Oh . . . one more thing. He's such a huge feminist, he tried to convince Papi to sign up for the Peace Corps and go with him to Afghanistan, long before war broke out between that country and the United States, only because he read somewhere what the Taliban government did to women there. He happily introduces himself as my stepmother, is proudly on top of things when it comes to *"la niña's"* affairs and is a great confidant and enabler. He's ultra-liberal, kind to disgusting extremes, and I adore him.

"Don't worry about us, *mi'ja,* we're really just here to keep you company," said Papi looking at my big messy house. "By the way, when's your appointment with your lawyer? Want me to go with you?"

Yeah, right. That was all I needed. Maybe this time the lunatic throwing things at people could be my father instead of me.

"Oh, that's all right, Papi. No need. Actually, why don't you tell me about that bolero you've been composing?"

"Ennhhhh . . . you know . . . it's going, it's going . . . not quite there yet. Sure you don't want me to go with you?"

"Of course she's sure. What do you want to go over there for?" said Benji, who knows my dad better than if he'd given birth to him.

"Okay, *Chico,* okay. When you're right, you're right," said Papi, walking over to me.

Looking into my eyes, he touched my cheek with his hairy, sunburned, wrinkled hand, then smoothed my eyebrows the way Mami used to.

"You're my baby girl, Erika. Just like when you were little . . . and you're going to be fine, you hear?"

For a moment, it was like being nine years old again and running into the house, crying because the neighborhood boys had baptized me "Erika, the hysterical."

"Gilberto, for the love of God, they're children," my mother would say, without looking away from the soap opera of the moment: *Cristina Bazán.*

But it was too late because my father had but to see a single tear on my face before immediately putting on his weathered leather flip-flops and walking out with the rolled-up newspaper he'd been reading.

"All right . . . let's see . . . who's the sanguinary smart-ass with nothing better to do than to mess with my little girl? Who is it? So I know whose father to go to, and see if he's going to mess with me when I tell him what a bully his son is that he has to bother little girls."

Needless to say, no neighborhood boy ever dared answer him, so he'd look at them all up and down with his scariest Tony Soprano face and say ominously, "Ah, that's what I thought."

Back home, Erika, the hysterical, would be rewarded with ice cream, Oreo cookies, hot chocolate, or any other treat found. Back then, he'd say the same thing he was saying now: "You'll be fine, you hear me?"

Only now, Erika, the hysterical, only knew to nod before escaping to the living room sofa. Papi and Benji followed me, sitting on each side of me like Buckingham Palace guards, and we stayed that way for a while, stiff as corpses, staring at the walls while we listened to the faraway street noises that seeped through the windows.

"Erika, you want me to quit . . . in solidarity?" Benji asked, breaking the silence.

"For the record, I don't support fuddy-duddy stay-at-homes," Papi tried to make a joke.

"No, don't do that for me, Benji. You love your work and I know that Martin appreciates you—"

"I've been thinking," Papi interrupted me, "that maybe this is for the best. It's not like I want you to get divorced, but if things aren't going well, then I tell you there's nothing worse than living a lie."

"My marriage wasn't a lie," I said with a little more force than necessary.

"That's not what he said, honey," Benji tried to interject.

"Papi, you think I'm capable of pretending everything's fine for years when it's not? There was nothing, absolutely nothing, different!" I said it more for myself than for them. "And I was very happy, okay? I mean, we were always kidding around," I said, counting off with my fingers as I propelled myself into my idealized version of the near perfect past. "We slept together every single night, we talked about everything . . . and we had so much fun with just about any old thing. . . ."

If there's something you should never do when heartbroken, it's to enumerate the good qualities of the life you miss or of the person breaking your heart. I had tried not to feel the emptiness, not to think about how much and how constantly I missed him, about his way of putting out his arm for me to hold on to, or of his way of greeting me when calling to make up after some silly fight *(¿Negrita linda? Mami . . . ¿Mamita? ¡Negri!),* or of the way he pulled me to him when he wanted me.

I sighed, forgetting that Papi and Benji were watching me intensely, identical troubled frowns on their foreheads.

"Well, maybe this had to happen so you could move on with your life. I'd like you to reconcile, but not if you're going to be like this."

I thought of Martin's message on my answering machine and decided to keep it to myself until I was sure there was a chance of reconciliation.

"Really, Eri," said Benji. "You can get any man you want, better, more handsome, with more money and without airs of superiority like Martin."

"I don't want another man, Benji."

"Well, like your dad says, 'other people . . . farther down the road. . . . My God, *Chiquita, mira que,* you're difficult to console sometimes."

"Marriages aren't perfect. Many couples go through crisis . . . and they recover. They make up and get back together, even after the divorce is signed, sealed, and delivered. Look at Elizabeth Taylor . . . and Pamela Anderson."

Benji looked at Papi. Papi looked at Benji and then at the floor, moving his head from side to side.

"Mi'ja, just tell me . . . what evil strain of cocaine did you sniff? Because the truth is slapping you hard in the face and you don't want to see it," he said still shaking his head as if he couldn't believe what he was hearing. "And what do you mean by Elizabeth Taylor and Pamela Anderson? Both of them got divorced again!"

I'd forgotten that little detail.

"Calm down and leave her alone, Gil. You know no one learns from secondhand experience, and then of course, tonight, you'll be the one unable to sleep with the ulcer acting up."

But Papi kept right on complaining and giving signs of being well on his way to working up his own temper. So Benji got up from the sofa, put both hands on his hips and stuck out his chest, the better to glare at him with.

"Oooooyeme, tú tranquilo," he said as if I weren't in the room. "Our girl's gone cuckoo? Well, that's that. What're you going to do? We'll be right here to pick up the pieces, but right now, nothing we can do, okay? You listening to me?"

See what I mean? They fight, but they love each other and are like two wild mother bears when it comes to protecting me.

"Your poor mother must be turning in her grave, Erika,"

Benji said to me now. "Poor woman didn't raise you to be a doormat to your idiot husband and, forgive me Gilberto, but Erika. . . . Erika, I have something to tell you."

"All right, all right. I'll be calm, but don't make her worse," said Papi nervously.

"Aren't you the one who said it's better this way? Erika, yesterday—"

"What do you want me to say?" Daddy interrupted him again. "I find her here in this house, stick thin and asking one foot for permission to move the other . . ."

When he realized I was listening, seeing myself through his eyes, he said, "Don't pay attention to me, *mi'ja*. I'm a stupid old man. Maybe you're right. Men go through these things, people remarry. . . . Middle-age crisis and all . . . Let's just leave it at that . . ."

I wished him right with all my heart. For myself . . . and for him . . . and even for Benjamin.

"These things happen to men? What kind of advice is that, *Pipo?"* asked Benji. "She needs to move on, find another man, period. Eri, listen to me—"

"You know, I'm getting hungry. Where's that *ajiaco?"* I said, trying to disperse stress by changing the subject.

"Erika!" insisted Benji placing his hands on my shoulders. "Martin got engaged last night."

The water in my crystal snow globe must've risen and soared like a hand-sized tsunami because suddenly my fingers were trembling as if electrified, the secondary effect of the lightning strike that had struck the exact center of my chest.

"What?"

"He got engaged yesterday."

"What?"

"He got engaged. Yesterday."

"What?"

"That he's en—"

"Stop, Benji!" Papi screamed at him, exasperated.

"Can't be," I said finally. "Today . . . a little while ago . . . he called me; said he wants to talk to me."

"The bastard," said Benji. "Of course. He's afraid you'll find out any which way and be so upset you'll put him out to dry without a penny."

"Oh my God . . ." I said walking to the nearest wall and proceeding to bang my head against it in hopes of cracking myself unconscious, traveling ten minutes . . . or ten weeks back in time.

"You see? That's what your chatty tongue does," Papi said to Benji even as he ran to me and held me so I couldn't move.

"I'm sorry, *pero la verdad es hija de Dios,* and it's not fair that you're here suffering while he celebrates an engagement he has no right to make until he brings closure to his engagement with you. Let me see, I think they call it marriage."

I had to calm down. I had to. I'd just allowed myself to get carried away by senseless hope. That was all.

"I'm all right. I'm fine now. I'm okay," I said touching my head. "But where's that *ajiaco* or were you just teasing me with it?"

Two hours later, after pushing myself to eat a whole plate of *ajiaco* in order to convince them I was perfectly all right, and promising to call them every night so they'd know I was, they left.

Then, finally, I allowed myself to think of Martin, not

crying or screaming. My marriage really was a horror. And this blood I called love was nothing other than a chemical imbalance, a big bunch of lies in a circularly arranged thread; nothing in the middle but a damn tornado I'd have to keep fighting to defeat.

{eight}

Later—much, much, much later—I lay in bed thinking about her, wondering who she was. Wondering, who was the bitch Martin had not been able to wait to kneel down on one knee for, in front of all his friends? Who was the woman who'd taken it all away when she accepted that ring? Not just my husband, but everything that came with him, like my home, and certain friends, who now had to be too embarrassed to call me or afraid of taking sides. Moments I used to treasure now seemed vulgar and unclean.

It was almost dawn and I hadn't slept; making and remaking the "other" in my mind. Last night, between Martin's call and finding out about the engagement so suddenly, I hadn't wanted to worry the old men and so I had asked nothing, not even her name. Now, with morning blooming everywhere but within me, I wanted to know so badly I almost called Benji, perfectly aware that after satisfying my curiosity I'd have to listen to endless advice and warnings of doom. But after picking up the phone and putting it down again a half dozen times, I finally said, "Oh, to Hell with her." Whoever she was, I hoped she drowned in her own saliva during sleep. Yes, to hell with her, but in the meantime, I couldn't stay here, swimming in my own shit pool like an unfamous Frida or an untalented Sylvia Plath, waiting for "her" to dive down into the Hell I'd carefully imagined for her.

I had to do something worthwhile with this state I was in, and I headed down to the main branch of Miami-Dade's public library determined to continue the search for the substance or substances that would cure love.

It's a huge old building and the reading room was almost empty. A couple of homeless-looking guys pretended to read in order to enjoy the air-conditioning and the silence of the room. Another, his stench strong enough to punch me breathless from across the room, slept placidly on a chair, out of sight of the librarians who, on the other side of the room, worked diligently on perfecting the required air of strictness, pointedly fixating on anything that moved with looks that ranged between inexpressive and slightly mortified, as if they were mimes or sentinels instead of librarians.

Six hours and thirty-seven minutes later, I was starving and my eyes hurt from reading selectively from seventeen books, one hundred and twelve documents, and seventy-three microfilms on everything from love scandals of the rich and famous to medical investigations about the tear duct system.

And just when I was beginning to think I was an idiot for wasting a beautiful Sunday in an old library, I saw something that made my brain flip.

It was a small book, old and tattered, written by Ryan Noah, a retired scientist. From the publisher's notes, I learned that he'd been diagnosed with a rare type of schizophrenia shortly after this recipe book of aphrodisiac cooking, which used regular food as well as chemical substances as ingredients, was published.

Going back to the microfilm archive, I learned that the originally self-published book had created quite a controversy in academic circles because the chemical substances it named had either not been discovered or not been produced outside the human body when the book was first published—in 1825.

One recipe was titled "Wine, Chocolate, and Soft Light" and listed three ingredients—wine, chocolate, and soft light—without preparation instructions. In fact, the only other words on the page were an author's note stating that wine, chocolate, and soft light could stimulate dopamine in the brain, producing a sensation similar to that of cocaine, which, curiously enough, had not been harvested from the plant before the mid-nineteenth century, a quarter century *after* the book was written.

Another recipe called for endorphins, the natural substance the body produces to fight physical pain. There were copious notes from Noah in the margin stating that the constant presence of a loved one was essential for those who wanted to use the recipe, because it stimulated the production of endorphins, while at the same time warning against dependency: *"Once you have the savage who can stimulate the production of endorphins in your power, you cannot let her go! Your body needs her to produce the equivalent of minuscule pills against bodily pain! If she leaves, you'll be like a wounded soldier without your morphine, crying out for your daily dose of the disgusting drug."*

I skipped ahead to the final pages and found a photo of the author. He looked totally, utterly, and absolutely crazy, and yet there was a certain kindness in his stormy eyes, as if he'd once been young, happy, and handsome and life or heartbreak had done away with all of it. I looked at the black-and-white photo for a long time, feeling connected to the man in it, as if he could actually understand me. As if he were the only one who could.

A recipe for potatoes oven-baked in cilantro sauce called for PEA, or phenylethylamine, the natural amino acid that shares in the addictive effects of amphetamines. According to Noah, a little PEA would season the potatoes, give his recipe a "special flavor." He advised obtaining it through either a touch of the hands or the "deliciously violent meeting of the eyes."

"But my naive readers should beware. If your hands sweat, your breathing agitates, or your pulse quickens, you could be in the midst of an overdose. Perhaps in the future, we will learn to rearrange this molecule's atoms, placing its destructive power at the service of this ghastly revolting human race."

I fixated my gaze on that word . . . rearrange . . . to move around, to restructure . . . which in chemistry is like re-creating, making new, since the placement of an element can change the core of any material that it's a part of.

That was it.

That was the starting point for my pill.

The key was in re-creating a PEA molecule, then mixing it with the right amount of endorphins. (Why hadn't it occurred to me earlier?) I'd been thinking about mixing existing substances to create a new one, but had not considered doing my mixing within an existing chemical. Adding the endorphins to a restructured PEA molecule would temporarily repress the euphoric-addictive effect of love, thereby diminishing pain and giving the brain time to "break the habit."

I was thrilled as I walked briskly through the narrow bookcase partitions, searching for tomes to check out the basic interaction between drugs and their receptor; the design, distribution and metabolism of drugs; neurochemistry; the chemistry of pain; and existing drugs that affect perception, behavior, and disposition.

Another good sign? I felt silly for carrying on about the demise of my marriage when my cure was just waiting for my heart and brain to put the puzzle pieces together.

Once I had all I needed, I decided to take advantage of the quiet, the computers, and my sudden burst of energy to do a quick search for a divorce lawyer. I had another meeting with Martin's attorney in two weeks and no idea of what I'd be up against.

I wrote "Miami + divorce lawyer" in the Google search box. There were 133,812 entries. The search "Miami + female + divorce lawyer" turned up little more than 806 results. After looking at geeky lawyer photo after geeky lawyer photo, I decided to play a little and added the word "celestial" in the search box; I needed a higher being with a law degree, a license to practice and a weakness for women suffering from a combination of sadness and anger.

The computer responded to my search with a message that said "0 results for Miami + lawyer + celestial." But I kept on trying, inspired by old walls and tall ceilings and the rows of knowledge and discovery around me. The normal way of doing things had not worked for me lately. What was there to lose? I typed "Miami + lawyer + magical." This time the computer didn't even respond; stayed frozen for a long time. Last one, I said to myself, and wrote: "Miami + lawyer + spiritual." The message on my computer showed one lone result: Attorney Consuelo De Pokkos, probably a cover for a porn site.

The next image on the computer was of a common woman, round face, definitely Hispanic, with pure white skin and teeth like lightbulbs in the middle of her comically broad smile. She had eyes that reminded me of an old Chinese woman and thick, black glasses. Her brown, curly, shoulder-length hair finished the picture: Attorney Consuelo De Pokkos, spiritual lawyer.

There were several testimonials from satisfied clients on the site. They all talked candidly about how Ms. De Pokkos had represented them in their divorce proceedings, helping them to obtain the feeling of closure that allowed them to move on.

Sounded good to me. My day in court. Maybe Consuelo De Pokkos was just what I needed. I printed her contact info and went home, where there were six messages from Martin regarding something important he had to tell me and wanted "to have the courtesy of doing it personally." I disconnected the phone.

The next morning, I sat in front of Attorney De Pokkos and marveled at the amazing similarity between the image in the computer and the one in front of me.

"Widow?" she asked

"No, just divorcing," I said.

"Same thing," she said, smiling wistfully. "Let's see, Erika, that's your name, right? Tell me everything."

Where to start? I realized that despite weeks of complaining, crying, bitching, and hollering about Martin and the terrible, horrible, very bad infamy perpetrated against me, I'd never told anyone "everything," not even myself.

Instead of responding with "I need a divorce and I want you to represent me," which would have been the logical thing to say, I said:

"My husband doesn't love me. He doesn't want me. He . . . cheated on me with another woman and now they're engaged. I feel humiliated, embarrassed . . . our families, our friends, the people at his work . . . and he . . . just treats it all as if our marriage was nothing, as if he can't wait to erase our life together and replace it with a better one. . . ."

I stopped talking for a few seconds, feeling the pain of each word, a pain I'd been carrying inside me for weeks and which now sprouted from me with the strength of water coming out of a broken pipe.

"Attorney De Pokkos . . ." I tried to continue.

"Oh, please, call me Consuelo."

"Consuelo, I—"

"No. Attorney Consuelo," she corrected me again with a weirdly placid smile that made me wonder about her mental health.

"Attorney Consuelo, I need legal representation, obviously, but I realize as I talk to you that I also need to know what happened. I want my marriage validated. It *was* real, it existed, and it was important to me. It wasn't some meaningless thing . . . and I, at least, valued it and respected it."

"I see," she said, not seeing anything at all.

"I don't want permanent economic gain," I hurried to explain. "But right now, It's the only thing that will make him stop and think. I don't want him to be able to destroy this marriage without giving me the opportunity to say what I have to say, without him having to tell me, to my face, what happened and why he did this and—"

"What in the world are you talking about?" she interrupted me. "You can't dictate what someone else will value or not. So your husband's a pig. That's reality. He's not the first and, frankly, I hope he's not the last because I'd starve to death. . . ."

She was silent for a few seconds, as if the idea of an epidemic of faithful husbands constituted the grand social quandary of the future.

"But back to your case, you don't want to understand or make anyone value anything. You want to go back to your husband, but not before teaching him a good lesson. You want to destroy him a little, don't you? You want him to suffer what you are suffering, isn't that right, Erika?"

"I don't think that's even possible anymore, and I really think your explanation is a bit simplistic," I defended myself.

"It is. You're human, you love, the person you love humiliates you, replaces you, forgets about you. You say you want to 'understand,' but if you really wanted to, you would have. What you really want is for him to have to continue to explain himself so that he can feel guilty, realize he's made a mistake, and come back to you."

Coño. Damn crazy logical woman.

"Is it so bad to want things to be the way they were?" I accepted finally.

"Of course not. That's just how stupid we all are. But even if you get back with him, you'll need your little revenge, and you know why? Because you don't want to feel you allowed the infidelity. You want to feel you did something about it, stood up for yourself, refused to be an accomplice."

"But I did . . ."

"But you didn't. Your worst-case scenario has already happened, and at some level, you allowed it to."

"But . . . what does that mean? That he has the right to go on with his life without care or pain? Without mourning us for so much as a single minute? It's . . . it's just not fair. I want this . . . ending . . . to hurt. We should both be hurting."

"I thought you just wanted to understand, to validate, thought you didn't want money . . ."

"I don't. Not really. But there has to be something I can do here because I can't live with this anger in my chest."

"Never fails: show me a woman who doesn't want revenge and I'll show you a woman who secretly hopes to reconcile with her husband. The minute they see the light . . ." she said, more to herself than to me. "Erika, fighting for more money than is due you or delaying the divorce is not going to help your self-esteem or your pride, and it certainly won't make you happy. It will just make you old . . . and fat, cause you more than one blister and a couple of bunions . . . but you can do that, if that's what you really want. Your decision."

"It's not about revenge," I said, standing. "I thought you were a real lawyer."

"I am. I thought you were a coward, and you are. Why aren't you embarrassed to admit you want your husband back, yet you won't admit you want your revenge first? Do you want it for free? Ah, you want Attorney Consuelo to do everything! You want me to ruin my 'karmic' record, get the wrinkles, gain the extra pounds, *and* the bunions! Well, I won't if you won't do your part."

This woman had to be drunker than a fly swimming in rum, but I stood there, unable to move, before sitting down again.

"Now then, do you want to take revenge against your husband, yes or no?" she asked moving her face close to mine and staring into my brain with her Chinese-like eyes twinkling like identical silver spoons.

"Well, yes," I gave up.

It felt strangely comforting to say it. Attorney Consuelo's way was unorthodox, and she *was* a bit heavy on the crazy, but I felt relieved somehow. And her way didn't mean she didn't know what she was doing, I convinced myself. After all, anyone who'd met me two weeks before would've said I was crazier than she, yet when it came to my job I'd been able to keep it together.

"Yes," I said again. "I want him to be sorry. I want him to beg, to admit he made a mistake. In fact, it'd be perfect if he tried to come back . . . only I'd have already gotten over him, rejecting him without a thought," I said, letting myself be carried away by my own fantasy. "Then, alone and confused, he'd try to get her back, but she wouldn't have him, afraid he could not sustain the lifestyle he wooed her with. And then he'd have no choice but to realize she was a piece of cowhide for whom he left a good woman who loved him," I smiled, satisfied. "And he would cry, feeling forgotten . . ."

Attorney Consuelo stared at me.

"Oooooh-key then, Erika . . . This is good. You've done good. I can't help you if you don't tell the truth. Sometimes it's ugly, but you still have to look it in the eye and show it you're not afraid. That's what you've just done. However, I can't give you revenge, much less guarantee your husband will come back, in fact, just the opposite."

She was quiet again, as if she were on one of the imaginary trips she seemed to take frequently, then added:

"What I can do is help you understand what happened and why, so you can move on. I can also negotiate a fair settlement for you. It won't be vengeance, but it'll bring you peace."

I thought about it for a minute and decided I didn't want to go through this with another lawyer.

"Okay, do it your way, no vengeance," I said with a show of hands, feeling exhausted.

Attorney Consuelo smiled as if she were filming a toothpaste commercial and the director had just yelled "action." Leaning toward me, she smoothed my hair with her long, red nails and I was strangely comforted, remembering my mother.

"Very good, Erika: divorce without vengeance. Receiving what's yours and nothing more. Of course, your husband will try to give you less than what's rightfully yours, so in order to achieve justice, we won't have any choice but to make the poor sap suffer a bit . . . for his own good, you understand . . . all to help him achieve a level of comprehension and sensitivity," she said winking at me before jumping up from her seat with such energy she startled me.

"Now, what do you say to some nice, soothing tea, huh?"

{nine}

"What are you hiding from me, you beastly piece of brain?" I said, in my best Wicked Witch of the West imitation.

For days, I'd been trying to come up with a practical way of extracting PEA molecules from every imaginable source. True, I could have just bought them from any of the laboratories that supplied chemical compounds to NuevoMed, but then I'd have had a lot of explaining to do if anyone in the finance department decided to do one of their random purchasing audits.

So I settled on my own sweat as my primary source, at least until I could come up with a reasonable explanation for buying a compound that had nothing to do with Varitex, and got down to the business of examining it under a microscope. Soon after, I recognized a formation consisting of two handsome carbons and one absolutely gorgeous nitrogen.

"There you are, my pretty, come to mama," I cackled, and

would have taken my witch impersonation to ridiculous lengths had I not been interrupted.

"Busy?"

It was Lizandra Salinas-Montes. The real witch.

"Not really . . . didn't hear you knock."

"I can't imagine 'not really' making you that excited?" she said, making her beady eyes so small, I fully expected her tongue to dart out at me with a hiss.

"Did you need something?" I asked, mentally adding, "you stupid microbe."

"Just the Daytime Varitex questionnaire. Is it ready?" asked the witch, scanning the counter space around my microscope; devoid of files, data tables, or other paraphernalia useful in keeping a record of chemical observations.

"It's still missing a few touches, but I'll email it to you as soon as it's ready," I said, thinking that it was missing so many "touches," it hadn't even been started.

"Uh, Erika, I'm guessing you already know but . . . we're considering several P.R. agencies . . . to help us with all the . . . government relations work, among other things and . . . I wanted to show a couple of people what some of the key points to address will be . . . you know, general consumer perceptions—"

"Lizandra, forgive me, I just really need to finish what I'm doing right now. Don't worry, you'll have it the minute it's ready," I said, cutting her off to deny her the pleasure of telling me she'd hired the husband who fired me.

"Well, it's just that one of the agencies we're talking to . . . is your ex-husband's."

In Spanish, we have a name for the constant itch in Lizandra's heart: *ganas de joder.*

"You mean my husband's. We're not divorced yet."

"Only a matter of time, I understand. And I'm sorry, of course," she said, still running her eyes over my desk.

"Of course. And you're right. I did know about it and I was curious . . . How exactly did they happen to end up on *your* . . . short list? I mean, they don't have a government relations division and they've never represented a drug company," I said, emphasizing the "you" so she couldn't hide behind the company "we."

Lizandra laughed, as if she now had me right were she wanted me.

"A mutual friend made the connection. Well, actually," she said, as if she were giving me a stock tip, "it was my sister, Marisol."

"Your sister?" I said, searching my memory and quickly finding the perky blond who'd asked to "borrow" Martin for a dance during the company Christmas party. She'd even thanked me later, saying I'd saved her from being a wallflower.

"The one I met at the Christmas party?"

"Yes, that's her. I'd forgotten you'd met," said Lizandra with a cautious smile.

I remembered her perfectly, the sister. She was one of those women whose main attractiveness resides in their ability to pull off the perfect dumb slut act. They wear low necklines and bright red dresses. They keep their eyes very open and their lips in a perennial pout. They giggle and act weak and in constant need of a man's support. What could she possibly have to do with Martin being about to land the NuevoMed account? Oh, God. It couldn't be.

"She's working on finishing an advertising and public relations degree and an old friend at the agency . . . oh, what am I saying, of course you know Fernando . . . he arranged for her to do an internship at the firm as a favor to me," Lizandra blabbed on.

I prayed I was crazy. I prayed what she was so obviously dying to tell me wouldn't be what I was thinking. I prayed I'd be able to fly if I flapped my arms. But even as I prayed, I went in for my own kill, unable to back off.

"Don't you have to be about to graduate . . . for an internship? And wouldn't she be a bit too old to still be 'working on finishing' a degree she started almost a decade ago?" I added.

"She did take a bit of a long break," said Lizandra without taking her eyes off mine. "You know, went to Europe, saw the world . . . but she's young . . . not quite thirty yet."

"Really? Go figure, I thought her well over. Must be the European water," I kept teeing the ball, inviting Lizandra to come at me, still hoping against hope she'd prove me wrong.

"On the contrary, Europe did her good," said Lizandra, unable to hide that I had finally succeeded in pissing her off enough to say what she had come to say. "She grew up. She became a woman. In fact, she just got engaged a few days ago," she added with her eyes dead set on mine.

Shit. I'd had the enemy close and her sister even closer the whole time. I completely forgot about Lizandra after that. I forgot she was there, didn't even hear her; my mind frozen on the image of her sister and my husband. Now that I'd finally put a face to the devil's body, my mind couldn't wrap itself around the idea of this being the kind of woman who'd managed to move into his heart before I'd had a chance to move out.

When Lizandra got tired of pulling at the scab on my wounded heart, she took one last look around the lab, still trying to figure out what I'd been investigating when she'd walked in, and left.

I knew it was important to keep her out of my business, so I pulled myself together and wrote out the damn questionnaire, printed a hard copy, locked my office, and went straight to my boss's office.

You see, in the pharmaceutical industry, the balance of power lies in knowing what other people are trying to find out before they do. Just like I imagine in the TV industry, it's about knowing which shows are being considered for air, and in the stock market it's knowing a company's financials before they're officially revealed. That's why Lizandra was so interested in finding out what I was up to. Because even though she was a senior vice president and had much more corporate clout than I, she also knew that in our business, the real power is in innovation. And that was my kingdom.

I found Santiesteban holding his head with his hands.

"Come in, Erika, come in. I'll be right with you," he said when he noticed me standing in the doorway.

We got along great, Santi and I. He was a good boss; smart, generous, an idealist of sorts. And although his role was more salesman than scientist, he had genuine love for science and for the company.

He always wore white and that, along with the thick eyebrows and the bushy mustache he combed constantly, made Papi nickname him "Mister Dandyman" when he first met him at another Christmas party.

"Something wrong, Santi?"

"The usual . . . numbers and more numbers. What's that you got there?"

"Questionnaire for Daytime Varitex."

"Ah, good, good," he said, skimming it. "This is very good. I just don't know if it's enough."

"I'm sorry?"

"Don't you feel there's something missing?" he asked, pointing out the window.

"Like what?" I asked, still thinking he was somehow referring to the questionnaire.

"Something . . . a big idea . . . something amazing . . . capable of motivating big capitals, something to energize the scientific community. Something worthy of our times."

"I can't believe it. Reynaldo Santiesteban . . . finally bored of promoting migraine as the smallest great big epidemic cursing humanity," I joked.

Santiesteban was known throughout the scientific circles of Miami for thinking about migraine 24/7. In fact, about once a month he'd saunter into the lobby cafeteria for Cuban coffee, spot us having lunch, ask to sit with us, and, within minutes, manage to switch any conversation to the topic of migraine.

"Us" was usually my lunch-eating posse of chemical technician friends: Ally, a recent grad with a sweet face and blue-green-purple hair; Rony, who we nicknamed "Testosterony" because he was always talking about sex and celebrities he wanted to sleep with; and Wanda, who couldn't forgive herself for having slept with him once and now thought Rony was the simplest man-pig to roam Miami—and frequently told him so.

And there we'd be, eating, listening, and watching Santi

transform himself into a bard on steroids and the cafeteria into the Nuyorican Poets Cafe, telling us it was up to us at Nuevo-Med to "live, breathe, and sing" the truth about migraine to the general public, before swallowing his coffee in one gulp and leaving as quickly as he'd come.

"Yo, Dude, you think the bro' talks about migraine when he's sticking it to his wife?" Rony would say.

"Why are you so gross? That's what I want to know?" Wanda would say then, rolling her eyes.

"What'd I do? I just said the dude has got to . . ."

"We heard you, Testosterony. Let Wanda eat."

So you can see how I'd have fainted if Santi had admitted boredom with migraine and Varitex the afternoon I went to his office.

"On the contrary, Erika. I think we have the best medicine against migraine. But now what? Do we stop? We create a dozen variations of the same thing and that's it?"

"Well, you're kind of preaching to the converted here, but I didn't know the company was looking to put some money into a little dreaming right now."

"It isn't, but you know me. Pay no attention. Just ignore me. Now go home. Good job."

I was almost out the door when he stopped me.

"Erika, one more thing . . . Has Lizandra told you she's considering Quintero, Silva and Echegoyén? I asked her to have the courtesy . . . How's that going?"

I shrugged my shoulders to say that it was going like any other divorce, except that it was my own.

"You know you can count on me, on Marta and on me, for anything you need."

"I know, Santi. I have to go now. I'll let you dream," I said, winking at him before I left.

When I got home, I had a letter from the president of the Democratic Party of Miami Beach, scolding me for my lack of contribution and my absence during the chapter's last two fund-raisers. She hoped I wouldn't take offense if she withdrew me from the activities committee board and knew I'd understand her need to reward those members who'd given themselves "body and soul" to the good of the country. In any case, she enclosed an envelope, in case I wanted to do my part for the future of the United States of America.

Great, Erika. You have no husband, children, or money. You're almost out of house and home, and now the Democratic Party, who rejects no one, has rejected you. What you have is incipient cellulite, bills to pay, and a divorce conference coming up in a week in which you'll be represented by a nutty, self-proclaimed spiritual attorney and face a husband who doesn't remember your name and whose future sister-in-law happens to work across the hall, in case you ever need a reminder of what's happening. Keep it up and one of these days you could win a prize. Oh, no, sorry. No prizes for failure.

I went to my bedroom in a funk and turned on the TV. They were rerunning the episode of *Friends* in which Ross tells Rachel that he cheated on her because they were on a break. I'd seen it a million times, but that night it bored me in a sad, empty sort of way.

I turned off the TV and got one of Lola's books from the night table. The first page I opened to said that whatever the situation is that exists in your life, you have to accept it, because if you don't, it will keep on happening in twenty different ways until you do. In other words, the Democratic Party thing was a duplicate of Martin's abandonment.

So either I accepted that Martin had left me or I'd suffer being left in a million little (or big) ways. I had to be careful. Maybe the next time I went to the bakery, the baker would tell me to go to Hell. "Erika," he'd say to me, "go to Hell. *Al carajo.* No bread for you."

I thought I'd made progress in the acceptance department, but according to the book, the fact that I was suffering these little rejections was proof I had to go further. It said that one way of dealing with our own resistance to accepting reality is to give thanks for everything we have, every day. And if you can't find something to be thankful for? You guessed it: you give thanks for your health.

"Warm up by writing down at least five things that you are thankful for." According to Sarah Ban Breathnach, this simple exercise would make me feel like the richest person in the world. Rich was better than sad, so I tried it.

 FROM THE DESK OF ERIKA LUNA

Dear God, I thank you for:

1. My good friend Lola
2. Papi and Benjamin

. . .

(Give me a moment.)

3. My work

. . .

. . .

4. My health

. . .

. . .

(Take it easy. I'm thinking.)

. . .

. . .

. . .

Coño.

{ten}

Attorney Consuelo advised me to move out immediately even though the only money I had access to at the moment, other than my salary, was a Christmas Club opened under my maiden name that contained five thousand dollars.

"Let's take care of Spirit first. Spirit will provide," she told me.

Of course, that's what happens when you get your advice from a woman who makes you recite positive affirmations and bless the check you're going to give her before accepting it.

"What do you want to be in such a spiritually dense environment for? Go to a friend's house instead. I'll let your husband's lawyer know to deal with me in the future and we'll confirm the date you already had for the one single mediation session."

So I put three business suits in my bag along with a couple of blouses, three panties, two form-fitting bras, a pair of faded cotton cargo pants, a shirt that declares me the planet's sexiest woman, a pair of jeans, a folder with the divorce documents, bank statements, my wedding photo album (just in case Martin or the demon sister he slept with decided to destroy it), and the blue artisan's glass cross we had bought for a dollar while vacationing in Mexico City.

Once in the car, I called Lola.

"What kind of idiotic lawyer tells you to abandon your home? If you're not living in it, it'll be more difficult to get the court to cede it over to you."

"I don't want the house."

"Then you sell it."

"Let him sell it. Either way, he'll have to give me half."

"Or he can stay living in it, the better to enjoy it with his new love."

I didn't answer because the words "his new love" knocked the light right out of me.

"I'm sorry. Forgive me," said Lola. "You know you're more than welcome to live with me, right?"

"Yeah, right. And be the third wheel between you and 'Bob, your friendly neighborhood Florida Power and Light guy?' Uh, no thank you. But by the by, how's that working out?"

"Let's see . . . In one word? Electrifying."

I laughed, happy for my friend.

"Well, you'll have to tell me everything when I go over. Right now, I have to do some major apartment-searching. I may need to stay with you, but only for a few nights until I find something and have it cleaned. Good thing there's not much to move."

"Well, if you really want to move, my friend Rolando just

moved to Barcelona and his apartment is not too far from your job."

"Wait, Rolando the astrologer-*santero*-psychologist?"

"No, Tía. The integrated spiritual solutions consultant."

"What do you mean? He's no longer an astrologer-*santero*-psychologist?"

"Sure, just now he mixes all three things. I'll give you his number. . . ."

The apartment was in Coconut Grove, a pretty yuppified section of Miami, populated by young professionals with too much money to spend on just about everything and a strange mix of low-rise luxury condos and renovated wood cottages.

I parked the Jetta where I could and walked until I found it: 3333 Rice Street was a small bone-colored building with a beautiful wrought-iron gate that looked like it might have been torn from its previous life as an entrance to an Arab mosque.

Someone with a green thumb had planted azaleas in a huge pot just outside the gate and they were beautiful, though still, as if lacking wind to dance, and instead decided to battle the hot Miami sun with a little afternoon nap.

I rang the bell and a short woman with purple-hued hair and Jackie Onassis–style eyeglasses appeared before me instantly.

"I'm here about the apartment that just became available?"

She looked at me as if asking herself whether I was worth missing the rest of the one p.m. *telenovela* for. She must've decided I was because she opened the gate wide, her smile still incomplete.

"For how many?" she asked looking fixedly at my face.

"Just me," I answered looking at her just as fixedly.

"Single then . . ."

This was the moment to answer proudly: "divorced."

"Yes, single."

I must have passed her secret test because she allowed her smile to complete itself, briefly showing me her fake dentures.

"Santa, at your service. Come with me," she said pointing to wooden stairs so clean you could eat on them. We were approaching the third floor when I asked:

"No elevator?"

She glared at me as if she'd let me in from a rainstorm and here I was complaining about a one-drop leak.

"It's a small building and quite old. Only two apartments per floor and space distribution is excellent. You can't find apartments like the one you're going to see. Plus," she said looking me up and down "you can use the exercise."

I pressed my lips together and turned my eyes into slits, but didn't respond because my mother taught me (*a cocotazos, no lo niego*) to respect the elderly, even when they were not respecting me.

After a bit of struggling with the key, the door opened and I was glad for my silence. Sunlight was everywhere. The walls had the texture of beach pebbles and the color of dulce de leche ice cream. The floors were polished hardwood.

I took off my shoes and walked on the bare floor, warm from its noon sunbath. I took off my jacket, loosening my bun, and let my brown leather hobo bag fall to the floor.

"Do you have references?" asked Doña Santa, looking alarmed at what must have seemed to her the beginning of a striptease.

"I'll take it," I answered.

The old woman hesitated, so I opened my purse and began to take out the crisp hundred-dollar bills I had withdrawn from the bank that morning.

"Well, all right," she said. "Let me get the rental contract so I can take down your information."

While I waited, I floated toward the kitchen. It was so small, it was more like a big armoire. The stove and fridge were avocado green and were at least twenty years old, but they were clean and it was true that the apartment was well distributed because, just then, a light wind came in through the open front door . . . and it made the cotton-and-lace kitchen curtains on the other end dance a slow dance from their place above the sink. For some reason, the sight made me happy.

The rest of the apartment consisted of a small bathroom with glass fixtures and Art Deco tile in several shades of blue, and two small bedrooms.

I walked toward the room that faced the street and looked through the trees over Coconut Grove's commercial district. There were boutiques and cafés and people walking hurriedly to have lunch somewhere before continuing to spend.

I was still there, looking at the place where I intended to escape from the life that had escaped me, inhaling the picture-postcard view inhabited by tourists, the well-off, and other worry-free beings, when Doña Santa put a ballpoint pen in my hand and I heard myself ask,

"Where should I sign?"

{eleven}

On the morning of the day I was scheduled to move out of Lola's apartment, where I had finally decided to stay, and into the Rice Street apartment, I awoke to find Lola and her morning meditative ritual:

"I am love. Love comes to me. Love sprouts from me and through me and reaches all humanity. Love grows. It pleases itself and expands within me. Love climbs my mountains. . . ."

I squinted to look at the orange, sunburst-like, George Nelson clock on the wall leading to the kitchen. It was six a.m.

Hours of that annoying thing she calls mantra and I was inspired to create one of my own and holler it back to her. . . .

"I hope love suffocates in you so normal people can sleep in peace."

Silence.

I smiled, satisfied, until I heard her padding to the bathroom, whispering:

"May love protect this house from ill and blackened auras, and from those who doubt the healing powers of the universe. Love lives in my home . . . despite ungrateful friends with an immediate, and hopefully temporary, lack of enthusiasm for life. Love . . ."

But it was Sunday, and after a while the litany began to feel comforting. I fell asleep again and this time, when I awoke, it was to Martin's voice. Martin?!

"She's asleep, Martin. I'll give her your message."

"You know, Lola, the fact that Erika and I are no longer a couple doesn't mean we have to turn our backs on our friends."

"I'm sure your friends will be happy to hear that. Erika's asleep."

I got up from the sofa quietly, licking my teeth and trying to smooth my tousled hair before going to the door, which Lola held open only about an inch wide, as if Martin were an unwelcome salesman or a Jehovah's Witness.

"What do you want, Martin?" I said.

"I want to talk to you," he said with a disapproving look at the old cotton pants and the T-shirt that proclaimed me the planet's sexiest woman when I looked anything but.

"Talk."

"Will you come out for a second, since it's obvious I can't come in?" he said, looking at Lola with his hurt little boy expression.

"Excuse me," said Lola under her breath, moving away from the door to let me through.

I stepped out and we stood there for a few seconds. It had been weeks since I'd last seen him and I couldn't stop looking and examining every detail: the little wrinkles around his eyes, the dozen dotted birthmarks on his face. . . . I noticed he'd just cut his hair and that there were three new white strands, still electric and standing away from the rest of his hair at rest.

"Erika, I came here to talk to you because . . . I don't want us to end like this. We're not enemies, at least I'm not your enemy. I'm a man who loved you . . . very much in fact, and all I want is for us to do this . . . the right way, like—"

"Friends?" I interrupted when I got over the "I loved you" said like that, in past tense.

"Well, yes, why not? Who knows where all this will go . . . who even knows if this is the end of you and me?"

"You certainly seem to."

He sighed, sat down on Lola's bench.

"I've been feeling . . . really terrible, you know? My mind . . . has been like a puzzle," he said as if I was still his favorite confidante.

"It must be cold feet. They say that happens to grooms before the wedding."

To which, to his credit, he got over quickly.

"Who told you?"

"Who cares?"

He looked out onto Lola's front yard jungle, held his head with both hands.

"I care, Erika, because I had things I needed to explain to you before . . ."

"Please don't explain anything," I said, realizing Attorney Consuelo was right: the only explanations I wanted were the ones that would allow me to stay with him.

"Why? Why does it have to be like this? Why can't we do things in a civilized way?"

"Did you do things in a civilized way? You've done what you wanted to do your way and now I have to be civilized?"

"Erika, listen to me: sometimes men . . . sometimes things . . . Okay, look, this situation got out of hand, I admit it. It got away from me and . . . you found out and . . . But, believe it or not, I still have feelings for you. I do. How could I not, after so much . . . life . . . together? And I've . . . I've missed you, and, but, now, there's something I have to . . ."

There. Almost the words I had wanted to hear. Almost, except for the fact that they felt strangely disjointed, as if two different Martins were each trying to say something different at the same time.

Suddenly, he'd lifted me onto his chest, pressing me against him and kissing me as if this were the beginning instead of the end. He surrounded me with both arms, pressing his mouth insistently, almost authoritatively, against mine, threatening to end my resistance as he opened my memories of us and willed me to take a snapshot and bring it to life again, be his once more, for this one moment.

I started to fight back even as so much of me wanted to give in and then, in a heartbeat of desperate intelligence, I stayed still and silent, rejecting him by inertia, while secretly clinging to whatever had made him want me. I felt him and smelled him and made an imprint of the texture of his arms around me, remaining very still inside the warmth of his embrace, all the time listening to the furious sounds of the storm we'd become, knowing it would soon be cold again, probably colder than ever.

He finally let me go, a puzzled look on his face.

"I'm sorry . . . I'm really sorry, Erika. Erika? Do you hear me?"

"No."

"Do you want to go somewhere and talk?"

"No."

"Do you want me to leave?"

I shrugged my shoulders.

"Your 'fiancée' must be waiting for you."

He sighed, getting up.

"This is how you want to end?"

I didn't answer. I saw him leave, unsure of what his real purpose in coming had been.

I realized as I watched him walk away that though he might not have stopped wanting me, he'd forgotten how to love me, and that one thing could not substitute the other. This man who'd just left wasn't the Martin I missed. That Martin had been stolen. Or he'd left of his own accord, using his own two feet. It didn't matter. He didn't exist.

I went back inside the house and looked on Lola's shelves. I opened *What Smart Women Know* by Steven Carter and Julia Sokol. It said: *"Smart women know that . . . even though crying the loss of a loved one takes time, the idea is to stop the pain as soon as possible, which means not looking back."*

I put it back to its place and opened another: *"It's important for your happiness to realize that you're never getting back with your ex, at least not in the type of relationship that you want. But there is a possibility that you will have that relationship with another person . . . as soon as you let go of those old hopes."* It was, *Letting Go: A 12-Week Personal Action Program to Overcome a Broken Heart,* written by Zev Wanderer and Tracy Cabot. I put it in its place, feeling sad I'd found what I was looking for.

"Attorney Consuelo?"

"Well, about time you returned your calls."

"I'm sorry. I didn't get your message."

"I didn't leave one, but I wanted to tell you there's a support group for divorcées meeting next week that I'd like you to go to."

"What? No, no, no, I don't have the time. I have a lot of work . . . and I have to move . . ."

"Of course you have the time. You need to learn about divorce from other people's experiences, and a support group is a friendly, confidential environment."

"Actually, what I called to tell you is that—"

"Oh, so we have to talk about what you called about and nothing more? You didn't call to talk about this, but I'm talking about it and—"

Since I've learned not to mess with people who are crazier than I, I just said:

"Big groups of people intimidate me."

"Who said it was a big group? But, okay. Fine. Everything in its own time. How can I help you?"

"How much money are we asking for?"

She paused for a second.

"Okay. Well, let's see . . . we're at . . . seven hundred and fifty thousand dollars . . . and counting."

"I don't want it."

"You don't want what?"

"I don't want this. Can you ask Martin's lawyer what they think is fair and leave it at that?"

I waited for her to scold me for being stupid and possibly curtailing her earning potential.

"Very good!" she said.

"Very good?"

"Yes, Erika. Very, very good. There's hope . . . there's hope."

And she hung up.

I opened another book and read: *"You will survive. You'll get better. There's no doubt about it. The healing process has a beginning, a middle and an end. Have in mind, at the beginning, that there is an end. It's not that far. You will heal. Nature is on your side and nature is a powerful ally. Tell yourself often: I'm alive. I'll survive. You are alive. You will survive."* The book I had chosen at random was *How to Survive the Loss of a Love* by Melba Colgrove, Harold H. Boomfield, and Peter McWilliams.

You'll think it's strange, but when I read those words I felt I wasn't alone. I felt hope. It was as if a tangible, superior force, instead of a mere book, were watching over me, telling me everything would be okay.

I decided to make it a day of endings, of letting go, and drove to Miami Beach to make sure the movers hadn't left any of my boxes behind and that the Salvation Army truck had taken all the pieces of furniture I'd been "allowed" to keep. I walked through the empty rooms until I was hungry, then made myself a shriveled ham and dried-up tomato sandwich, which I ate in my favorite corner—a small terrace behind the garage.

There I thought about that morning and what had happened between Martin and me. I thought about marriage and divorce, about love and science, and about how precious even this little bit of relief was, knowing it was over and there was nothing I could do.

I wanted others to have this relief I was only beginning to grasp was possible, and as I thought about my pill, my heart filled with something beautiful because I knew the science I loved with all my heart was the tool I needed to help humanity. I would liberate it from stunted passions, rearranging the brain's chemical balance in order to reach the well-being we all have a right to. And who knows, maybe there'd be more love everywhere when heartbreak was no longer something to be feared. Tomorrow, I thought with renewed resolve, I'd go to work early to avoid the witch, her helpers, and their curiosity, and I'd begin the task of finding and restructuring that PEA molecule.

I got up and shook off the crumbs that had fallen on my lap, ready to drive down to Coconut Grove and begin organizing what few things I'd taken with me. As I turned to leave, I was hit full force by the beauty of the garage wall that faced the terrace. It was covered with unmatched vintage tiles, their only common trait being that they all had a bit of lapis lazuli in them. Martin and I had spent months scouring tile depots and salvage stores for them. The terrace floor was tiled in Mexican Saltillo and there was so much greenery surrounding the cozy little deck that it was easy to forget we had neighbors.

Standing on that spot, I said good-bye to the life I'd always been afraid to lose and quieted the doubts of my heart, begging it to forget and look forward because it was gone and nothing could bring it back.

{twelve}

I awoke at dawn the next morning with the intention of getting to NuevoMed before everyone else. But most of my things were still in boxes and waking up in a strange room after more than seven years of living in the same place was so disorienting that it was eight o'clock by the time I walked out of my apartment with my finger-brushed teeth, blue jeans, white T-shirt, and a wrinkled black blazer missing at least one button.

A tall guy with longish hair and a neat-looking beard walked out of the apartment across from me at the same time. He looked a bit like Gael Garcia Bernal. You know, the guy from *Amores Perros* and *The Motorcycle Diaries?* But he was taller than I, so he must have been at least six feet, and he had that bit of a preppy-bohemian, intellectual air.

"Hey . . . How's it going?" he said.

So fucked up it's not even funny, I thought.

"Good, and you?" I responded as I looked for keys I wasn't

sure I had, among the seven hundred and sixty-five things in my purse.

"New neighbor?"

"Yes," I said with a courtesy smile I hoped reflected how little I felt like talking.

"Nice meeting you. Pedro Juan."

"Hi, I'm Erika. Erika Luna," I said and shook his hand, which was warm, as if he'd just gotten out of bed.

"Can't find your keys?" he said after a moment of standing there with no apparent intention of leaving.

He looked to be thirty, with thick eyebrows, a teasing smile, and, from what I could see, great talent for stating the obvious.

"Well, no, it's just . . . moving is a mess . . . with all the boxes . . ."

"Only five, I heard, and a mattress," he said. "My aunt owns the building," he added sheepishly.

I swear it. They smell me, lunatics do.

"Oh, well, in that case . . . I mean, if it's only my landlord going around discussing my business with other tenants, then I have nothing to worry about," I said emptying the contents of my purse on the floor before realizing that I'd be showing my new neighbor about three quarters of my ass if I bent down to sift through the mess. I stood there like an idiot wondering what I'd have to do to make him leave to do whatever it was he'd come out of his damn apartment to do.

"You know how old people are," he said, ignoring my bitchy tone. "Besides, I think she likes you, because I'm her favorite nephew and she wouldn't have rented you this apartment if she thought you'd be a 'bad influence,' " he continued.

"I'm sorry . . . Bad influence? How old *are* you?" I asked, pissed he wouldn't leave me to get my keys and close my door.

"Thirty-four."

"Well, there you go. I don't think you can be influenced at this stage of the game, my friend."

"Agreed," he said, smiling. "But you know women . . . manipulative, controlling, never find anything because they carry whole houses inside their bags," he added, pointing to my things strewn on the floor.

"Okay, what do we have here?" I said looking him over in mock detainment. "A sexist . . . smack dab in the middle of the twenty-first century."

"Well, it's not exactly the middle. . . . Hey, wait a minute, you wanted to say sexist pig, didn't you?"

"How did you know?" I asked before I could stop myself.

But he just put his hands on his waist and bent his head, chuckling softly before answering me.

"So I've been told before. But I direct a domestic violence shelter, even though I graduated in chemical engineering, a field in which I could be making obscene amounts of money. Instead I have few pennies to my name, and live with my aunt, who spends her days trying to set me up with the first neighbor who catches her fancy, on top of which I risk the threats of virulently abusive husbands and the monthly possibility of having my nose, a rib, or, God forbid, other things, broken for me. As a result, I have to say your comment is actually . . . quite interesting."

Okay, I admit my mouth dropped open for a few seconds.

"Then why do you go around acting like a retrograde jerk, saying those things about women?"

"I was . . . trying to make conversation. It's called flirting.

Pathetic, I know. But are you always that quick with your man-hating shotgun, or is it just nosy neighbors who get under your skin?"

I had to smile. He was my neighbor, after all, I thought, deciding it wouldn't hurt to be friendly.

"What do you do?" he asked.

"I work for a drug company."

"Interesting."

"I suppose."

"I'd reach for your keys, but you'd probably accuse me of sexism," he said with his teasing smile.

"You know, I think it's a miracle the women at your shelter aren't the ones beating you up," I said finally bending down for my keys, deciding that if I continued to worry about his seeing my behind, I'd get nothing accomplished today.

"Not that they haven't tried," he said, unable to keep from sneaking a look.

"Well, good-bye now," I said, trying to pull my pants up circumspectly, then quickly locking the door and heading for the stairs. "I hope you have a great day, Pedro Juan, was it? Stay away from violent attackers."

"I will, thanks. Erika?"

"Yes?" I said, already a landing below him.

"Welcome. I hope we become good friends."

Not if I learned to leave my apartment on a parachute, I said to myself as I waved good-bye.

You can imagine how late I was getting to work. Once there, I asked Naty to take my calls, then I locked myself inside the lab and got to work.

First, I jumped rope for about ten minutes, but the damn air conditioner was so strong I couldn't sweat a drop. So I turned on the radio to 95.7. A guy named Daddy Yankee was singing "Lo Que Pasó, Pasó." It was perfect. Not that I knew how to dance Raggaetón, but the point was moving and sweating, so I danced as if I were self-exorcising until I felt the first drop of sweat on my previously sterilized and plastic-wrapped forearms.

I kept dancing as I looked for a sample-taking slide and then, there it was: my beautiful formation composed of two carbons and one nitrogen unit. I began to alter the order of the elements over and over until I realized I'd have to add something to achieve it. But what?

A couple of hours later, Vico C sang a duo with Gilberto Santa Rosa, but I wasn't dancing. I was extracting endorphins from roses I'd sent Naty to Publix for, trying to make them adhere to my molecule and thinking if this didn't work, I'd give up, at least for today. I'd already tried with a splinter from a small lemon tree I have in my office to counteract the sterile lab atmosphere, with an orange peel and with the last three hairs from a small laboratory mouse and I was beginning to lose faith that I'd be able to achieve anything significant using these home grown methods.

I made a tear on one of the petals of the smallest rose in the bunch. Under the microscope, it looked like I'd made it bleed, its particles set into sudden movement, as if in pain. I added the drop of sweat and watched it run to where I'd cut the rose, extending the pinkish formation and turning it a purplish atomic blue. Only now there was one carbon, one nitrogen, and two more carbons, and I couldn't breathe. The floor opened under my feet like a red sea of pure, transforming emotion and I thought, My God! I did it. . . . I think I did it. . . . Can't be . . .

it can't be this easy. . . . It can't be . . . but it is because I'm looking at it. . . . I've reconfigured a PEA molecule!

I repeated the process twenty-two times, and twenty-two times my molecules left behind their pink innocence to assume their night-blue dress. Then, one by one, I transferred them carefully into a presterilized crystal flask using a dropper as I watched breathlessly to see if anything changed when I put them together. Nothing appeared to. Only that in my hand I now held what was possibly the raw material for my heartbreak pill. I put the flask in my purse and happily began to rewrite the messy notes I'd taken while dancing, sweating, tearing, and mixing, when my cell phone rang. It was Attorney Consuelo.

"Where are you?"

"Working," I said, realizing it was entirely possible she'd forgotten I worked for a living.

"And here I've been waiting for you for the last half hour."

"Why?"

"Uh, the meeting? With your husband and his lawyer, remember?"

"Oh my God, what do you mean? When?"

"In exactly one hour."

"No way! My God . . ." I said, wanting to shoot myself.

"Yes way! Absolutely yes way, ma'am!" she said with in a ghetto drawl that made me wonder how many personalities she was given to channeling.

When we got there, the receptionist told us to wait in the small lobby right outside Attorney Chavez's office. There were several offices on each side of the long, wide hallway and several small receiving areas every three to four doors just like where we sat. Two black leather Swan sofas down, a woman flipped through magazines. She looked familiar and I kept looking at her, noticing she flipped magazines as tensely as if they were death row summaries, as I ignored Attorney Consuelo's last-minute advice and my own butterflies over what awaited me inside of one of those offices.

Actually, everything there seemed familiar and I realized there wasn't much difference between those offices and the ones where I'd screamed my lungs out just three months ago.

But I was different. Calmer. Maybe it was true time heals all wounds. Without intending it, every morning I'd woken without Martin next to me had made me stronger, not to mention what focusing on something more important than the two of us was doing for me.

Yes, it was all going well. That is, until I caught her stealing a glance at me. It was her! Lizandra's sister. I got up and resolutely began to walk toward her, leaving Attorney Consuelo in mid-sentence. The fear in her face as she quickly got up to knock urgently on the door closest to her, immediately confirmed my suspicion. Not only was she a bitch, I thought, she was a cowardly one.

In seconds, I was face to face with her; my lawyer right behind me, demanding to know the reason for my rudeness just as Martin came out of the office door on which she'd pounded, Attorney Chavez behind him. God knows what sick trick they'd been planning while they made me wait in the opposite lobby.

But at the moment, I only had eyes for her: the woman my husband had left me for. I could already see his influence on her. The same short blond hair, but now she carried it in soft waves framing her face. Her eyes were a very light hazel, surrounded by long, straight lashes, and she wore a lot less makeup than I remembered her using at the NuevoMed Christmas party. I guessed her to be about five feet, three inches to my five feet ten, which made me feel like an ungraceful giant to her delicate wedding-cake doll. She had lost weight, and was the real life image of a modern-day Cinderella in her long-sleeved, knee-length denim dress, adjusted at the waist with a wide silver belt and black ankle boots.

It was a strange sensation I had then. As if I were driving down a steep road with my head wrapped in a dark shawl, my car unresponsive to my foot on the brake pedal. I heard the voices around me, but was unable to find my voice to answer.

"Erika, I didn't know you were waiting. Why don't we go into the conference room? You must be Attorney De Pokkos."

"Pleasure to meet you, Attorney De Pokkos."

"Likewise, follow me, please . . ."

"Erika . . . Erika, what's wrong?" asked my attorney, when she tried to usher me into the office behind Martin's lawyer, and saw that Martin, the cake doll, and I were still petrified into place, staring at one another.

"I suppose you must be Mr. Echegoyén," said my attorney, finally getting the picture. She adjusted her humongous eyeglasses before asking cake doll, "And you are?"

"Marisol," she replied after looking at Martin, as if requesting permission to speak.

"All right, Marisol, what brings you here?"

"Excuse me?"

"Yes, I find it appropriate of you to excuse yourself. What kind of woman attends the divorce conference of the woman whose divorce she's precipitating? And what kind of man brings her?" she asked turning to look at Martin. "Erika," she said without taking her eyes off him. "You must forgive and forget this man quickly. He's just not worth carrying negative karma around for more than one life," she finished as if the others couldn't hear her.

"Why don't we all calm down?" said Chavez nervously.

"I'm calm," I said, surprised to have my voice back.

"Of course you're calm, honey," said the crazy lawyer I'd hired. "To lose it for you, you've hired Attorney Consuelo. That's me," she told the others as if they had just floated down from heaven and had no idea who she was.

"Please," said Martin, "we are wasting time standing here in the hallway."

"Why did you bring her, Martin? Why continue to hurt me?"

We looked each other in the eye. The only two people who should know what'd happened, but didn't. Martin looked at me like a little boy who knows he's done something wrong but doesn't know why he did it or why it's so wrong that he should feel bad about it.

"She hasn't been feeling well lately. We were coming back from the doctor and . . . I didn't want to leave her locked up in the car. I never thought you'd cross paths or recognize each other, Erika."

"Ah, and I thought you might want to repeat yesterday's scene in Lola's house when you held and kissed me," I said glancing at Marisol, because I am not Mother Teresa, and I don't have to protect the feelings of a woman who didn't give a damn about mine, and because it hurt to see him be as solicitous with someone else as he'd once been with me.

"Erika, I went to Lola's house to try to tell you that Marisol is pregnant . . . and that, as you already knew, we're going to get married."

Pum . . . pum . . . pum pum pum. . . . That's the sound my body made as it fell down imaginary stairs.

"I'm sorry . . . I really am . . . I didn't want to hurt you, but I didn't want you to find out from someone else, like you did before," he continued, explaining himself to my astonished face.

Pum . . . pum . . . pum pum pum.

My face felt hot and I knew I was crying and my calm had gone to hell.

"Martin," I said, hating myself for crying. "How can you . . . be so sure? This . . . I . . ."

Yes, I know. I'm a masochist, but I couldn't stop searching for his eyes and when they finally met mine, I knew my voice had finally gone through with it's threat of extinguishing.

"There's a lot of love that will always be there, Erika. But this . . . happened . . . it's happening and—"

And there was no amount of oxygen to clear my head. "Excuse me," I said, taking my purse and walking out of there.

FROM THE DESK OF ERIKA LUNA

The process . . .

Phase A: It can't be. This can't be. I'm being paranoid. Elmer, Charlie, Juan, or whoever would never cheat on me.

Phase B: He cheated on me! I'll kill him . . . and I'll make it hurt.

Phase C: He cheated, but . . . I can't help missing him. Maybe there's a way to forgive and forget.

Phase D: Being cheated on? I thought that was the worst, but no. The worst is knowing he doesn't love me anymore. I have to make him love me again, even if just for revenge.

Phase Z: It's over. I have to accept it. He doesn't love me or never did. I accept it. I'm done fighting. To Hell with him. I'll die alone, eating soup in a robe surrounded by cats. To Hell with him!

That's where I had thought I was, at "to hell with him!"

When I got to the apartment, I threw myself on the mattress that passed for a bedroom set for now, and looked at the dulce de leche–colored walls, earnestly trying to see the bright side of things, and stop my downward slide into the dark. Now there was no way to lie to myself. (Oh, God! How can he marry her and have the children we dreamed of with her instead of me?) Now there was no limbo. (I'm never again going to be with him.) This was perfect. Now I couldn't continue to kid myself that he'd come back, think things over. (Oh my God, he's really marrying her.) There was nothing to continue to wait for, nothing to keep me stuck. (He's not coming back.) I now had the opportunity of creating a whole new life. (Without him.)

I knelt on the mattress in front of the window. Down on the street, couples walked. Cars carried the remains of a light and playful rain, and the lights coming from inside the cafés, restaurants, and exclusive shops of Mayfair mall were beginning to fuse under the filter of dusk.

I thought about Martin and felt a strong need to say good-bye, to be in his arms and relive everything one more time. But I could also imagine her, with her head on his chest instead of mine, occupying that space, watching TV while he stroked her hair distractedly, a besotted smile on his face. And it was my heart that hurt. Literally hurt, as if Mike Tyson in his prime had punched me hard in the chest.

Wait a moment. In my purse I had the active ingredient for a pill against bad love. And what was Martin if not a huge case of big, bad love? I thought of the rose petal I'd made bleed and the atomic blue color of the molecules I'd so lovingly placed in the small glass flask. How would I ever know if my idea worked if I didn't test it on someone with a truly broken heart? And what was my heart if not broken into a billion microscopic little pieces?

I got the purse and held the flask of my insanity in my hands for a long time . . . maybe thirty, forty minutes, I'm not really sure. I only know that during one of those minutes, I swallowed the mixture whole.

The effect was immediate. The walls started to change color and then disappeared as I flew around the apartment, or at least it felt like flying as I zoomed out of control, crashing against the walls like a bumper car with wings and no brakes.

Far, far, very far away, I heard someone knock on my door. It didn't even occur to me to open it, but the engine in my body jet propelled me to it and my whole body crashed against the door. When I opened it, my impertinent neighbor stood there, his hand ready to knock again.

"Hi! I came to apologize. I didn't mean to be rude this morning . . . I was just—"

"Shut up," I told him. "Apology accepted."

After which, I proceeded to vomit on his chest before fainting in his arms.

{thirteen}

At first, I feel nothing. Just a deep sleep coming over me like a thick quilt. There's a sudden urge . . . I remember I'm supposed to document this, but I'm just too sleepy; feel pulled from below as if by death, or very strong anesthesia.

My eyes are closed and yet it all looks so bright . . . a forest of orange and pink branches similar to the reproduction of hair shafts and follicles on commercials for deep-conditioning hair products. There are also blue wires I imagine are the neurotransmitters in my head; my brain communicating with my conscience in spirals as blue and vibrating as the sea.

I've taken my own invention of rose petals boiled in sweat, goaded by pain too deep to face, a hate-message to conscience, which doesn't know anything. It doesn't know you're dying. It thinks you're being dramatic or that you just want attention. It doesn't realize how sick you are. I tell Martin all this but he doesn't believe me; tells me he's having a baby and that it's all he knows.

I make myself focus, try to become aware of where I am again, try to hold on but I'm falling, then fleetingly realize it must be the pill working and that makes me happy because it means I am a scientist and not some woman doing something crazy in the name of love. No. This is my work. I've done this for science.

But when I try to raise my hand to wave good-bye to him, I feel like crying and I put my hand down. Someone tells me there are other men. I don't know who. Or where those men are. But I don't want them. I don't want anyone. I try to concentrate, to bring him back into my consciousness, where I can at least touch him with thought. I give him words and I tell him, "Speak."

So he comes closer and when he does speak, I'm surprised, even though I gave him the words, retrieved from my own memory, probably the only place where they still exist.

"Not everyone has to have children," he says now. I say, "We are not talking about everyone," at the same time as the Erika in my memory says, "I know, but maybe we can start thinking about it."

Now we're having sex. The weight of him almost jolts me out of my stupor . . . the weight of his hips on my thighs, of his shoulders . . . the curve of his neck . . . I inhale, try to sniff him . . . like a dog, reject the realization that it's a memory, forget I can only smell him with my brain now.

I say, maybe out loud, "You're going." And he responds, "I don't want to go," as he comes into the house, drops his keys on the lap of my sitting rounded woman/goddess statue by the entrance, takes off his soccer shoes, wipes his sweat and heads upstairs for a shower.

"You've got to go," I say, standing next to him, inside the shower stall.

"Why? I can change and be the same."

"But you don't want to."

He doesn't listen; he's on the patio with Julian, the neighbor who has a sailboat like the one he wants to buy. He doesn't hear me.

"Why did you do this to me?" I say, hugging his back as he cooks. "Why, when I loved you with all my heart?"

"I didn't do this to you," he says, tasting the mole we always make for Thanksgiving dinner at my father's. The *arroz con gandules* we take to Thanksgiving lunch at his mother's is next to it, covered with tinfoil instead of a proper top. "I didn't even think about you."

"I don't think of you either," I tell his back.

And for one second it's true. For one second I feel a great relief, an absence of pain, an emptiness where there was great weight. A great nothingness that makes me neither happy nor sad because it's just nothing, and for that one second I can imagine life without him. For that second, Martin is only a man to whom I was married, who I loved, and nothing more.

He's still there, by the stove, and he smiles at me as he tastes, but everything around him is going because I know what he means when he says he didn't think of me, having now seen the possibility of not thinking about him.

Only there's this gnawing sensation, like someone calling me. It sounds urgent . . . and I don't know why, but suddenly, I want to care, aware that I'm about to lose something precious. Something hurtful, but genuine and true.

"Stoooooooooooooooooooooooooop. . . . No, no, no, no . . .

Don't go . . . stay . . . I'll deal with it, I'll just deal with it . . . stay here . . . the weight, I need the weight again . . . I don't want to float away . . . It can't just go like that . . . stop, come back . . . wait."

But he's gone . . . even though he's still there, which is as if he weren't because I can't feel him. The mole is just plain chocolate sauce and has no steam, and his smile is frozen and I don't really care. Life will go on and he'll be some guy I used to be married to, lived through.

I sleep now, not wanting to be that animal that rolls around in its own blood, while the driver who ran it over continues on his way, forgetting about it after a few blocks.

No. I'm not that. I am a scientist. And I've done this for science.

{fourteen}

When I opened my eyes again, it was morning and a comforter I'd never seen before covered me and my vomit-riddled clothes.

I recalled opening the door for Pedro Juan the night before and thought that, among other things, my neighbor had great talent for catching me in the most embarrassing situations. He must've thought I was drunk, maybe even pitied me, comparing me to the women he helps at the shelter.

Good, I thought. "Maybe he'll leave me alone now. Maybe everyone will just leave me alone," I said out loud, covering myself from head to toe, wanting only to sleep, even though, judging by the amount of light coming in through my windows, it was probably time for work.

That was the beginning of panic for me. Instead of being afraid of the consequences of drinking potions that hadn't been analyzed adequately, which would've made sense, I suddenly began to experience a fanatically consistent fear of life's small challenges. I began to be afraid of bills, even if I had enough money to pay them; of the newspaper, of broken appliances, because they meant I'd have to call some customer service line and initiate contact with strangers who now made me nervous; of crying children and dogs without owners, of days, and nights and the past and the future, but above all the things I was now afraid of, I was afraid of the present. I was so screwed up by fear that even the phrase "global economy" would set off shivers that lasted for hours.

I'd also put aside my pill and all research into PEA and its possible antiheartbreak effects. I was exhausted from fear, incapable of a clear thought. The sense of relief that my reengineered molecules had produced in me when I took them after the last divorce conference had been short-lived. The pill left behind side effects that pointed to more questions than answers, questions that made me even more afraid, questions I was unsure I wanted to answer.

Attorney Consuelo told me it would all go away once the divorce went through, that it would be like burying a corpse that had been reeking for too long. She prepared the final proposal, which Martin accepted in my absence. I'd receive my lawyer's expenses at the end of that very week, when the agreement was notarized, and the total value of the house minus taxes and real estate fees, once it sold. Martin kept his piece of the agency, valued at one point two million dollars, his brand-new Lexus, and his investment portfolio, undervalued at one hundred and ninety-eight thousand dollars.

According to Attorney Consuelo, the four hundred thousand dollars I would receive was about half what a judge would've granted me, but fighting for more would have taken months, if not years. I didn't have time to waste with more fighting. And besides, no one had asked about the things that really mattered and which I'd taken with me: the pictures of our vacation in Venice, my wedding dress, and a few sketches of me that Martin made on napkins—when tired of lovemaking on rainy weekends, we'd walk to any open South Beach bar to get a drink and philosophize about love, war, and the secret meaning of life. Within a month, I'd sign a piece of paper and that would be that. White out and a fresh sheet of paper.

But that would be then, and this was now. With the divorce settlement signed, all claims on my credit card accounts had been dropped. They were active for the first time in weeks, and the hours extended, seemingly endlessly, before me.

Since moving into Doña Santa's flat, I hadn't been to the beauty salon, hadn't bought clothes or furniture, hadn't even been to the supermarket. Not even once. I just went to work, ate out every day, and, of course, steered clear of my neighbor at all costs. Who needed the embarrassment?

That morning, I felt money plus time called for a little extravagance, so I decided to go to Bal Harbour mall, favorite hangout of the obscenely rich and the fabulously famous; where better to scare fear away? I deserve these things. *I should celebrate the changes in my life*, I said to myself a couple of hours later, as I tallied my purchases over a glass of wine at the Bal Harbour Bistro.

 FROM THE DESK OF ERIKA LUNA

A marine blue chiffon skirt by	
Erin Fetherstone	$749.00
(For the new me, so new I had no idea what she'd wear)	
La Perla silk bustier and panty ensemble	$289.00
(To show Lola, and the world, that I *could* look sexy for myself)	
Clarins Body Firming Cream	$57.00
(Because faith is the last thing one should lose)	
Professional makeup application	
by Laura Mercier artists	FREE
Laura Mercier products I felt compelled to buy after	
professional makeup application by her artists	$142.00
Tiny Louis Vuitton monogram canvas bag	$290.00
Parking	$15.00
Brunch at the Bal Harbour Bistro	$68.15
Three cups of coffee and a biscotti	$13.12
Total spent in less than two hours:	$1,623.27

Now all I needed was a raise.

I began to dream of a particular newspaper headline that would read something along the lines of:

HEARTBROKEN SCIENTIST INVENTS DRUG THAT PUTS AN END TO THE WORST EPIDEMICS OF THE NEW MILLENNIUM: LONELINESS & HEARTBREAK

Puerto Rican chemist, Erika Anastasia Luna

> Morales, received the Nobel Prize for Chemistry from Alejandro Sanz and a fifty-million-dollar reward from Argentine actor Darío Grandinetti in a ceremony celebrated for the first time ever in Istanbul.

Biririri. Biririri. Biririririiiii.

"What're you up to?"

It was Lola.

"Running toward bankruptcy."

"What? Where are you?"

"Bal Harbour!" I said, mimicking her drill sergeant tone.

"I don't know how you can hand over your money to these designers, these . . . dictators, really, who enslave women in their 'fashion etiquette' schemes, and, you know what? I'm coming over. I'm coming over there right now."

And she came. Over frothy cappuccinos (four dollars apiece, plus taxes) I told her about my empty apartment, about my pill and the "progress" I'd made before fear had set in, and about my face-to-face with Martin and Princess Di the other day.

Lola listened attentively. I thought she was going to tell me I was absolutely insane and I was prepared to accept I was and declare I didn't care. But she just nodded silently a few times before saying,

"I'm proud of you. In fact, I'll go further and tell you this: I was wrong. I think your pill could work, or at least bring about some important discoveries about love in human beings. I'm sorry I was skeptical. You shouldn't give up."

"You see?" I hugged her. "This is why I worship you."

"Well, don't worship me so much. Now tell me what are all

these things," she said, pointing at my bags; as usual, her moment of pure tolerance and understanding was short-lived.

"I decided to do something for myself."

"And you interpreted that to mean that you should spend the money you have along with the money you don't have yet?"

"Well, yes, that . . . more or less. I deserve it."

"You deserve to keep sitting on the floor, in order to buy things that will not lift your spirits for more than five minutes, but for which you'll be paying with hours of insomnia?"

"Yes, Lola. That's what I deserve. Exactly that," I said, forgetting I worshipped her.

"Would you trust me . . . for today?"

"I always trust you."

"But today I need you to trust . . . *and* do what I tell you."

"And that means . . ."

"Return everything."

"Are you crazy? It's embarrassing . . ."

"They're the ones who should be embarrassed, selling things at these prices."

"Hey! Everyone has to eat, right? Besides, it's all good, quality stuff."

I was about to say I deserved them, but Lola was already walking toward Nordstrom with the bag of Laura Mercier cosmetics. I hid behind a pillar and looked the other way when the girl who'd done my makeup turned toward the general area of where I stood, looking like a schizophrenic patient in advanced state of paranoia.

"They need the receipt," Lola came to tell me.

I gave her all of them and in less than an hour, she'd returned every single thing I'd bought.

We then went to my apartment, where she made inventory of the bare walls and the unoccupied floor, measured my windows, inhaled the cold air inhabiting the dance hall in my fridge, and examined the mountain of self-help books she'd been lending me and the journal in which I'd written down anything that left the slightest imprint on my brain. She opened it to the first page and spent long minutes looking at the sketches I'd made of Martin, my former home, and myself. She then looked at my notes and drawings on the pill and read the conclusions I'd drawn from all I'd read in my medical journals, which were spattered with the photos of women sporting happy faces, an air of success, or just relaxing, that I'd cut out of magazines.

"You know, I think you just might have something . . . really great here" was all she said.

Then she glanced at the mattress I'd been sleeping on for over a week now and sighed. It was almost two in the afternoon by then. We sat on the wooden floor and counted the money we'd recovered: a total of fifteen hundred twenty-seven dollars.

"Let's go," she said.

"Where?"

"Shopping."

"We just got back from shopping . . ."

And off we went. First, to Antiques Row, a street filled with antiques shops, factories, and loftlike warehouses full of architectural salvage. In the first one we entered, we bought a carved wooden angel the size of a toddler. It was painted in several tones of chocolate brown, guava red, and vanilla and was so well made it seemed to be about to take flight after some good deed, a satisfied smile on his pale pink face.

"You girls setting up house?" asked the nosy shop owner, all the time applying her lipstick with a mirror stationed on top of the cash register. "You know, the artist is a Nicaraguan sculptor. She threw a fit, sold me all her work. Said she was tired of starving and having her art go unappreciated."

The sculptor was right because, thanks to Lola's bargaining skills, the angel only cost us thirty-eight dollars. On our way out, we saw a white metal bed that belonged in a World War Two infirmary. The lady assured us it was a rather large French daybed, but when we told her we didn't really care where it was from, she sold it to us for only fifty dollars.

A few stores down, we saw a sofa that had been part of a set in some off-Broadway play that had come to nearby Fort Lauderdale for only one season. It looked like an analyst's couch, made of wood so dark it was almost black and upholstered in dark, creamy, chocolate-colored velvet.

"Come on, we don't have all day," said Lola, pulling me off of it and snatching it, along with a fifties, bronzed office lamp, a desk chair like the ones you often see detectives sitting on in movie sets in the forties and fifties, and two small clamp lamps like the ones contractors use to light scaffolds at night.

The shop owner, a bald, burly man with a sweet voice, let us have it all for two hundred and fifty dollars and promised to deliver it that very night for an additional thirty-five. We gave him fifty to pick up my angel and bed from his neighbor, the Revlon lipstick cover girl.

Next stop: the Salvation Army Thrift Store, where we found an authentic vintage French seamstress's mannequin, the kind with the linen-wrapped wooden body and an iron sphere for legs. We bought a yellowed lace nightgown to go with it, as well as a selection of mismatched plates, utensils, and wine goblets. A pair of linen napkins brought our total to eighty-seven bucks.

"We need light," said Lola, as if she were Sherlock Holmes and had just solved the crime.

So off we went again, this time to the candle factory off Twenty-seventh Avenue, where we bought fourteen of them in green apple, brick red, mango yellow, and cerulean blue.

At the Home Depot we bought house plants, a prefinished oak-wood plank, and some pink lightbulbs for another sixty dollars.

As we waited to pay for two black, two-drawer, file cabinets at the Office Max next door, I called a discount mattress shop and ordered a full-sized, pillow-top mattress with a chenille cover, and charged the whole thing, even the delivery, to my suddenly busy MasterCard.

"Can I request a stop?"

"You have to go to the bathroom?" asked Lola.

"No, *chica.* I want to go to Target," I said like a mischievous little girl. "You know, design for all? Plus Martin hated it."

"To Target it is," said Lola immediately.

There, we bought sheets. All white because, according to Lola, they aid the thinking process. We also bought an Isaac Mizrahi plastic shower curtain; transparent except for these big orange and pink gerbera daisies embossed on it, and a Polaroid camera with several cartridges. I had an idea for informal pictures of dusk, my favorite time of the day.

For our shopping finale, we trekked off to Out of Africa, the best little ethnic décor store, right at the center of the Coconut Grove Mayfair mall courtyard, which features great Hindu and African artifacts. There we bought several cotton saris and a beautiful pewter tray with carved spirals highlighting its rim.

Once back at my block, we proceeded, tired as we were, to photograph anything and everything that caught our attention: a tree, a boutique store window, the street sign for Rice Street, a mailbox, a city sewer top, the cutest Beagle puppy with hot male owner and everything, a waitress cutting flowers for her tables on top of an empty table, my own building façade.

We also took photos of the sky as it changed from bright, light blue to violet blue, to rose, then yellow-orange . . . until it finally morphed into a seventies tie-dyed T-shirt.

"This is fun!" said Lola looking thirteen.

She looked beautiful and I felt lucky to have her.

Later, we went to the Wild Oats supermarket on U.S.1 and bought healthy foods because Lola insisted that feeding my body well is what I really deserved. So it was figs, mangos, fresh spinach, wine, mineral water, French bread, olive oil, feta cheese, and a half pound of prosciutto ham for me. I also bought several pints of Ben & Jerry's ice cream and three magazines and Lola bought several bouquets of white, pink, and red roses and a white orchid. Total spent at the market: one hundred and thirty-three dollars, after which we ran to the apartment to wait for the furniture we'd bought. The man had told us we'd have to wait till the end of the business day or nine-thirty p.m., so we waited, sitting on the floor, leaning against the tight-spaced balcony railing, drinking wine and looking down at the late-closing shops and cafés of Coconut Grove and at people, either alone and hurrying past, or accompanied and happily strolling by.

"I foresee very good things, Erika," said Lola, taking a sip of wine.

"When?"

"Now. It's the start of a new life," she said, just as we heard the ring of the doorbell below us and dusted off our behinds to go open the door downstairs. "And I want you to trust your heart. It's nuts, but sooner or later it'll lead you home."

"What heart, *chica?* What I have here is a deep black hole," I told her half kidding, half drama queen.

"Your heart isn't a black hole, Erika. The hole is inside your head. And that one, my friend, is huge," she said, giving me a playful push down the stairs.

We stayed up till two that night setting up the apartment, drinking wine, and eating delivered pizza. We covered the white metal daybed with the new mattress, the white sheets, and one of the saris. Next to it, I placed my pottery barn brushed-nickel floor lamp with its big translucent glass lightbulb. In the corner, facing the bed, I placed my mannequin dressed in its yellowed-lace nightgown. The feeling went with the building, romantic and a bit bohemian, and it made me smile. The room I'd shared with Martin had been on the masculine side with lots of dark wood and shades of olive green and earth tones. This one was soft, as if dreaming, even though there weren't any curtains, not that they were necessary in a fourth-floor flat. I placed three elongated candles on the window ledge and the room was set. We then hung the plastic shower curtain and the bathroom immediately became happy; the blue tiles splashed with big orange and pink gerbera daisies.

We put the fainting couch in the living room and draped it with the other sari. The angel went in the corner facing the balcony we'd overfilled with just six or seven green plants. I piled up my bigger books in front of the sofa and put the spiraled, pewter tray on top. It still didn't look like a living room, so I placed the rest of the candles on the tray and pink lightbulbs on the industrial-looking clamp lamps I'd affixed to the back of the couch. They looked like metal wings about to lift off, and reminded me of Ingo Maurer lamps. For art, we tacked the thirty-plus Polaroids we'd taken to the wall like an urban mosaic and it was magical.

"This way, you'll always have nice pictures to look at and you can change them as you change," said Lola, loving it all.

"What makes you think I'll change?"

"You already have," she said, placing plates, glasses, and napkins on the white, wooden, wall to wall, open kitchen shelves.

In the second bedroom, below the window, we placed the two file cabinets with the oakwood plank on top and the forties "detective" chair in front of it. My reference books journals, microscope, pencil collection, and laptop completed the new "home office." The rest of my books, I stacked in columns against an empty wall, before looking around to see if we were done.

"There's something missing," said Lola.

"Like what?"

"A feminine detail . . . such as this," she said, pulling the slender wood statuette of a dancing woman out of her enormous handbag. "I bought it in Mexico and was waiting for your birthday to give it to you, but I think you'll enjoy it more now."

"It's incredibly beautiful," I said, touched.

The woman was arching her delicate waistline as she pushed her chest forward passionately, one leg airborne, the other on tiptoe, arms raised toward the sky in rapturous euphoria.

"Oh, Lola . . . it's really, really beautiful. Thank you . . ."

"You're welcome, fool," she said.

"Oops, one more thing missing," she said, running toward

the bathroom with the roses we'd bought on her arms. "I read in *Rolling Stone* that Barbra Streisand demands her toilet bowl be filled with flowers daily, so that all of her, and I do mean all of her, will always smell like roses."

"And you believed it?"

"Why not? Sounds to me like a great way to pamper yourself," she answered, undressing the roses and letting their petals fall into my just-deodorized toilet before cutting the stems off the rest and putting them into an empty can of stewed tomatoes with a colorful vintage-looking label.

"Maybe . . . but I don't see the point of wasting beautiful flowers like that."

"Waste? Did you say waste? Erika, you listen to me. What matters here is the message, the symbolism of the matter. Didn't you want to do something for yourself? And you deserved this and you deserved that . . . ?"

"Well, yes . . ." I answered.

"Then listen carefully: there's no such thing as waste when it's for a queen. You're the queen and this is your castle."

"For now."

"Time is immaterial. What's important is that queens love themselves and treat themselves like queens wherever they are."

I fixed my gaze on the mini-perfumed pool my toilet had transformed into, dozens of cream- and crimson-colored rose petals floating on the now deep blue, deodorized water. I thought it was one of the most beautiful things I'd seen in my whole life.

"So I'm a queen even though I've lost the way back to my kingdom?" I asked.

"And you'll continue to be one, even if you never return."

{fifteen}

And life went on.

Exactly one month later, Martin and I were legally divorced. In fact, in a no-fault divorce state such as Florida, the defendant doesn't even have to appear in court. The person who sued for divorce just waits in a room with other miserable people until they call her name and her lawyer takes her place to her left.

"Name?"

"Erika Luna."

"Address?"

"3333 Rice Street, Apartment 7, Coconut Grove, Florida, 33133."

"Now, please answer yes or no to the following questions. Is your marriage irremediably broken?"

Can you imagine asking anything crueler to someone who is seconds away from being officially divorced?

"Ms. Luna, the court will ask you once more. You need to answer yes or no, loud and clear, for the record. Is your marriage—"

"Yes, yes, yes! It's broken, all right. Absolutely ruined . . . destroyed, not so much as a rag left, you happy?"

Attorney Consuelo made an apologetic gesture to the judge and pushed me out of there in a hurry.

And the thing is, at this point, divorce annoyed me but it didn't hurt me. I'd finally gone from the false "to Hell with him" of a month before to an "I could care less" that cared so little it was barely there.

How did I do it? Well, I'd love to tell you I did it by being the courageous, strong, integral woman my mother raised me to be. And I do admit it's true what they say: time does heal. Every day *was* a bit better than the one before. But what did it matter when nights continued to be a humungous piece of apocalyptic shit?

After the disaster of that first time drinking my own chemistry mix from Hell, my intention was to leave well enough alone. I said to myself that it was crazy to think I could invent a new drug, and such a complicated one at that, all by my misguided self. If others with more resources and know-how than I had not done it, there was probably a good reason for it, and that all I'd manage to do would be to turn myself into the town's scientific laughingstock for trying to "make a career out of my divorce," as Martin had accused me of doing.

But science is nothing if not persistent. It began to stalk me. Suddenly, Helena Fish and her book turned up everywhere. I counted at least five movies, six TV shows, and nine advertisements in which people asked for relief against heartbreak in some way or another. A highway billboard announced: "Yvonne Montero no longer suffers for love. Find out why, Monday through Friday, at seven, eight central, on Telemundo."

But the last straw was my father, who called me one night to tell me of the death of the Puerto Rican announcer who used to recite a popular Christian commercial in the seventies that went something like this: "Loneliness hurts. The twentieth-century man is a lonely man." I heard this as a personal reprimand from twentieth-century man for my lack of courage and commitment to humanity and to my career.

Between that and the dark, insomnia-induced circles under my eyes caused by how very much I missed sleeping with my now ex-husband, I'd decided to give the heartbreak pill another try.

(It still amazes me. I no longer wanted to go back to Martin. I was divorced and I understood and accepted that it was a done deal, but the habit of sleeping with him was still there, like a second skin, preventing me from spending so much as twenty-four hours without remembering that I'd lost something.)

I started to prepare and consume cocktails made with endorphins I'd either realigned or mixed with various quantities of phenylethylamine, dopamine, norepinephrine, and even oxytocin, which caused an eruption that looked as if I'd been in a swamp without insecticide, not to mention diarrhea that got me to my high school weight of one hundred and twenty-three pounds.

Relief was not immediate. I found that for my recipe to work, I had to ingest it in quantities exceeding sixteen hundred milligrams, and that even then, my body seemed to absorb the remedy so that eight hours after taking it, I'd have a strong headache coupled with deep sadness that made me feel like an empty water pail turned upside down.

Little by little, I improved the formula. The feeling of emptiness was still there, but every day it became more and more like that shirt you haven't worn in years. You know it's there, somewhere in your closet, but since you never see it, most days you don't even remember it exists.

During the four weeks that followed, I literally turned into Dr. Jekyll and Mrs. Hyde. During the day I worked hard at NuevoMed's. At lunchtime I ate at my desk in the lab as I either ordered or organized whatever chemical compounds had arrived that day so I could take them home without compromising sterility, and always being careful not to buy too much of anything in any one order to avoid having the supplier feel the need to alert the general purchasing manager at NuevoMed. (The quantities I was working with made it impractical to keep using my own sweat as raw material, plus it was just too third-worldly. If I got caught, so be it.)

If I spoke to anyone at all, it was either Naty or Santiesteban, and then only if he requested my presence.

The rest of the time at work went fast, between avoiding Lizandra and the rest of the insects with superiority complexes in her department. During the night, I let calls from my father, Benjamin, Lola, and Attorney Consuelo go unanswered. One night even Pedro Juan, the neighbor with the great (or horrible, depending on how you look at it) sense of timing, knocked on my door and I was silent till he went away. All I wanted was to work on my spell in my pajamas, my hair falling loose and unruly down my back, and enjoy the conspicuous absence of tears and painful memories.

Once in a while, I'd go to Tu Tu Tango, the tapas restaurant on the corner of Cocowalk, to pick up the *sofrito*-sautéed mushrooms and the southwestern chicken egg rolls made with black beans, corn, and guacamole that I'd ordered by phone, and that was that.

By the end of the month I'd taken eighteen versions of my potion, bounced off every wall of that apartment, and taped myself shouting, weeping, and muttering without pause while under the effects of the mother of all chemical cocktails.

"You shouldn't drink so much. Or whatever it is you're doing."

Damn it, damn it, damn it, damn it, daaaaamn . . . it! My sautéed mushrooms were ready and waiting for me and I had to get trapped between the door I'd just shut tight and my neighbor, who was just coming up the stairs. Damn it!

"Oh, I don't drink . . . and by the way, how are you?" I said pretending all our interactions had been polite and . . . normal.

"Look, I just want to help you," he said seriously, not a trace of teasing or mockery.

"No, no, really, I don't drink. Or smoke . . ." I said, pausing where I'd been about to add "or do drugs," which had the effect of immediately convincing him that I did.

"No one is worth what you're doing to yourself," he said, scrutinizing me from top to bottom, which prompted me to scrutinize myself to see what it was that was causing so much concern.

"When was the last time you brushed your hair?" he said, taking a tousled (okay, dreadlocked) lock in his hands and showing it to me before I had time to protest. "And, what happened to your hands?"

"Nothing, and when did I hire you to become a cross between Joan Rivers and my mother?" I said, noticing my fingers full of purplish spots, the result of all that mixing of the red, blue, and green substances, as well my overgrown cuticles and total absence of contact with a nail file.

He was thoughtful for a few seconds.

"You know, you're right. Don't pay attention to me. What I am is *tremendo come mierda,* excuse my Cuban. For some screwed up reason, I think it's my duty to save the world," he added, smoothing the beard he no longer had.

"You shaved."

"What? Oh, right. Yes. You're just now noticing, huh?" he said with a bit of a little boy's pout.

I felt bad. He had no reason to care, yet had still made the first move to make sure I was okay; had even offered to help.

"It's just . . . I've had a lot of work. I'm in the middle of some very, very important research and . . . stuff. That's why I have all these stains, by the way."

"Okay," he said. "I guess . . . Sure."

"You don't believe me?"

"Why not? Besides, it's none of my business, right?"

"I never said that. And, believe it or not, I'm just like you."

"Really?" he said, looking me up and down exaggeratingly, which came off quite seductive, I have to say. "You *are* a woman, though, right?"

"I didn't mean that."

"So how are you just like me? Nosy?"

"An idealist . . . wanting to save the world."

"Ah, that," he said, the teasing smile coming back, up front and center. "I see. I see. So, if you're perfectly okay, and nothing's wrong with you, and you like to help others," he was saying, as I stupidly nodded to everything he said. "Then you will come to the shelter with me on Saturday."

Men are all the same: capable of recuperating and turning the tortilla on you in two seconds flat.

"Maybe."

"Okay . . . okay . . . Maybe's good. And, if I swear to you I've never bitten anyone, will you stop avoiding me?"

I almost denied it before realizing there just wasn't any point to it.

"Maybe."

He laughed heartily.

"At least you're honest."

"Unfortunately."

But I did stop avoiding him. And although I admit the lack of sex made me mentally measure his back, arms, and chest on more than one occasion, there were four reasons that make clear why, in the course of the month that followed, Pedro Juan and I were able to develop a flirty (combination of slightly morbid compliments coupled with heated intellectual debate), yet comfortable (platonic), friendship:

 FROM THE DESK OF ERIKA LUNA

Reasons not to get involved with Pedro Juan:

1. He's my next-door neighbor and I don't want to have to jump out the window every time I want to leave my apartment without bumping into him.
2. I'm not ready for an affair—not even with a vibrator.
3. He can be insufferable, but he has a good heart and I don't want to hurt someone like that.

4. I want to keep free of entanglements with the potential of muddying the results of my heartbreak pill observations.

And that was that. The day I knew my pill would be a reality someday, was the day I realized how much my life had changed in the last eight weeks. The closer I came to achieving my dream, the less I thought about Martin, and everything began to normalize. The fear began to disappear along with the insecurity and the constant desire for solitude.

I began to stop for coffee with Doña Santa in the mornings before work. During the day, I concentrated on Daytime Varitex, and for the first time in a long time I stopped ditching the innocuous, thousand and one staff meetings at NuevoMed. (Torture! This is torture I tell you. You people are frying my brain!!!!!!)

At night I'd have dinner with Lola, Pedro Juan, or Attorney Consuelo, and once in a while I'd even have it with all three.

One night after we'd all had dinner on a sari anchored on the floor with pillows, Lola called me from her cell as she drove home.

"Please tell me you're aware that he's into you."

"Nope. I haven't noticed any such thing, and I've told you: I don't want to get involved with anyone."

"Okay, okay, but I'm telling you, he's cute . . . and he's got that sexy, deep bohemian guy mixed with political activist good boy with the dash of street bad boy charm thrown in that you like. I think he's just what you need right now, and the fact that he's dry from all that drooling over you is not a bad thing."

"I can give him your number if you'd like."

"Funny. Would you really want Carlos to kill me? But you really should . . ."

"No."

"You should think about it, is what I was going to say. From all that banter at dinner, it sure looks like you enjoy watching that ten o'clock soap opera with him," she said suspiciously.

"I like soap operas, and I like having someone to talk with about them after they finish. When it's over, he goes home and that's all."

"Nothing happens?"

"Nothing happens," I said listening to Lola opening her noisy front door.

"Maybe you're afraid."

"And maybe I'm sleepy and don't want to listen to you."

"Okay, but at least listen to what the great philosopher Erich Fromm has to say about this: *"The practice of faith and courage begins with the small details of daily life,"* she began without giving me a chance to object. *"The first step, is to notice where and when one loses faith, to look through the rationalizations, which are used to cover up this loss of faith, to recognize where one acts in a cowardly way, and again how one rationalizes it. To recognize how every betrayal of faith weakens one, and how increased weakness leads to new betrayal, and so on, in a vicious circle. Then one will also recognize that while one is consciously afraid of not being loved, the real, though usually unconscious, fear is that of loving."*

"What do you think? Great, isn't it?"

I feigned snoring.

"Gghhhhhhhftpzzzzzzz. . . . Gghhhhhhhftzzzzzzz."

"You're just—"

"Ciao."

"Ciao," she said, muttering under her breath.

Weekends were spent with Papi and Benji, at the movies, or reading in my apartment. But it was night, just before going to bed, that I'd mix a new, thicker variation of my potion. I'd mix until I had a creamy paste, spread it on one or two Hershey's chocolate squares so it tasted good, then wash it all down with half a glass of cold milk.

This, I soon learned, helped counteract the extreme effects of the drug. There was no more bouncing, shouting, or murmuring. I'd just read a little to make myself sleepy, and if Morpheus, god of sleep, was late in coming, I'd look out my window at the dark night sky, and allow myself to think about Martin, knowing indifference and oblivion would now arrive long before sleep did.

{sixteen}

Love is a drug—equal parts mania, dementia, and obsession. It's an instant instinct, like lightning; visceral, unmistakable, and corrosively addictive. An illness society uses for the purpose of making drama, television, poetry, criminal anthology, and even journalism, only now beginning to suspect its devastating physiological effects, despite the thousands of anecdotal clues scattered throughout the annals of medicine, history, anthropology, and art.

A woman, five months pregnant, is abandoned by her husband. A month later, her baby decides he'd rather be born early than live in a sad uterus; forgets to bring the ability to talk and the desire to communicate with the world around him.

In the midst of unbearable frustration, a woman tells her mother she's tired—tired of caring for her, tired of her constant complaints and her negativity. She tells her that since she's had to take care of her, she hasn't known a day of peace and quiet in which her feet, back, and head don't hurt.

That night, the mother uses a candle to burn sections of her arms, circularly, almost in a pattern. Not because she wants to hurt herself, but because the physical sting she feels as she burns her old body is the only relief against the pain she feels at the thought that her daughter doesn't love her.

A man meets a woman and decides that he doesn't love his wife anymore. He kicks her out of his life. He forgets that she exists. At first, the wife feels sorry for herself. She sees herself as grotesque, ugly, clumsy, not enough or very little. Months later, she starts taking a drug, using herself as a guinea pig, without taking precautions, without taking violent side effects into consideration, without telling anyone about the dangerous extremes into which she has taken her experiment. Despite the risks, there is a level of relief. One drug weakens the other.

But love is like cancer. If you leave it unattended, it comes back when you least expect it. And when someone, maliciously, leaves the newspaper with the announcement of her ex-husband's wedding announcement wide open over the sink of the women's bathroom of the company she works for, love's old physiological symptoms come back, suddenly and violently.

MR. AND MRS. RAUL SALINAS-MONTES
ANNOUNCE THE WEDDING THIS SUNDAY
OF THEIR DAUGHTER, MARISOL,
TO MARTIN ECHEGOYÉN

Renowned Miami publicist Martin Echegoyén and Marisol Salinas-Montes will receive the blessings and good wishes of family, friends, and associates at an intimate ceremony, this Sunday, at the exclusive Doral Country Club Resort in Miami.

I was still holding the newspaper when someone opened the bathroom door. It was Lizandra. She took the newspaper from my hands and said,

"Oops. Sorry. I left this behind."

She left along with her assistant, who was already in the bathroom when I got there. I bet they planned it together as a joke/wedding present for the future Marisol Salinas-Montes *de* Echegoyén. A prank they could use to calm her as she got dressed before walking down the aisle.

Well, so fucking what? I already knew Martin was getting married. I'd known for months. We were already divorced. And I was already cured. So why the intense shaking? Why these feelings of being on board a turbulent plane? I turned on the water faucet and let the water run, allowing myself to feel whatever I felt, looking for the monastic peace I'd gotten used to in the last few weeks, or, at worst, a piece of "I don't care," small as it might have been at that moment.

That Martin was getting married was a *crónica de una muerte anunciada,* but feeling like digging a hole in the ground to lie in because of it only meant one thing: my pill was a failure.

I went back to my office, blocked caller ID by dialing star 67, and called his cell phone.

"Hello? Hello? Hello . . . !"

Click.

I knew I wasn't twelve years old, but the need to hear his voice was so strong, and the relief of hearing him so great.

Coño! Coño! Coño!

I began to look through the files I'd accumulated in my personal folders regarding the pill. They all showed my name and the date.

- Erika Luna 5/13/06
- Erika Luna 5/27/06
- Erika Luna 5/30/06
- Erika Luna 6/02/06
- Erika Luna 6/03/06
- Erika Luna 6/04/06

Of course. How could there not be a problem? I was the only patient; the investigator and the investigated. But I had no choice, at least until I could advance my formula enough to tell Santiesteban and become the crazy woman who was fired for putting the company's credibility at risk.

"Are you okay?"

It was Lizandra, who had slithered into my office, whistling and spitting like the snake she was.

"Please refrain from coming into my office without knocking."

"It was open."

"It was semi-closed."

"My God, Erika, this isn't high school. I didn't come here to fight; I came here to say I'm sorry. I don't want you to think I left the newspaper in the bathroom on purpose."

She was talking and I was looking at how her thin little red tongue darted in and out of her mouth as she talked.

"Sure," I said, quickly picking up and closing all the folders I'd had open and scattered all over my desk.

"Are you sure? Because I want you to know that I really respect your work and I don't want this situation to affect our blah, blah, blah. . . ."

All this without once taking her eyes away from everything that was on my desk, her diminutive eyes trying to catch a word, some phrase that would allow her to piece something together while I continued closing folders as if there were a hurricane warning in effect for my desk.

I couldn't risk anyone finding out at this point, so I kicked her out of my office with the minimum requisite diplomacy, took all the folders containing information about the pill, and put them in my bag. I also shoved all the little flasks with my name on them in there, along with all my clippings; a mystery when read one by one, but able to point to what I was investigating if put together. I finished by printing all compromising documents and sending the originals to the desktop trash bin before emptying it, and went straight home after a stop in the purchasing department to pick up my escort of ten very small white mice.

When I got there, my first impulse was to put on some old pajamas and go to sleep to avoid thinking about Martin and his stupid, stupid, stupid wedding.

I imagined him on his honeymoon. Ours was in Italy.

Surely now they'd go to Paris to make everything more romantic. In my mind, I saw the two of them, happy, looking at houses, choosing one close to good schools and a park, searching together for a baby name. . . .

The pill! I should think of the pill. I needed to think about this FUCKING PILL! Now there was something worth thinking about. Yes, sir, had to save humanity and all that hogwash, gosh darn it.

So, I put on some shorts and a T-shirt that wouldn't have fit me three months ago and opened all the windows. I put on my favorite Habana Abierta CD, turning the volume all the way up. Then I made a drink out of equal parts club soda and orange juice, a little lime and sugar, and lot of ice, and I got to work.

Four hours later . . .

Problem: The compound doesn't create the temporary immunity needed against the illness's when outside elements are present.

In other words, if after a flight you have a headache and you take some aspirin, the pain will go away. And during the duration of the pill's effects, you could probably take other flights and not get a headache. The aspirin would make you immune during the approximate eight hours its effect lasts.

Not the case with my pill. I'd taken a dose less than eight hours before I'd seen the announcement of Martin's wedding. But as soon as I realized what I was reading, the pain was unmistakable, intense, and convulsive.

And then there was the relief when I heard him on the phone, followed by a feeling of desperate anxiousness to continue hearing him, all after weeks of not thinking of him . . . or not too much anyway.

I thought that if love was a drug and the result was addiction, then, I'd have to do what drug addicts do: break the vice. No touching, smelling, seeing, or listening to the cause of my disgusting illness. But in order to give a heartbroken person the willpower needed to stay away from the person causing the heartbreak, my pill had to be capable of changing his or her brain's messages. Just like diet pills can make you feel so full you can't eat another thing, my pill had to create a feeling of already being in love so the bad love would have no effect.

I kept on reading, writing, measuring, and mixing, and it was already getting dark when loud knocks on my door fused with the "Ahora sí tengo la llave" of Habana Abierta. It was Pedro Juan.

"What have I done to you to make you want to deafen me, where can I buy that CD and . . . who . . . what . . . beauty salon from Hell has ruined you like this?"

"What are you talking about?" I said, turning to the little mirror that hung facing my makeshift lab and the wide open door I'd forgotten to close before opening the apartment door to Pedro Juan.

My hair was somewhere inside a two-foot-high afro completely covered with whitish dust, while my face showed traces of a sea blue stain, product of the high temperatures at which I'd had to boil the PEA to achieve combustion.

"Mother of God!" yelped Pedro Juan, who'd bypassed me to enter the restricted confines of my mini-lab and was looking at the 343 flasks, 3 microscopes, 16 measuring instruments submerged in sterilizing liquids, 10 white mice, the 103 colored folders, and me, as if he were before Dr. Frankenstein and the laboratory of death.

"Tell me the truth. Are you a terrorist?"

"No, dummy."

"Freelance for the CIA?"

"No."

"Then what's happening here? And don't tell me there's nothing going on."

I kept silent as he observed everything, already somewhat recovered from the shock. Finally, he said,

"So . . . you're not an alcoholic?"

I shook my head.

"You don't do crack?"

I shook my head again.

"Then what are you doing?" he said with such compassion, it broke my heart, or my brain, which felt like a wildly thumping heart, so that it was a few seconds before I could answer.

"I'm trying . . . to create a pill against heartbreak."

"Okay. Okay. Okay, don't move. I'm going to look for my car keys and we're going to go to the hospital right now and get that head fracture examined."

I didn't move. I didn't say anything as he stared at me as if seeing me for the first time until he understood I wasn't joking.

"Okay. I get it . . . I get it . . . Do you have beer?"

"For what?"

"Because I'll need it to listen to every last detail of what you're going to tell me."

And I told him, enjoying being able to break free of so much secrecy and self-doubt about what I'd been trying to do.

"It's official," he said. "You're completely insane."

"Thanks."

"But I think I can help you."

"Help my pill how?"

"Not your pill, you. Come to the shelter this Saturday."

At first, I refused. But when Saturday came and I needed to stop thinking about the pill that wasn't working even more than I needed to forget that Martin was getting married to another woman in exactly one week, I caved.

"You sure you have the stomach for what you're going to see?" he said to me while driving there that Saturday.

"It's not like I was born yesterday."

"Oh, I know, but you need a lot of courage to see the broken lip of a fifty-year-old woman. Especially when you know it was her husband who broke it."

"I have more courage than a few men I know," I said, wanting to goad him.

He ignored me.

"And even more courage to look into her eyes and know how much she hates herself for being in front of you, letting you look at her broken lip."

I watched him drive and decided not to answer. But I liked knowing that there was a sensitive, committed man behind his bad boy, player pose.

Casa Julia was on the southwest side of Eighth Street and Fifth Avenue. The site of the famous street festival was almost vacant now and the only noise came from the domino-playing old men in the park. As soon as we were inside the purposely nondescript building, Pedro Juan gave me a robe, gloves, a first-aid kit in a bag, and two generic-brand disposable cameras. We entered an infirmary of sorts where there were already two other girls with robes similar to mine and a guy dressed in jeans, a tie, and a white shirt with the sleeves rolled up.

"On Saturdays we receive ambulatory cases," Pedro Juan explained. "Marcos provides legal counsel and we document their wounds in case they decide to press charges later on. Migdalia, Frances, and I cure their injuries, if needed, and offer them shelter."

"What if they talk to me? What do I say?"

"Most won't. Few come here ready to leave their abuser. If they talk while you're treating them, listen, but don't put yourself in their place."

"Why not?" I asked.

"Because if you put yourself in their place, you will be in a place from where you will not be able to help them. All right? All right then, let's get to work," he said, slapping my butt playfully, and then disappearing before I could protest.

Soon after, a Miami-Dade County bus arrived with a dozen and a half broken dolls. Most of them were there because a neighbor or a police officer had seen the abuse and, in compliance with new domestic violence laws, had made the complaint on behalf of the woman. Before the women involved in a complaint could go back home, the county required they at least listen to their options at an authorized counseling center. In this case, Casa Julia.

And I, who'd wanted to die because of infidelity, just didn't know how to look into the eyes of these women, whose beauty hid behind the rubble of broken noses, fractured clavicles, swollen lips, and bloody blouses.

I'd barely been there an hour when I had to accompany one of them to the bathroom because she was convinced her husband could be hiding there, behind the shower curtain, under the toilet seat, or on the other side of the tiny window over the sink. While she peed, she looked from side to side and held on to my hand, all the time apologizing for being afraid.

I spent the rest of the day cleaning wounds with hydrogen peroxide and rubbing triple antibiotic on people so destroyed, physically and psychologically, that it felt like walking into a flood with a pail. They were like me, loving the one who broke them. Except they were only able to breathe in, their purple mouths always drowning in saliva and fear, skin constantly working to rebuild itself. Still, I knew there was that thing we had in common: I couldn't completely let go of love that was hurting me either.

In one or two occasions, my gaze settled on Pedro Juan as he worked on a girl named Amelia. She was sixteen years old. Her mother had been thrown down the stairs during the night and was at Jackson Memorial Hospital. Amelia's mouth was bruised and blue. She'd made the complaint against her father, had nowhere to go, and would stay at the shelter. I watched as he cleaned her wounds with such tenderness, that I felt like hugging him, like hugging everyone, because just like there was a lot of pain there, you could also feel the love and hope of those working.

A couple of times I noticed Frances, Migdalia, and Marcos looking first at me and then at Pedro Juan with curiosity, but there was no time to talk, much less to ask questions. When it was time to go, I said my good-byes to everyone and went to the car to wait for Pedro Juan . . . and to cry.

"If you cry, I won't bring you again," he said, opening the driver-side door.

"You only say that because you don't have a uterus."

"Well, you got me there."

"Sorry. I just don't know how you can see so much . . . violence . . . day after day and not be affected by it."

"It does affect me. But I know they'll remember that I didn't ask questions, that I didn't judge them, and that they can come back and stay any day they want, and that they'll be able to bring their children and start over. And then I'll be able to help them because they'll be ready, having decided they will not be hit again," he said, wiping off my tears. "Besides, if I cry I'll just get ugly."

"Who said you were pretty?" I said amid the tears.

"Listen, lady, considering I've seen you dressed up like the town drunk, like the bitchy neighbor with the wrinkly clothes, and as Madame Nostradamus just a few days ago, I wouldn't talk if I were you. By the way, what're you going to do with your pill once you get it to work?"

"Talk to my boss, beg him not to fire me for working secretly on company premises . . . and trust that he'll support me so that the board of directors at least considers analyzing the possibility of financing viability studies."

"Well, something tells me you're going to do that and more," he said with this weird, proud husband expression.

"What makes you so sure?"

"That the good ones always win . . . and you don't look it, but you are one of those—you know, good ones."

"Is that why you brought me today?"

"I brought you to torture you, of course. What do you think?"

"Seriously."

"Okay. I wanted you to see you're not the only one who suffers. That everyone has their own Hell they don't know how to get out of," he said with a smile. "Maybe one day you'll tell me about yours."

"I don't have one."

"Of course not . . . In addition to everything else, you're now going to turn out to be a liar."

"In addition to what else?"

"In addition to beautiful," he said, running his hand down my cheek before turning on the ignition.

Oooookay . . . now I'm screwed, I said to myself.

Going to Casa Julia with him had been good for me. At any other time in my life the experience would have made me look at him with different eyes, maybe even consider the possibility of being with this man who could be laughter and stillness, sensuous and innocent, simple and complex, all within that one body and at the same time.

But it wasn't another time. It was this one. And as Benji liked to say, *"mi horno no estaba para galleticas,"* meaning my "oven" wasn't, and didn't want to be, up for baking cookies with anyone, and that included Pedro Juan.

{seventeen}

They say that when it rains with the sun still shining brightly over the sky, a witch is getting married.

I believe that when it rains just before dawn, and the stars are still twinkling visibly through the fading blue translucency above, a chemist is turning into a magician.

That's why I studied chemistry. I wanted to be a magician, and magic is nothing more than what begins when medicine, alchemy, chemistry, and physics come to a halt.

What was once considered evil witchcraft—the transmutation of metals, atomic disintegration—is really the work of some scientifically inclined Robin Hood extending his faith in humanity further than logic wanted to allow.

The night of my visit to the shelter of broken dolls, I didn't sleep at all, and the following night, a Sunday, was even worst. I began to have nightmares as soon as I closed my eyes, and they continued until I managed to wake myself up when the alarm clock on my night table told me it was four o'clock in the morning.

I closed my eyes again, resolved to get some sleep, but in that place between waking and sleeping, the bridge between my mind and my unconscious functioned as a View-Master where I saw a backlit word: balance.

I opened my eyes. I closed them again to see if it was still there, under my eyelids. It wasn't. Balance. What did it mean? To balance means to level out, to make things equal on some level. I closed my eyes again and went back to the day I saw a PEA molecule under my microscope for the very first time. I remembered the pinkness of the formation, the two carbons and the dashing but lonely nitrogen. I opened my eyes for good this time, feeling myself sweat.

Balance. Two carbons and one nitrogen wasn't balance. One nitrogen and one carbon was balance, and in this way I could take the molecule to its simplest form, without losing any of the components that made it magical.

How the refreaked out hell hadn't it occurred to me before? I put on a knee-length jean jacket over my sleeping sweats and drove over to NuevoMed. I'd need microscopes more precise than the ones I had at home to see the subtle changes that eliminating one carbon would cause.

It was five in the morning by the time I got there and Charlie, the security guard, greeted me with a disturbed, puzzled look.

"Something wrong, Mrs. Luna?"

"Not at all, Charlie. And it's no longer Mrs."

"Ohhhh . . . I'm sorry to hear that. You go right ahead now."

"Thanks," I said rushing to open my lab, where I was welcomed by the hum of the ultra-cold air conditioner needed here to keep unstable chemical substances as unadulterated as possible.

When I began my work with the pill, I did it with two carbons and one nitrogen, which is the way the human body makes PEA. I mixed that formula with endorphins, adding one carbon and then two carbons, then adding one nitrogen, which was one way of achieving balance. But that had given me the shakes and caused hallucinations, so I had varied the quantities of each component a thousand and one times with horrendously unstable results.

But now I saw clearly. PEA doesn't work on quantities smaller than sixteen hundred grams. All I had to do now was to eliminate one carbon and elaborate a pill with eighteen hundred milligrams of the restructured molecule, effectively keeping it from being voraciously metabolized by the body, neutralizing heartbreak without causing secondary effects.

I finished the procedure and mixed and stored enough batches of it to last me a week. Then I pushed aside a pan full of sulfuric acid and a liter of glycerin to reach the very last Orangina in my lab's mini fridge. I dissolved the almost two thousand milligrams of the first batch of my antiheartbreak concoction into my fizzy drink, put a Lila Downs CD into the computer, and sat on the window ledge to watch the sun come up over the corner of Kendall Drive and U.S.1 before drinking my invention.

As I drank, the day began to dawn ever so slowly, inside and outside of me. I could still see the stars shining despite the incipient brightness of day, and I began to dance among the jars, the mice, and the microscopes; inundated by intense joy and the rapturous optimism permeating the conditioned air of my little gray lab. I sang and danced until, exhausted, I let myself plop down among the medical journals and folders spread out on my desk, realizing that for the first time in a long time, I was happy.

{eighteen}

I'm going to ask you to be as honest and direct with me as I've been with you from the day I hired you."

"You're scaring me, Santi. What's going on?"

He'd sent his assistant for me. He, who always called me directly, or dropped by my office unannounced. Then he'd made me wait outside his office for twenty minutes before calling me in, and Norma, his longtime secretary, usually so courteous and friendly, hadn't even offered me coffee. To say this didn't bode well would be an understatement.

"Sit down," he said as soon as I entered. "Would you like a Pepsi? Water?"

"I'll take the Pepsi. With ice."

He served it in silence from the improvised mini-bar at the other end of the office. That area looked more like an ode to the mid-century modernist design on which he was an expert, than an office. All the furniture was from his personal collection: a

Paul McCobb bookcase, a George Nelson credenza, an Amelia Pelaez painting and another, more contemporary one, by Nereida García-Ferraz.

"Has another drug company made you an offer?" he asked in dramatic point-blank fashion, handing me the glass and going to stand by the window like they do in soap operas.

"I don't know what you're talking about, Santi," I said, knowing exactly what he was talking about.

"Someone came up to me, about a week ago, to warn me about instances of strange . . . behavior on the premises."

In the drug industry, "strange behavior" is code for exchange of privileged information, the insertion of corporate spies, or the theft of prescription medicines.

"Santi—"

"No, no, no. Let me finish," he said, acting more and more like soap opera actor Andrés Garcia as he sat on his black leather Eames lounge chair. "I didn't believe the reports. You have, after all, been like a daughter to me. I hired you when you'd just graduated from college, I've mentored you, and here you are. But this morning I get here . . . and I run into Charlie, the security guard. The overnight security guard who hasn't gone home because he needs to talk to me . . ."

"Santi—"

"And he tells me you were here at five in the morning last Sunday . . . in your pajamas. Then I enter my office, haven't even put my suitcase down, and what do I have in front of me if not Purchasing's monthly balance breakdown? The same one that shows . . . that you've spent your six-month budget in three, buying compounds that have absolutely nothing, nothing, nothing to do with Varitex!"

"I was going to pay it back, but they wouldn't let me buy what I needed in big quantities without the company license number and . . ."

Santi shook his head as if asking "What compounds?" but I knew he just shook it because he couldn't believe what he was hearing.

"And as if that wasn't enough, you've been avoiding me, and everyone else here, for months. You don't have lunch in the cafeteria; you don't speak up at meetings . . ."

"I hate meetings."

"Yes, but you're paid to contribute your knowledge and perspective to the company business and lately you've done neither. It's not like I want to toot my own horn here, but I think I've been a good boss, haven't I?"

"You've been a great boss, Santi," I confirm.

"Aha . . . 'a great boss.' Then, I ask, what is happening, Erika? And please, don't lie. Obviously, I'm going to have to fire you. . . . And I'm sorry. But I give you my word that I'll do everything in my power to keep the company from pressing charges against you. All I want from you is the truth. You owe me that much."

I hadn't even thought about lying. Not even now, shamed that my boss, who'd always respected my work and treated me with genuine affection, would have to threaten to fire me.

I crossed my arms and looked away to keep from crying, my eyes resting on the seventies orange poster that showed a group of hippies making bubbles while looking at the sky with a "far out" expression. It read: "Drugs are beautiful." For some reason, it made me more confident that Santi would understand. So I took a deep breath and . . .

"Santi, remember when I gave you that Varitex questionnaire a few months ago and you told me that something was missing? A great discovery, something that would energize us?"

"Sure, I remember," he answered, scratching his head anxiously.

"I think I have it."

"Erika, don't give me . . ."

"I do, Santi. I can feel it," I said, placing my hand on my heart to emphasize. (I knew how to be dramatic, too.)

"I don't understand . . . what is it you have?"

"The heartbreak pill."

You'd think he'd be surprised, or that he'd at least ask what I was talking about. But nope.

"The heartbreak pill . . ." he repeated, scratching his chin. "You mean an antidepressant?"

"I'm talking about a new technology, based completely on the principles of chemical biology. Processes that our body was made to execute and that could balance the effects of love, or rather, the aftereffects of bad love."

"You're . . . serious . . ." he said, getting up and out of the lounge chair, doing away with the formal distance of the desk between us.

"I've been taking the most recent formula for a week now and, judging by how I feel, I think it works. It's as much as I can say until I can do things the right way, and test on other humans."

"A week? A week . . . the morning Charlie saw you?" he asked, beginning to put the two and two of my seemingly irrational behavior together.

"Yes."

"What do you mean you've been taking it, Erika?" he said, reverting to his usual self for a minute. "I don't even have to tell you the risks that involves. There are procedures for these things. You've put your health and the company's credibility at risk."

The scolding was long and torturous, but by lunchtime, he was making excited little jumps and his mind was on the future: he wanted to make a presentation to the board of directors, he wanted a first phase of lab tests, he wanted clinical tests . . .

"We'll call it Elle, or something like that, something sophisticated. It'll be the discovery of the decade," he said eagerly. "Erika, do you realize this could win us a Nobel prize?"

"Too controversial, Santi."

"You're right. Then it'll be the designer drug of the year. Remember controversy equals sales. We'll be in all the newspapers. . . . Maybe we should call a meeting with Lizandra's group . . ."

"*Ay no, Santi.* No, no, no, please. Give me some time. Let's wait before talking about this. Let me take the formula a little longer before I have to start defending it to the world."

"Will you stop taking it if I forbid it?"

I shook my head.

"All right. You're the boss, then. One week," he said as if he'd said a year. "In fact, take a few days away from the office. Go to the doctor. Have him do a complete physical—heart, blood pressure, CAT scan, etcetera, then just concentrate on observing and noting the effects of the compound. When you're ready, we'll revolutionize the scientific world," he said, brushing his big mustache with his fingers. "And Erika?"

"Yeah?"

"Can I ask a personal question?"

"Sure."

"Is this . . . about Martin? I mean, is it because of him?"

"It's because of me," I said to his skepticism. "Because of everything, I guess," I admitted after a few seconds. "But now I'm the one who has a question to ask," I said, wanting to change the subject.

"Like I said. You're the boss now."

"Were you really going to fire me?"

"What choice did I have? I have a responsibility to the board and to this company . . . and to Reynaldo Santiesteban, damn it, who's spent his life here working," he said, without looking at me. "But I assure you that it would have devastated me to do it. And it hurts me now that I didn't realize how hard the divorce had been on you. Maybe I should have helped you, helped you both, more . . . especially with his business woes and all that's happened recently."

"What are you talking about?"

"Well, you know, they just lost Wendy's and South Miami Hospital."

"No!" I said, thinking Martin must have been going crazy. Those two clients were his rice and beans, representing more than fifty percent of his business.

"How did you find out?"

"Lizandra told me . . . her sister, you know, this Sunday . . . well, you know."

"Yeah, I know."

"She told me about it when I refused to approve her choice of them as agency of record."

"Conflict of interest?"

"Please," he guffawed. "If I had a son, I'd make him vice

president. This is about the fact that they've been slacking off, Erika. The big advertising and public relations agency is a thing of the past. Now it's all about 'creative workshops.' Places full of young ideas, flexibility, and better prices. I don't have to tell you things would be different if you were still married. Everything would stay in the family, Martin would have had a vested interest in our continuing to do well and we'd be paying favored-client rates. You know what I mean?" he said tapping his temple with his index finger as if saying the world belongs to those who use their head. "But that ship has sailed. Plus, NuevoMed doesn't need to associate with anyone to stay up to date. We have innovation to spare here," he said, smiling so wide he could've bit his ears.

As Santi talked, my doubts about the pill were renewed, outlined by a strong feeling of compassion for Martin. That agency was his life, and after the first few moments of shock, I strained to focus and remind myself that he was no longer the center of mine. What *I* had to do was take care of *myself,* keep a check on *my* feelings, and make sure Elle worked.

"Santi, remember, you promised me more time."

"More time, yes."

"And you won't tell anyone."

"No one at all."

"I'm serious."

"I've never been more serious."

"That's what worries me."

"Well, don't worry beforehand, worry after there's something to worry about, which would make more sense."

What didn't make sense was continuing to try to have a serious conversation with a boss whose soul had abandoned his body, his corporate self's fear of risk now tempered with scientific exhilaration at the thought of actually making something new, if not by visions of architectural blueprints for a bigger building for NuevoMed, with twice the scientists with whom to revolutionize the industry until the end of his life, if not mine.

{nineteen}

I decided to be a good girl and have the physical Santi recommended. I also had an electrocardiogram, a CAT scan, a PET scan, and every other scan he was able to get NuevoMed Pharmaceutical to pay for. What can I say? I owed him.

So as agreed, I took notes of everything, from what I dreamed to what came out of my body when I went to the bathroom.

If Martin happened to come to mind, I'd write it down, wanting to be able to pinpoint the exact moment my memory of him ran out of batteries, no longer able to invade my caudate nucleus. In fact, every morning I'd conduct a little test: I'd look at one of his pictures for at least thirty seconds, taking my pulse before and after. Even though my pulse did accelerate while I looked, it always went right back to normal as soon as I put the offensive photo out of my sight, giving new meaning to the phrase *"ojos que no ven, corazón que no siente,"* which means "eyes that can't see, heart that doesn't hurt."

Better yet, no more cravings for his voice. No more tormenting myself listening to Gilberto Santa Rosa's rendering of Pablito Milanes's classic or torturing the neighborhood by singing it . . .

Muchas veces te dije
I told you many times
que antes de hacerlo,
that before going forward . . .
había que pensarlo muy bien
we'd have to think it through

No more pacing my apartment, clinging to the walls, dragging myself across them to pour his memory, like salt, on my wounds.

No doubt about it. I was much better: my little apartment looked as if it had come out of the style sections of *Lucky, Dwell,* or *Domino* magazines. I ate less and better and I exercised more, I read more books and less tabloids, I watched more foreign movies and less television. I spent Saturdays helping Pedro Juan at the shelter, and on Sundays I'd buy roses, even if only to throw the petals in the toilet when they withered.

Despite all my progress, my family and friends still felt entirely free to tell me how to manage my life.

"Listen to what John Gray says," said Lola, opening his book wide, right there on the table of the organic restaurant where we were having lunch after a Pap smear that reminded me that we are women in a man's world in the tactless form of the forceps-like contraptions used to execute it.

"John who?"

"The one who wrote that women are from Venus and men are from Mars?"

"Oh, yeah, that John. I'm sure he has a clue."

"The first attribute that makes a woman most attractive," she ignored me, "is self-assurance. Most women have noticed some special women who have men wrapped around their fingers. They wonder how the special woman does it: That man will do anything she wants. These special women always exude an air of grace and trust. They are self-assured. They respect themselves and assume others will respect them. A self-assured woman trusts that others care and that they want to support her. She does not feel alone. She feels supported by friends and family and by men. In her mind, almost all men are likable until proven otherwise."

"Well, that's just shameless," I said.

"Shameless because?"

"Not only does he declare all men good and pleasant, but he dares publish it."

"Hey, are you sure that heartbreak pill of yours has no obnoxiousness-inducing properties? You're a hard pill to swallow today, my friend," said Lola, shaking her head while taking a huge bite of organic salmon. *"Wah chu nehed ee chu eet eople."*

"Eat what?"

"What you need is to meet people," she repeated, swallowing. "Especially men, and prepare yourself, because you're going to have to kiss a lot of toads before you find the prince who will replace Martin, who, while we're at it, was the biggest toad of all."

"Can't my prince arrive with all his evil spell issues resolved and ready to ingest?"

"Look, not that you have to fall in love tomorrow, but at

least look around you. Notice someone . . . the doorman, the waiter, the mailman, even Pedro Juan, for crying out loud."

"Oh, no. Nah. Uh-uh. As in heeeeeeell no."

"Why not?"

"Because."

"Good answer, 'because.' "

"I don't need someone who's going to complicate my life, Lola," I said, spitting the carrot and alfalfa smoothie blend I'd ordered.

"Erika, you were born complicated. Let's not blame Pedro Juan for that, okay?"

"Oh, ha! Ha, ha, ha," I mock-laughed. "Lola made a joke. Have some pity people. Laugh. You, ma'am . . ." I said in the direction of a woman whose family must've forgotten to tell her she died five years before, so slowly did she eat her avocado sandwich. "Please, laugh. It's not that hard, we promise you."

"Very funny," said Lola. "Good thing she can't hear you. And I insist: get out and meet people."

"Don't you mean *eet eople?"*

But it was as if she'd cursed me.

The next day I woke up at six in the morning, tired of resting and taking notes, resting and taking notes, resting and taking notes. It was raining softly and a street cleaning crew swept what was left of the evening with big mechanical brooms and resigned faces. I observed it all from my minuscule balcony on the fourth floor of 3333 Rice Street, while the neighborhood was still sleeping.

I decided the moment was tailor-made for café mocha and a newspaper, so I put on some flip-flops, denim shorts, and a white macramé halter top and walked to the Starbucks on

Grand Avenue. Once there, I ordered my coffee, paid for it along with a copy of the *Miami Herald,* and sat at one of the little tables they put out on the sidewalk, ready to enjoy the self-created, touristy feel of my morning.

But I hadn't gotten past the front page when I noticed a young guy with a nice tan and dirty blond hair in a crew cut. He was somewhat thin, though wiry, and he had strong arms and a firmly set jaw below the greenish eyes now looking at me, unabashedly. I decided to scrutinize him with the same intentness so he'd feel embarrassed and look away. No such luck.

He smiled, coming over immediately, like a child who's been offered cake.

As he walked toward me, I couldn't help focusing on his smile. It was beautiful and reminded me of religious portraits of Madonnas with fresh, powder-white skin smiling kindheartedly.

"Speak Spanish?" he said smiling the smile.

"Sí," I answered.

"Then tell me your name and the names of the two people I should thank for making you so beautiful," he said, relieved there were no language barriers to his Don Juan strategy.

"Venus," I said to tease him. "And why are you not in school, young man?"

He seemed taken aback as he answered.

"I'm twenty-six."

"In that case, hasn't anyone ever told you it's dangerous to talk to strangers when your mom is not around?"

"Actually, my *mami* did warn me about strangers . . . just forgot to tell me what to do if the stranger looked like you. For the record, I'm flirting. We don't have to get married if you don't want to."

He was right. I'd lost all sense of the harmless notion of flirting, and if I was ever going to "eet eople" as Lola had advised, I'd better begin to practice with a breathing specimen *pronto*.

"You're right, I'm sorry," I said.

(Five minutes and I was already apologizing. What is it with us women and the "sorry" thing, anyway?)

But he just smiled; his incredibly white teeth illuminating everything, from his tanned face to the huge sign above him that read "trouble ahead."

"What's *your* name?" I asked, seriously starting to entertain the possibility of very, very, very bad behavior. After all, I *was* on vacation and abstinence had been obscenely long and cruel.

"Icarus."

"Really . . ."

"If you can be Venus, I can be Icarus."

I detected his accent: Cuban. Same as my neighbor. In other words, not just trouble. Really big trouble.

"Erika," I said, quickly erasing the image of Pedro Juan, before I could worry about what he'd think of this and stunt my natural flirting inclination.

"Erika . . . Erika," he said as if trying it on for taste. "Well, Erika, I'll say this: if you could see how delicious you look, sitting there, reading your newspaper without a care in the world, with your hair a mess as if you'd just woken up and your face just washed like a little girl's . . . I think you wouldn't make things so difficult for me."

"Wow. You're really good," I said in English, a bit sarcastically even, while my head noticed how easy it was to forget about his age with every word that came out of his mouth.

"You'll have to translate the actual meaning of that. I'm terrible when it comes to English-language double-meanings. I put up a good fight in Italian though, and I won't go hungry in French, but English . . ." he said, letting his eyes roam down my neck, clearly letting me know the words were just there as background for the real conversation going on live though nonverbally between his eyes and my neck.

I was doing a lot of looking, too, as I thought about the one million more important things I could be doing at the moment without the slightest intention of doing any of them.

"Forget it. It wasn't worth repeating. So, tell me, really, what is your name and what do you do when you're not flirting with harmless strangers?"

"Darien, and I used to be a manager here, at this Starbucks."

"Not anymore?"

"Nope. Approximately sixty minutes ago I became a citizen of the world, free from the oppression of labor caused by turbo-accelerated modernism," he said with a satisfied expression, before rushing to clarify. "Not that I was fired. I quit. Leaving . . . for Italy."

"Oh. What will you do there?" I asked, looking down distractedly to direct his gaze to my breasts.

"Paint."

Why am I not surprised? I thought. A bum.

"I have a scholarship to continue my art studies in Rome . . ."

Oh, well, in that case . . . said Erika, the snob, to herself.

"What kind of painting do you do?" I asked out loud.

"I'm inclined toward surrealism."

"Like Dalí?"

"I wish," he said, staring intently at my face. "Are you married?"

"Yes . . . No . . . I mean, no . . . I mean I just got divorced. But don't worry; nobody wants me enough to be jealous over me."

I meant it as a joke, but as soon as I'd said the words, they were real enough to touch, to feel so true.

"I think we can fix that," he said, smiling the smile again. "And it occurs to me that you should spend the rest of the day with me."

What did I tell you? She cursed me, Lola did. Not only had I *"eeten eople,"* but the *"eople"* seemed to be exactly what the doctor had prescribed: simple, without complications, and the perfect way to find out if my pill had been able to erase Martin from every last neurotransmitter in my brain.

When I finally said yes, I waited, expecting to see a trace of triumph in his face, something to tell me that he was thinking something like "Got her; a sugar mama to tide me over until my trip," because that's how I felt: ancient and wise, but pathetic and vulnerable at the same time.

But if he thought it, he hid it well.

"I just sold my car. You mind if we go in a taxi?"

"No problem. It'll be fun. Expensive, but fun," I said.

"Oh, don't worry about it. Let me take you out in style. . . . Well, actually, my style," he said looking intently at my face before asking, "You really want to spend the day with me?"

"Yeah, really," I smiled.

"Then, just wait a bit. I'm waiting for my last paycheck."

"Why don't you pick me up in front of that building over

there in about fifteen minutes?" I told him, writing down my address on a napkin, but leaving out my apartment number, before rushing off.

"Erika!" he called out to me after I'd already crossed the street. "Don't take too long."

It was a quick, soapless bath. My pessimist mind saying: "Take a bath if you want one, but know it's highly unlikely he'll be waiting when you look out the balcony."

Of course, my extremely horny, girlish-romantic mind defended me: "Shut up, idiot. Does it bother you so much that she should enjoy a moment of peace?"

"Oh, come on, we both know the last thing she's looking for in that one is peace."

I left them arguing in the bathroom, put on a green cotton baby doll dress, some low-heeled, dark leather sandals with delicate rhinestone details, let my hair down; curls, tangles, and all, added a woven purse with bamboo handles, amber earrings, and out I went, closing the door ever so carefully.

But not carefully enough.

"Hey, you! Good morning. Going to get breakfast? Want me to go with you?"

It was Pedro Juan.

"Hi, oh . . . no. No, no. I'm just . . . going toooooo . . . run some errands . . . with my father . . ."

"This early?"

"Yeah, you know . . . county things . . . papers. You know how government agencies are . . . I'm actually late so . . . ciaoooo," I said, taking the stairs two at a time so he wouldn't insist.

The taxi was already waiting and I liked that Darien never

doubted I'd come. I wanted to be like him, confident, secure, never sad over the man who'd left, or guilty for the one who couldn't see I had nothing to give at the moment, other than the most uncommitted of flirtations. Besides, why the hell should I be guilty? Pedro Juan wasn't my boyfriend, or my lover, or my anything.

Unaware of my internal contradiction, Darien gave the taxi driver the address for the Miami Art Museum downtown.

It was the strangest cab ride ever: we were silent the whole way there, probably feeling the strangeness of what we were doing, me sneaking peeks at him as he looked out the window, as if he'd never seen Miami, thinking I wouldn't have believed the Virgin Mary herself if she'd told me the day before that a couple of hours later I'd be on my way to a museum with a sexy young stranger six years my junior, and that I'd be glad I had. Once we got there, I got to see Darien's inner child in action and couldn't remember the last time I'd laughed so hard.

"Did you know Edward Hopper's wife was so freakishly jealous that he took pains to avoid painting anybody else?"

"Maybe he loved her so much he didn't want to paint other women."

"No, I don't think so. I think it was to avoid getting beat up by her . . . look at those wrestler arms—she could have beaten him up and taken all his painting money. Okay, don't believe me. I swear to you, it's still *the* rumor of the 'international art world,' whatever that means," he added when I laughed at his story.

In between this painting and that one, he took my hand and I let him. But when he tried to kiss me in one of the few corners hidden from the mimelike museum security guards, I put my hand between his mouth and mine.

"Let me make myself clear. This is as far as you're going to get with me . . . today. I mean, not that you're going to get somewhere after today. I mean, I'm not saying it will or it won't, I mean, what I'm trying to say is . . . this is . . . let me know if it's a problem." I gave up reciting what could pass for the most incoherent contractual clause ever spoken by someone who'd wanted to "be clear."

"No problem at all," he said, looking straight into my eyes. "Does it bother you that I tried?"

"Well, if I were your age, it might've. But I understand what I've led you to think by coming with you and . . . look, I know I'm not some fifteen-year-old virgin, but," I said, hearing myself sound ridiculous and feeling painfully aware of the fact that it had been almost a decade since I'd dated anyone, never mind picked up a complete stranger. "Just forget it."

"Listen: age doesn't matter."

"Of course it does."

"To get to know each other, to share art—here, now—it doesn't. And I was having such a good time looking at that cute face you make every time you like a painting, hoping you'll look at one of mine like that some day," he said with a syrup-dripping gaze. "That's enough for me. You know, for today of course," he finished with a wink and a little smirk.

"Sure you're only twenty-six?"

"Let's go," he said, pulling me with him. "We have a lot left to see."

We talked about everything. About Cuba and Puerto Rico and about the plight of Latin America in general; about art, about dreams and regrets, likes and dislikes. Then we took a cab to Miami Beach where he had frog legs and I had lobster crab cakes. Appetizers that wouldn't interfere with our hunger to get to know each other. When I told him I'd never had foie grass, he promised he'd take me to a great place for it and I thought it was sweet of him to pretend to make plans that included me, though I was sure I'd never see him again.

I asked him what he thought of the possibility of a heartbreak pill, as if I'd read it somewhere.

"You can't eliminate love's pain."

"Why not?"

"First, because it's the noblest pain there is. Second, because through it we learn to grow as people. And third, because . . . what is art, poetry, and music but the transformation of an artist's pain into a present for humanity? The artist delves into what hurts him and releases it as an offering for the uplifting of those who come after him. It's like . . . like the supreme sacrifice or something like that, *me entiendes?*"

After hearing that, as you can imagine, if there were any saliva left in my mouth, what didn't fall on the floor evaporated between my open mouth and the horny vapor seeping out through my dress.

We walked on the beach and seven times he tried to kiss me. Or rather, he kissed me. Every time I took longer to separate and look at him with my strict-teacher look.

We got to a place where there were ten white beach loungers, one over the other and tied with a chain. Darien put his hands on my waist and lifted me up onto them.

"Hey! Hey! What the . . . Hey!" was what I heard, and it appeared to be coming out of my butt.

I jumped down just as the voice said, "Go away, man. I'm trying to sleep!"

It was a homeless man, sleeping under the seats with the same abandon one might sport at a five-star hotel. Darien laughed hard, and ten yards away, once over the scare, so did I.

"I have an idea," he said suddenly. "Let's go dancing."

"You know how to dance?"

"I'm Cuban," he said as if that fact alone preempted any discussion.

Night was fast approaching, and I thought, what the hell.

"So let's go," I said.

We went to a place called Café Mystique and danced for hours before taking a rest, watching the scene in silence, smiling at each other across the noise whenever they played a slow, voluptuous salsa song and the old man sitting close to us got up to show off with his sexy, white-haired, octogenarian wife. By the time we went back to the dance floor, I was ready to make the semi-dark room my ally, to kiss and let myself be kissed.

The way to "some place" where we could be alone (his study) was short and calm. He opened the door and invited me in. I declined his offer of coffee and took the time to observe every detail while he opened a bottle of wine.

"You like tulips?" I asked, pointing to three that had begun to wither in a flower pot next to a smallish, honey maple futon bed. "Me, I'm crazy for poppies. Before, I used to like lilies, but not anymore. Poppies are a lot more beautiful, and sometimes when I'm a little down, I buy sunflowers."

"Actually, I bought those to paint them, but I do like tulips. And now I like you, who are much more beautiful than a poppy . . . or a lily . . . or a sunflower," he said, coming closer to me with each flower he mentioned, a glass of wine in each hand.

When he finally kissed me, it was a long, open-eyed, hungry kiss that made us laugh self-consciously when it was over.

Then he closed his eyes and pressed me against him and I envied him for being the kind of person who could dive into a swimming pool without worrying about his clothes, or the cold, or whether he'd be able to swim.

As I thought, trying hard to focus; he just touched, his hands alternating between the small of my back and my hip bones as if redrawing instead of undressing me.

When he tried to move forward, I stopped him; with little conviction at first, but when his breathing quickened and I felt him losing control, my protests became forceful and, I'm ashamed to say, a bit on the hysterical side.

"Darien, stop. Darien . . . stop . . . Stop!"

He stopped, giving me a puzzled look.

"What's wrong?"

"I got scared," I said to avoid saying "I remembered" or "I still feel married," "I'm confused," or "I don't know what I'm doing."

He laughed and said, "Don't be scared, *mami.*"

But he slowed down after that; a delicious, deliberate, torturous slowness, kissing and holding me tight at the same time, bathing me in wine he later drank from my skin, making and unmaking me with strength and certainty. And when my screams threatened to wake the whole neighborhood, he just held me, rocking lightly on top of me and whispering, *"Calladita . . . así . . . calladita, niña linda,"* which made me even crazier, wanting to bite into his thoughts, search wildly for his center.

We were resting when I heard my beeper somewhere. I got

up to see who was beeping at that hour, but he pulled me back and we fell to the floor.

"No, you're with me now. Come here," he said.

And that's all I'm completely conscious of, except for the charge of electricity coming from his skin, warm to my touch, and the feeling of being full and alive and suspended somewhere on the ninth floor between fantasy and reality and thinking that if stopping time were possible, I could have found hidden truths in that corner of existence.

Which is just what I tried to do: stay there, suspended even as we lay facing each other on the floor, our bodies cool and warm and sticky from wine and sex, my heart filling me whole, to judge by the heartbeats making the lifelines of my palms pulsate; his seeming to teeter on the flutter of the dozens of butterfly kisses he placed on my eyelids during the "after" of that night.

"You feel that?" he asked later, a hand between my breasts.

"What?"

"Your heart . . . it is shaking," he said, smiling. "I thought . . . I mean, I don't know, but a little bird told me I wouldn't get any further than a hug today . . . well, actually, she meant . . . not really today . . . not that she was saying . . ."

"You making fun of me?" I asked, eyes closed.

"No, *mami,*" he said. "But believe it or not, I hadn't spoken a single word to you and I knew, somehow, that I'd reach you . . ."

"Conceited," I said sleepily.

"No, it's not that. It's just that there's no such thing as one-dimensional access, and you were inside of me so quickly, so powerfully. You sitting there, beautiful and just . . . this vision of strength, and I just knew."

I saw myself as he saw me then and it felt like resting after running. I looked inside for the words to explain what I felt, then opened my eyes and just offered him my arms, wanting to thank him for taking me to meet the "me" I'd always wanted to be.

{twenty}

It was the kind of beautiful Sunday morning that wraps itself around you like a thick, sun-warmed towel after a cold swim.

In another part of the city, in the Doral Golf Resort to be precise, Martin was, at that very moment, making the last adjustments to the suit in which he'd marry that afternoon; his beguiling bride probably in a nearby room, surrounded by gushing women who'd repeat how beautiful everything was, only to later spend hours criticizing what they'd praised, with merciless envy.

Meanwhile, in another sun-bathed Miami neighborhood, I moved my hips to the rhythm of merengue, singing *"Nadie se muere por un amor que no le conviene . . . Nadie se muere . . . nadie se mue-e-reeeeeee,"* which means that nobody dies over love that's not good for them, although if you know me a little by now, you know I don't really believe that.

But it *was* the perfect song for the day, as I swept, sang, danced, and moved furniture out of the way in preparation for

DIY day with Lola, Pedro Juan, and even Attorney Consuelo, who'd agreed to come and help Papi and Benji paint the living room for their anniversary dinner next month.

My father and Benji live in the Sabuesera, affectionately referred to by Latino Miamians as the *sous wes* of the city. At one point it wasn't worth the land where the houses stood, but now it's *the* neighborhood for professionals, enterprising self-starters, and other capitalist mammals; its streets stuffed full of Mediterranean lies, as I call the boxes posing as luxury condos, higher-than-thou gate-protected mansions, and the smell of fat-free, latte, eggnog, chai, mocha, frappe, machiatto, and expresso-whipped coffees courtesy of the many Starbuck's that proliferate like gas stations, selling their sugary energy source for well over the three dollars a gallon we're all in an uproar about.

So you walk down this or that street, go up another block on that other one until you get to a dead end, turn right, hang a left, and continue slowly so you don't miss a street that looks more like an alley than an actual street, and there, in the middle of this nonplace is the time machine, circa 1940, a.k.a. my father's house.

It's a small frame-and-concrete cottage with a sloping roof and a balcony guarded by two ancient rocking chairs. Inside, a dining room, a kitchen, a bathroom, and two small bedrooms, one of which is always full to the ceiling with all the things people need but can't get in Cuba. Benji buys it all to send to his mother and brothers who still live there. Things like sweaters they refer to as "pullovers" regardless of style; *zayas,* which means skirts; all kinds of medicines; underwear, *pitusas* (denim jeans) for the *chamas* (little kids), perfumes, lotions, makeup ("because everyone needs a bit of glamour to avoid dying of boredom and disappointment in islands where nothing ever changes"); toys, razor blades, flat-heeled shoes for all that walking and . . . you get the picture.

The second room is unusable, not just because of Benji, but also because of all the people who beg him to take things to their loved ones when he visits his family every year: a letter for Alicita's grandmother; a video of someone's niece's *quinceañera;* photos of Rafael's newborn girl; or a video game for Alfonso's nephew who just turned ten and has never met his uncle in person. People send themselves in bits and pieces to keep the habit of love alive across the ever-widening ninety-mile stretch that separates Miami from Havana.

There's a small, plant-filled deck behind the kitchen where my father gardens, reads, and composes his boleros. It's connected to the living room by white French doors, and on the day of my ex-husband's wedding, I was trying to protect them with blue painter's tape as I sang, swayed, and sashayed to the music of Miami's El Zol 95.7.

"What? What's the problem?" I asked Benji, Papi, Pedro Juan, Attorney Consuelo, and Lola that afternoon, when I caught them staring at me between puzzled and worried.

"No problem, just . . . We thought you'd be feeling a little down today," said Lola, pulling trays and roller sponges out of a Home Depot bag.

"Why? Because Martin's getting married? Well, wrong conclusion. I knew this whole 'have to paint the living room this Sunday, bring your friends, I'm old and tired' thing smelled fishy," I said, looking pointedly at my father. "Listen everybody: don't worry about me. I feel fabulous. It's all perfect. Martín doesn't exist. If you don't believe me, ask Benji."

The Mexican protagonist of the Sunday Afternoon Movie chimed in to say "That bastard" at that precise moment.

But nobody noticed. Their attention was now successfully redirected at Benji and the possibility of his knowing secrets the rest of them didn't, leaving me free to sweep, move furniture, stretch sheets of canvas cloth on the floor, think about Darien, and feel ridiculously guilty.

The worst had been that first morning. Maybe it's happened to you. You wake up next to someone for the first time and realize you were dreaming. That this man snoring beside you just cannot be. You rise to the surface of your body and choose to remember that you have a life to go back to. That you can't just decide to become Mrs. "Mr. Twenty-Something-Year-Old," have his children, and live a good life supported by his very talented painting of skulls, regardless of how tempted you might be to trade in your lived-in life for one so fresh with possibilities.

FROM THE DESK OF ERIKA LUNA

I'm a whore.

I'm a really big whore.

But I refuse to regret it.

That's a lie.

I'm not really a whore.

And I do regret it.

Even though I'd do it again.

And I did do it again. During the two-week sabbatical Santi gave me, I woke up late, took my pill after lunch; then read, drew diagrams, and noted my observations in the afternoon. But as soon as dinnertime rolled around, I'd throw everyone off my scent and run out of whatever restaurant, domestic violence shelter, friend or family home I was in to meet Darien in his studio—a small room with a bath in the back of a private home in Silver Bluff. Once there, I'd bathe in his attentiveness, using his desire like a balm against the mosquito bites of divorce, forgetting everyone and everything, letting him sketch me, talking life and nonsense, and experimenting with single-girl freedom until . . .

"What would you think if I didn't go to Italy?"

"What do you mean, if you didn't go?"

"Well, I have some savings. I could get a job giving art lessons here, and continue my studies with a private teacher."

"I don't get it," I said, alarmed.

"I want to be with you."

"You *are* with me."

"No, I mean *be* with you . . . be . . . with you."

"Please say you're kidding."

"How about I'm in love with you, instead?"

"You'd have to have known me for a bit more than two seconds to say that."

"Two weeks," he corrected me.

"And to even think about throwing your future away, you'd have to have known me one hundred years, or the sufficient time to go insane," I said, really alarmed now.

He stared at me, looking struck, for what felt like a very long time, then turned away, gathering his brushes.

"I think it would take a lot less than one hundred years for you to drive someone crazy," he said finally, mixing brown acrylic paint with limpid white to match the tone of my skin. "*Ya* . . . forget about it, *Mami.* Wipe off that tragic face and cross your legs like I showed you before the paint dries."

So I sat down and posed, for the first time since meeting him realizing the consequences of what I'd done . . . and regretting it. A regret that had nothing to do with Catholic guilt or with the hypocritical sexual restrictions of approximately fifty percent of this society, but with the fact that I'd used him. I'd used another human being to fill my need to feel beautiful and be desired, recruiting him blindly for confirmation that my pill was working, despite knowing from the start that no matter how wonderful he was, and he *was* wonderful, I didn't want to share my life with someone with so much yet unlived. Even worse was the fact I hadn't given a thought to the possibility of his becoming attached and harboring hopes of a relationship, creating with my self-involvedness the very suffering I'd been trying to cure.

The strange thing was, even after weeks with Darien, each night better than the last in every sense, I only felt the warmest of affections for my bright, young painter. Even stranger? The past no longer had a name, a scent, or a taste, just weeks after I'd wanted to die because "it" was marrying another woman. There could be only one explanation: I was on the right track with my pill . . . and my life.

So it was in that spirit of affection—and cowardice—that I tiptoed out that Sunday morning to go to Papi's, leaving Darien to sleep late next to a note that read simply: "You're a beautiful person. I've loved being with you. Please believe I wish great things for you and hope life delivers all that you desire. *Besos,* Erika."

"You couldn't have broken up with him if he was sleeping, Eri," said Benji when he was done scolding me for exposing him as a confidant in front of the others and threatening me with revealing anything that caused him a problem with Papi.

"Shush, Benji. Papi might hear you and then you're the one who'll have to deal with him, *sin comértela, ni bebértela,"* I said, concentrating on the coffee that had served as the pretext to go into the kitchen. "You change your hair color?"

"*Niña,* only you could go from the most absolute respectability to an affair with a twenty-something stud in a matter of days," he said, emptying sugar into a canister to protect it from ants. "You like it? The gray made me look older, and you know Gil always says he's not one for old men, so . . ." he said, running his hand over the new dark brown shade. "But don't change the subject, what's with picking up a man one day and dropping him two days later with a note, no less."

"Two weeks," it was my turn to make the correction.

"There are vibrators for that, you know, and they look like the real thing these days. Men aren't objects."

"I knew there was something going on," said Lola coming into the kitchen and scaring the life out of us.

"*Ay,* forgive me, Lola. I haven't had a chance to tell you," I lied. "And the only reason Benji knows is because he calls at all times of the day and if I don't tell him what's going on, he doesn't keep Papi off my back whenever I don't come over for dinner for more than three days," I said, looking at her doubtful expression. "You think it was wrong?"

"No, *Tía,* please. What would worry me is if you'd done it for revenge."

"I did it for me. I swear it."

"Then everything's fine," interrupted Benji. "And you just relax because I can't speak for Gil, but my motto is live and let live. But wait a minute girlfriend, 'cause you've been saying a lot and not much at all. Now tell us, the painter's tools . . . they work?"

What to say? The sigh that escaped me was such that Benji and Lola went into a fit of laughter and Papi began to ask what the commotion was in the kitchen, putting an end to all the indecent conversation.

"So that's why you got so stressed out at happy hour the other day," said Lola as we headed back to the living room with coffee, garlic toast, and a huge pot of fried chickpeas and chorizo that were all the more delicious for being a day old.

Lola was referring to what'd happened a few nights before, when, after much insistence on her part, and beginning to think it would be good for Darien and me to spend some time with other people, I went along with her to happy hour at a Coral Gables bar called Chispa.

"The problem with living in a world of couples, is that there aren't too many places where one can feel happy to be single," Lola had said, though she was doing so well with her electrician I wasn't sure she could still be considered single. But that was her opinion of the Happy Hour Phenomenon . . . and this was mine.

<u>Happy Hour:</u>

6:00 PM–6:05 PM: The Scrutiny

You walk in and immediately twenty pairs of eyes land down hard on you.

6:05 PM–6:10 PM: The Initial Examination

Of the twenty, ten proceed to check you out discreetly, so as not to alert the girl they're currently trying to pick up.

6:10 PM–6:50 PM: The Calm Before the Fool Storm

This is the apparently quiet time in which remaining contenders try to decide whether to go for you as they surreptitiously glimpse your way every 45.3 seconds, while absorbing huge quantities of liquor.

6:50 PM–6:55 PM: The Weeding

Six of the ten will decide to go after more accessible (read: slutty-looking) prey and three will be too drunk to follow anything other than their own behinds back to their house. (Where waiting for them will be either a spouse who prays every day for a divorce, or a longtime girlfriend who believes he'll finally decide to marry her if she can just give him a little space.)

6:55 PM–7:00 PM: The Obstacle Course

The owner of the last pair of eyes begins to walk toward you, resolute and determined despite the push and shove of the human obstacles in the process of fermentation that surround him. This, by the way, is where the evening is supposed to begin for you.

7:00 PM: The Disappointment

He smiles and you notice his dental health is not the best. In fact, now that he's up close and personal, you notice that what's anchoring him to the ground is the thick gold chain complete with Indian chief pendant hanging around his neck, without which he'd be floating around like an astronaut, so light is his brain.

You think I'm exaggerating? In all, three men came up to me that night. Five minutes after greeting each with a "nice to meet you," the first one told me that the sexual fantasy of his life was to make love to two women at the same time. The second confessed he'd been married to a police officer who made him afraid of women. But the third one dropped the ball and splintered the bat, as we like to say in Puerto Rico.

"Baby, I love you. I *has* to tell you."

"Excuse me."

"No, no, don't go. Stay here, baby, 'cause I may be a little drunk but I know what I saying."

"Right."

"Yeah, 'cause I'm a cool guy, ye know?"

"Un-huh."

"I lov yu. Is ment to bi. Das it, o'aight? Remember what I say: I'm goin' to marry you, baby. Remember."

Of course I left him standing there. What was that, anyway? I found Lola, grabbed her by the arm with my mad woman expression out for everyone to see, and asked her to never, ever, ever again take me to another *horror hour.*

"They aren't all like this," protested Lola.

"We're leaving."

"We got here too late. Everyone's drunk."

"Right now, Lola."

"It's just a matter of experimenting with a few places."

"I'll wait for you in the car."

"Erika!" said Lola, trying to shake me into the present.

"Sorry . . . What?"

"You were on the moon," said Pedro Juan, taking the paintbrush out of my hands. "And you have some paint all over you."

"Some paint all over you" was an understatement. I looked like something out of a Pottery Barn's catalog, my legs now the same light yellow hay color of most of its pages.

"Sure you're okay?" asked Attorney Consuelo.

"Sure. Look, by this time Martin must've married his new Barbie, so if I'm not all right by now, it's getting late for me, don't you think?"

"Barbie, you said? The only 2007 Barbie here is you with your chocolate ringlets and your well-shaped national patrimony, you understand?" answered Benji.

"What's the national patrimony?" asked Attorney Consuelo who, like Pedro Juan, looked right at home among the lunatics I call family.

"Ave María purísima, 'licen,' " said Papi. "The national patrimony is the 'Jennifer López' of *boricuas,* the buns of steel, the luggage, the lobster tail, the big bumper . . ."

"Aaaaah, I see," said Consuelo. "The national patrimony is the trailer, the whole boat, the house with the yard and all."

"There you go!" shouted the others in unison, applauding.

I was glad they'd come. Thanks to my pill, my heart wasn't in pain, but my ego was, and for that there's nothing like being around friends who think you're the holy and perfect victim of that satanic devil, your ex-husband, and who try to cheer you up as you all drink beer, *materva,* or coffee and eat seafood spread, cheese, olives, sausages, crackers, and whatever else your father is able to find in the kitchen.

"But you tell me the truth, and forget that Luis Miguel singer guy for a second," Papi was saying to Pedro Juan. "What bolero written in the last ten years is worth listening to? None! None. Now, see here and listen to this little thing I'm composing for sugar cube over there," he said, puckering his lips at Benji, who blushed like a young girl.

Please wait, I have something to tell you
Don't want you leaving with the doubt
Thinking that in my life you've been
Refuge from storms . . . and bitterness

To which Pedro Juan chimed in, improvising:

It's true . . . you blew in with the rains
But you are . . . the magic of my daaaaays

"Eeeeeeeso," shouted the others, cheering.

"That's a great voice you have there, *Tío*," said Lola.

"Sometimes I don't have an answer for the lack of balance in the universe," said Attorney Consuelo, without rhyme or reason, as usual. "I see it every day with my clients: Martin's already marrying someone else, and here you are without a decent prospect to compose a bolero for you, or sing you a song, or maybe just take you out on a Saturday night," she concluded looking in the direction of Pedro Juan with stupendous obviousness.

But Lola didn't catch on and replied: "The problem is that she doesn't meditate, she doesn't commune with her inner self, and she doesn't let anyone help her. In fact, not too long ago I introduced her to this hottie who works with Carlos, I'm talking major catch, and she didn't even thank me."

"What?" said Papi.

"Ohhhhh, no. Wait just a minute here. Let me tell you all about this so-called 'hottie,' " I said before they all ambushed me.

His name was Néstor and he wasn't ugly. Worst than that: he was pleasant. Like soup. He picked me up dressed in corduroy pants and a silk shirt.

Minus 10 points.

He took me to the The Knife, an Argentine restaurant where the food is great and the service impeccable.

Plus 10 points.

And then, everything went to hell.

"So, you're divorced."

"Yes."

"Me, too. Let me tell you, I know just what you're going through."

"You do?"

"Yes. My wife got married again right away."

"Really?" I said, thinking that being fashion-challenged wasn't a crime.

"But you don't know the worst," he said, lowering his voice. "The worst is she refused to return the breast implants I gave her for her birthday. Now that idiot enjoys them while I get to pay the surgeon's bill for the next three years. I tell you, the next time I give a woman implants, I'll make her sign a contract so she has to return them if we divorce. Fair, don't you think?"

"And as if that wasn't enough, he fixated on my breasts as if he were measuring them with his eyes," I said to the others now.

"And for such a little thing, she discarded the poor guy and didn't speak to me for two days," said Lola.

"I didn't speak to you because of your false representation and blatant misleading," I answered. "That was anything but a hottie. What's more, and I'm reading to you now, for a change," I said, pulling from my bag *What Smart Women Know* and reading. "A smart woman believes any man who tells her . . . He has a problem with commitment . . . He's never really loved anybody . . . He may be moving away soon . . . His ex-wife or ex-girlfriend has reasons to hate him . . . He hasn't found himself . . . He found himself, but he doesn't like what he found . . . He has trouble settling down to a steady job . . . or . . . He needs a team of therapists to keep him functional. In other words," I finished like a politician asking the others to vote for me. "All men. Am I right or am I wrong?"

Everyone admitted I was right. Everyone except Pedro Juan. But since he had a habit of keeping a straight face, only to surprise you by guffawing or making one of his sardonic comments, I waited.

"So you feel ready to meet new people, date?" he asked finally, scratching his chin, still missing his goatee and surprising us all with this question.

I examined his seriousness, the wavy hair, and thick eyebrows à la Brooke Shields.

"I don't know," I answered, omitting that I'd already done a lot more than "go out" with a new man.

"You're still hoping your husband will come back?"

"No!"

"So no one has to fix you up. Go out with someone *you* like."

"I don't like anyone."

"Maybe you haven't looked."

"That's what I keep telling her," observed Benji.

"So just say you think Lola's right and be done," I said.

"On the contrary, I'd tell Lola not to meddle," he said.

"Excuse me?" jumped Lola.

"Who said that? You, meddle?" answered Pedro Juan looking around as if searching for the real culprit. "I meant interfere."

"That's funny."

"Or at least to mind your own business, stop being so nosy, or if you're going to meddle, at least get the girl a decent guy. 'Judge, I want my implants back?' " he finished, his shoulders starting to shake signaling the beginning of one of his seismic laughs. "Judge, I think I'm entitled to the breasts!"

This while grabbing his belly to control his laughter, infecting even my father—a difficult thing to do.

"Miss, I'm sorry, but you're going to have to yield the breasts," said Papi, surrendering.

With which both just let themselves fall on the floor, laughing so hard they looked to be on the verge of crying.

"No, no," said Lola, "make the other guy pay; he's the one using them!"

I'm surrounded by comedians, wouldn't you say?

"Case number three hundred six: hottie versus breast implants," chimed in Attorney Consuelo, so as not to be left out.

I must've done something really bad in another life, because everybody who comes near me is missing a screw or two.

"Stop laughing already, Pedro Juan, it's not funny!" I said later as we drove back to Rice Street together.

"So don't tell me things if you don't want me to laugh."

"Either there're few men worth two cents or I have met all the pigs."

"Hey, don't insult my species."

"Sorry, but you're not normal."

"Are you flattering me now?"

"It's possible."

"Erika, listen . . . One of the things I've made a point of in my own life is to stop explaining myself to others, but I want . . . I'd like you to think about this."

"You going to get serious on me now?"

We'd arrived at our respective doors and stood, centimeters apart. He was giving me a slow look. He began at my hair, which he rumpled lightly as if playing, then my eyes, and finally my lips, where he stopped briefly, before turning his gaze brusquely to the wooden plank floor.

"Love . . . is knowing you are a unique being," he said, ignoring the chemical short circuit we'd just experienced. "You are unique. And you deserve to be with someone who'd die to be with you."

"And if the person I chose didn't love me back?"

"Then that person couldn't make you happy, because he'd make you doubt yourself, who you are and what you're worth."

"Pedro Juan—"

"You and I are already who we need to be. We don't have to change anything for anyone. And we don't have to get involved in 'easy to manage' relationships, or avoid apparently complicated people as an insurance policy against pain," he said looking straight at me.

"Look, I'm just a woman like any other," I said, defensively, remembering Darien existed and wondering just how much Pedro Juan knew about him. "And like any other woman, I'll eventually learn what I need to in order to be a better person," I added, half-turning my back to him to search for my keys.

But he just whirled me around and embraced, or rather engulfed, me, holding me very tight against him.

"Don't learn anything, *bebé.* Just realize you're already perfect. And if you want to improve something, do it, but not so someone will love you. Whoever loves you, will love you no matter what."

I was surprised by the affection beneath his outburst, and even more by his calling me *bebé,* as if I were his sweetheart.

"You're right, I know," I said, stepping away, startled.

"Sermon's over. See you tomorrow," he said, entering his apartment before I had a chance to say good night.

When I got into mine, I had fourteen messages from Darien.

I remembered the note and felt sorry for having behaved the way I wouldn't want anyone to behave toward me. I was afraid to end up hardened and hidden behind the role of a woman so bitter, she's more of a man than a man. "I take them and I leave them. I do to them what they do to us."

The phone rang like an answer.

"It's me."

"I know."

"Something wrong?"

"No."

"Sure?"

I didn't answer.

"Are we seeing each other tonight?"

"No."

A few seconds went by.

"This it?" he asked.

"I think so."

More silence.

"My age?"

"Everything."

Yet another silence.

"And I'm sorry," I added gently, thinking how difficult it is to reject someone who doesn't deserve rejection. No wonder men, instead of facing you, will tell you they're going to the store for onions and never come back.

But when I hung up I felt relieved. Why hurt him and risk confusing myself? This was for the best. I'd continue as I had, free to pursue myself, to move forward with my work, my pill, and my life.

I left Darien to sleep in some corner of my mind so he could get up and leave when he was ready, and I was surprised to find space for him there where once they'd been only rage and pain. There was also space for Pedro Juan: a shady, complex corner . . . mysterious, but with the possibility of being wonderful, a possibility that terrified me.

There in my brain I also found the image of a young Martin, looking just as he had when I'd first met him, with the same hunger for success, with dreams, doing the best he could with what he knew, like me, like everyone else. A Martin I imagined married already and whom I thought of with a peace bordering on oblivion, knowing, nevertheless, that he was my history. That our love, our marriage, and our failure would be part of me for a very long time and that, pill or not, I would never be able to hate him.

{twenty-one}

Once upon a time, there was a Puerto Rican witch with big, coffee-colored eyes and a coil of long unruly curls the color of bark in wizened, old trees.

This witch had suffered terribly. And if she had been a man and a cowboy instead of a woman and a witch, she'd have said she had cured herself by her *cojones*. But she had none. Balls, or cojones, I mean, or even *cajones*, as former political witch, Madeline Albright would say.

All she had was a degree in chemistry and a romantic heart/brain. Her cave was really a lab and her magic potion was a simple formula made of hormones and chemical neurotransmitters.

Her wizard had left her for a sorceress, giving her the perfect reason to become the cliché of the antiman bitch witch; wrinkled by a repugnance resistant even to Botox, using water of distrust as perfume and carrying breasts rotted by hatred in her Calvin Klein bra.

Instead, our witch chose to remain a child, live light and trusting in the land of love as tummy ache, something to be solved with warm milk and pill-shaped chocolate candy and forgotten once over. To do it, she concocted a recipe, her very own witch's brew, using the only magic she had available, better known as science, and in the spirit of the good healers of our grandparents' time, she dreamed of giving her cure away to the world, making it easy to get for any heartbroken soul who needed it.

"Do you need anything else?" Naty asked from the door, purse in hand.

"Thanks, go home, I'm almost done."

"Don't go home too late; remember you didn't eat lunch today."

"Yes, *mommy dearest.* Now get out of here and go home to your husband."

As soon as Naty left, my laboratory/office turned back into a cave, courtesy of the pictures I'd ripped from magazines and pasted any which way on the walls with transparent tape. There were images of distant places, couples bewitched into love by the latest trendy perfume and fabulous models with even more fabulous shoes and faces full of life, or at least full of light from a photographic flash. There were jungle landscapes, reinterpretations of the sun, and ads for luxury yachts and hotels framed by opulent dawns. There were also pictures of flower markets, a happy boy eating a mango so juicy its liquid dripped down his chin, and blue-green broken-down buses filled to the brim with excited, hopeful missionaries. In other words, the mix of what the heartbreak pill was to me the desire to live fully in pill form. The want to live even when you know you're missing a piece of yourself, a sense of confidence in the fact that you're a lizard and trust that your tail will grow back and the pill is just there to help you do your regular running and scurrying around until it does.

In front of me was the notebook that had accompanied me through the long journey with the pieces of my broken heart/brain, and beside it, the most sophisticated presentation I was able to put together: from video interviews and an interactive model of the brain made of rubber and tiny electronic circuitry, to an animated computer slide show with sound effects and a few instances of morphing for spark.

As for the pill, I'd managed to perfect my formula, achieving immediate and consistent results in thirty-six mice as well as in myself. But that was only the beginning. Now I'd have to believe in it enough to win the opportunity to try it on other broken hearts. I had to dare discover that what sustained me through the pain of losing Martin was real and had the power to help people . . . or that it had all been a scientific illusion, a socket without a lightbulb, a firefly without a tail.

I left everything on my desk as if it were a scale model: flasks organized with their labels on, color-coded portfolios for each member of the board of directors of NuevoMed Pharmaceutical reading: "Elle, the Heartbreak Pill" on crisp aluminum-framed white labels, the CD with the animated presentation and my model of the human brain. All the necessary data so they could decide if they wanted to invest in clinical tests, the first step in the long journey to bring a drug to the market in the United States.

"Santi?" I said from his doorway.

"See you tomorrow," he waved at me, before going back to the mountain of paper on his desk.

"I'm ready," I said.

He looked up, tedium replaced by a wide open smile.

"You sure?"

I nodded my head several times, so nervous I could barely speak.

"Calculations?"

"Ready."

"Finance? What do they say?"

"The estimate works. I've already incorporated it into the presentation."

"Then . . ."

"I sent most of the elements to your email. Check them and tell me if you have any questions or if you think I'm missing anything. The rest is just you telling me when the board can see us, and I was thinking if we keep this quiet a while longer it would give us . . ."

The reason I stopped talking was my boss—he looked at me with such pride that I was touched to the verge of tears, as much by his confidence in my ability as by his idealism, his willingness to risk his career along with me.

"Well, we'll have to continue celebrating all night," said Benji later that night when I told everyone about the conversation with Santi during the small birthday dinner party Papi organized to celebrate Benji's fifty-fifth. The same one he'd been celebrating for at least the past three years.

"Not that it isn't an excellent idea, but I was thinking of taking Erika out tonight," said Pedro Juan.

Everybody stopped looking at me to look at him, who chose that moment to hold my inquisitive stare so intensely that the rest couldn't find anything better to do than examine the cracks in the wood of Papi's big old dining room table.

"I have to go to the shelter to leave a copy of the keys—they're installing a new air conditioner tomorrow morning—but I'll be right back to pick you up," he said without waiting to hear whether I wanted to go out with him or not.

"What about everyone else?"

"If they'd like to, they're welcome to come."

To which, of course, one by one, they all excused themselves with translucent alibis, making it clear to me that this had taken more planning then Benji's birthday dinner. Oh, but as soon as Pedro Juan left, I interrogated them.

"What's going on?"

"Nothing."

"Nothing."

"What do you mean?"

"What could possibly be happening?"

"Don't look at me, Erika," said Papi. "I like the boy. And you're both young . . . and single, and I don't see why you can't go out."

"And because we're young and single you all conspire against me?"

"Because of that and because you're stupid if you don't give a man that handsome, nice, and vice-less a chance, not to mention how obviously really into you he is," said Lola. "That enough or you need more?" she finished.

"I'm not ready."

"Precisely why you should go," said Attorney Consuelo.

"Chill, baby," said Benji. "It's just a date. It's not like you're going to marry him, although I'm not going to complain if you decide to screw the—"

"Benji!" said Papi.

"Oh, all right, Gil. *Cualquiera diría.* Sex is necessary and it's been proven that a good fu—"

"Benji!" shrieked Lola and Attorney Consuelo, making fun of poor Papi.

So I went. We walked through Lincoln Road, ate sushi, and listened to jazz at the Van Dyke's second-floor lounge with its red rococo couches and little red candles everywhere.

When we got there, a beautiful, tall, black man sang with a thin white-blond girl as couples looked on, holding hands and drinking martinis. I felt at home surrounded by all these strangers, and to judge by Pedro Juan's happy-comfortable expression, so was he.

"It's the kind of night I'd have planned," I said.

"Glad you're enjoying yourself," he said taking my hand. "And I'm glad you came, even though I had to put my food down in order to get you here," he said teasingly.

"Put your foot down?"

"You know, *meterte el pie,* as they say in good Cuban."

"Oh, okay. I get it. But it really wasn't necessary; it's always good to spend time with friends," I said, softly pulling my hand out from under his and emphasizing the friend part. "On the contrary, thanks for helping me get my mind off things."

"Not why I did it," he said, frowning.

I smiled then, telling him he looked very handsome, which left him speechless for quite a while.

And it was then, as we listened to song after song that seemed to seep in like water, that something strange happened; strange, perhaps, because it's so common. . . .

There you are, minding your own business, not paying much attention to anyone, until you notice (or others make you notice), that he *is* interested in you. Pretty soon, even if only for a few seconds before you discard the possibility, you actually consider it. Precisely because it is a possibility and because it means that maybe, if you dare, something could happen. And that makes it exciting. That's how I interpreted what I was doing by looking at Pedro Juan through the semidarkness of the jazz club with half-closed eyes, detailing his big hands with the hand I'd taken away from under his an hour (and two martinis) before, noticing his mischievous eyes, his strong neck.

Afterward, we walked around South Beach and talked. I told him about the books Lola had lent me and how, despite my skepticism, they'd helped me digest the past.

"I'm not saying I've converted to the self-help movement, but I do think it's possible to extrapolate very valuable lessons from some of these books."

"Maybe you can write a manual to go along with your pill. Something like, 'buy one and receive free, with your purchase . . .' "

"And I know exactly what I'll call it: 'Men are from Earth and they're here to screw us up.' "

I said it to tease him, to flirt, or maybe just to see if he was real and not just a compulsive good Samaritan.

"Well, I have a lesson for your manual, but you have to promise you'll change that horrible title."

"Let's hear it."

"You also have to promise not to get defensive."

"Speak now or forever hold your tongue."

"Learn to accept the word 'no.' "

"What?"

"The great problem facing intelligent women today is . . ."

"Yeees?"

"That they fall in love like idiots. Love and passion is everything. Their own intelligence? Out the window."

"That . . . is a very sexist comment."

"That . . . is a truthful comment."

"That's your lesson for my manual?"

"No, my actual lesson is a complicated concept."

"I'm listening—barely—but go on."

"A woman falls in love with a man. That man gives her a hundred and one reasons to leave him, and just to take care of any possible doubts, another hundred reasons why he's not the right one. And what does that woman do?"

"You seem to have all the answers . . ."

"She lies to herself. She says: he only says that because he doesn't know me. He doesn't know how special I am. When I get him into bed and I do this and this and a little more of that to him, Gumersindo, Jacinto, Jirimillo, or whatever he's called, will fall desperately in love with me," he said, imitating a woman's voice and not a very attractive one at that.

"And it's not true. 'No' means no. You may convince him to the contrary, but you'll be sorry you did. If Martin, for example, or whoever, didn't love you anymore . . ."

"Martin is history."

"Liar."

"How would you know?" I said beginning to feel something very similar to anger.

"Want me to tell you something? Fine. I don't know if it was your pill, or the many times you crashed into your apartment wall—waking me up in the middle of the night more than once by the way—but it's been a while since you suffered for Martin, the actual man. But you're as hardheaded as the most hardheaded of women and you want the one who says 'no.' You want to fix the one who can't be fixed, you want to make the one who left come back, etcetera, etcetera, etcetera."

"Since when are you an expert on what I think and feel?"

"Since I see you in every woman who suffers for love."

I breathed deeply, controlling the urge to kill him.

"You have no right to tell me what I feel."

"No, and you don't have the right to tell Martin what he feels. If he says he doesn't love you anymore, he doesn't love you anymore."

"He already said it."

"But you don't believe him."

"I do believe him."

"But you're still waiting for him to come back so you can shove it in his face that you don't love him anymore."

"Not at all."

"Then pay attention to the person who cares for you."

"When he shows up, I will."

"If you don't pay attention, you won't know when he shows up."

"Oh, right, because men are so subtle: 'Yo, baby . . . yo . . . looking good, Latina,' " I said, mimicking scratching between my legs to complete my characterization.

We were already driving back to my apartment and my mood was such that if someone dared smoke me, they would've been able to kick the habit, right then and there—forever.

"Perhaps," continued Pedro Juan, unaware of my murderous thoughts. "But stop trying to prove yourself right, that your ex did love you and that if he doesn't anymore, it's because the idiot doesn't realize you are the most wonderful woman in the world."

This is the problem with being friends with a man before you've so much as French kissed. We were at the entrance to our building and he was beginning the process of parallel parking in a minuscule space when he finally noticed he was killing romance that hadn't been born yet with every word that came out of his mouth.

"I'm sorry, *bebé.* I'm an idiot," he said. "I just want you to be over him."

"It's okay."

"It's not okay; I wanted you to have fun."

"I did have fun."

"Go out with me again? Start over?"

I smiled at him.

"Maybe I can give *you* some advice," I said.

"Shoot."

"Don't try to save me. Don't try to help, fix, or guide me." Just be and feel when you're with me so I can see you as a man instead of a counselor or a missionary on a rescue mission.

"Believe me, that's the last thing I want, but I don't know what happens when I'm around you. I want to get inside you and keep you from suffering . . . and I want you to notice I'm here. And sometimes, I try to be patient, but blah, blah, blah, blah, blah. . . ."

The blah, blah, blah was because at that exact moment, I looked up toward the building's façade. There was a man leaning sideways against the gate. He looked like he was waiting for someone and there was something familiar in his posture.

"Blah, blah, blah and I want us to get to know each other as two people who could blah . . ." Pedro Juan went on.

The man looked up, the light from the lamppost lit his face and my heart stopped.

It was Martin. The King of Rome.

{twenty-two}

"No one becomes such a woman,
a woman who loves too much, by accident."
—Robyn Norwood, *Women Who Love Too Much*

Of course it's not by accident. Unless the fact we all seem to have a stupid gene that activates the minute we fall in love is an accident, I thought, diving into another one of Lola's books. It was the classic of seventies feminine self-help literature in the United States, *Women Who Love Too Much.* Unfortunately, I was reading it a week too late. *"The following characteristics are typical of women who love too much. . . . Typically, you come from a dysfunctional home in which your emotional needs were not met."*

Well! I mean, it *is* true that my mother took as much after General Patton as my father did after Elton John. But I distinctly remember that their amount of "love and attention to my needs" would've been enough to make brats out of a trio of third-world toddlers.

Of course, only now do I understand my mother's frustration when, about once a month, she'd lock herself up in her room for hours, emerging with a new hairdo and sexy-for-her-housegown; seduction weapons destined to fail. My mother walking around in her long mesh and silk gown, even standing in front of my father, playfully modeling whatever she had donned, only so he could ask her if she'd eaten plastic pork chops and would she mind not blocking his view of the television. He'd continue to be fascinated by José Antonio Cosme, a chef with bulging eyes and a chin as protuberant as Jay Leno's, who'd explain how to prepare Turkish-style meat pies in between jokes on his *Friendo y Comiendo* show. Maybe Robyn Norwood knew what she was talking about after all.

"What're you doing here?" I said to Martin's back that night, after interrupting Pedro Juan's misarticulated declaration of love and making him drop me off at the old News Café at the corner of Rice and Mayfair with the pretext of needing a newspaper for my presentation.

"How're you, *negrita?*" he answered turning around, perfectly composed and relaxed enough to use his usual endearment for me, which, in general terms, means "little black girl," but coming from him always meant "we belong together."

I objected to his choice of a nostalgia-inducing term by raising my left eyebrow with as much skepticism as is possible to fit into a single brow.

"It's good to see you again," he continued.

"Shouldn't you be on your honeymoon?"

"I didn't get married, Erika."

I chortled out a laugh, as sardonic as it was false.

"God, you're incredible! Now tell me, Martin, what . . . can I . . . help you with?"

"Damn it, Erika. Are you deaf? I didn't get married! I

couldn't," he said, pacing to this side and that, as if telling himself instead of me, still unable to believe what was happening to him. "I needed to see you, to talk to you, hell, even to fight with you . . . to have something of. . . ."

There they were, the words I'd searched for like a mother looking for her firstborn inside a packed department store.

"And your wife? And you soon-to-be-born? How can you forget everything and everyone so easily? Oh, that's right: you've had practice."

He breathed deeply, always the publicist searching for the right thing to say, while I got busy putting up an imaginary brick wall between us, plastering it with cement for double safety.

"Listen, when I told Marisol how I felt—that I had doubts, that I thought of you after all that'd happened—she, at first, she threatened me with an abortion . . . and then I understood, and later, she understood that marrying would be a mistake."

"You're crazy," I said, attempting to escape before the words not yet out of his mouth could hurt me.

"I miss you with me, Erika. I miss your craziness, I miss that face you're making right now, your practical advice whenever there was trouble at work," Martin continued as if he hadn't heard me.

But he'd heard me all right. Why else did he keep moving closer to my building's entrance gate, effectively positioning himself between it and me with every word he spoke, all while never taking his eyes from mine, even touching my cheek with his hand once or twice?

What're you feeling, Erika? I remember asking myself, trying to listen to my brain above the noise made by the rush of words to which, by the way, the correct answer would've been (a) I don't give a damn *what* you miss, (b) Don't you ever again dare make the entrance to my home reek with your presence, you unworthy piece of shit, or, (c) Why don't you go seek the support and advice of the female mongoloid for whom you left me?

But of course I didn't say any of those things, because to do so would've been logical. And rational. And that was impossible when his words were making me remember the extent of what we'd had together. I was remembering nights spent on the bedroom balcony when he'd excitedly test his latest publicity strategy on me while I'd play devil's advocate. The two of us against the world, drinking wine and agitating the night with our philosophical debates.

They were powerful images, but I put my mind on pause and said:

"Are you going to tell me why you're here, or are you planning to keep playing the repentant ex-husband?"

"I'll tell you whatever you want to know, but do you mind talking privately? Could I, maybe, come in?" he said, gesturing upstairs with his jaw.

"No," I said abruptly before taking a deep breath to calm down and remain in control. "There's a café around the corner. I'd rather go there . . . if *you* don't mind."

Martin's face showed annoyance for all of a second before he corrected his expression and gave me a playful hug.

"What can I say to help you believe me, *negrita?"* he said, taking my chin in his hand. "I'm here . . . and I've come for you."

"What planet do you live on?" I said, pushing him away.

"Erika, she herself freed me of all obligation to that relationship when I told her how I felt. *She* decided, against my better judgment, that she doesn't want to be a single mother . . . and I can't promise her that I'm going to be there as she wants, when I'm still in love with you, when I can't think about anything other than getting you back. It was a mistake, Erika. I see it, now, and I'm so sorry. Please . . . forgive me."

I'm not going to deny it. For a sublime instant, suspended between vengeance and revindication, his words made me happy.

"I have so much to tell you," he went on despite my silent gloating. "So much to talk to you about. Would you at least do that for me? Ten minutes?"

If only I'd read this then, I wouldn't have gone with him anywhere: *"You respond deeply to the familiar type of emotionally unavailable man who you can again try to change, through your love."*

"We're here. Now speak."

"You have no idea how much I've needed to talk to you," he said, hanging his coat on the back of the seat.

"Then talk."

"I've been, I don't know . . . lost, I guess, depressed . . ." he said, ignoring my tone.

"Because?"

"I can't explain it. Everything, well, business, you know? It hasn't been going that well. You probably won't believe this, but every day I have less energy to go to dinner with clients, laugh at their jokes and do pirouettes to convince them our strategy is the right one."

Oh, what a relief! I had nothing to worry about. This was

the same old Martin. First comes business, then business, and then . . .

"So leave the company. You'd lose money, but if you don't love it anymore, leave it. Look for something else, something . . . more challenging. You know how to do it. You did it with me not so long ago," I said, unable to resist placing my little dig squarely in the middle of his right eyeball.

"Erika, please."

"Well, okay," I gave in. "But understand the message: maybe it's time for change," I said, not believing I was giving him advice again, as if nothing had happened.

"Start again at this stage of the game? Impossible," he answered.

"Why not? I mean, it's true you have a piece of splattered shit for a heart, Martin, but you're a brilliant publicist. You can do whatever you put your head to, without anyone's help, and be very successful."

He looked at me for a few seconds, a mild smile on his face. Then he lowered his eyes and looked at the floor for God knows how long.

"Well," he said finally, "at least you can still see a little good in me."

"One thing has nothing to do with the other."

"Yes," he conceded, "but what good is any of it when you've risked and lost what you should've protected the most," he said, putting his hand on mine.

Of course, he needs you, I thought stupidly, feeling triumphant. You are an intelligent woman, his intellectual and spiritual equal, a woman who loved him with all she had without caring if he was rich or poor. He's lost you and it serves him right.

The result of having my ego compensated? An extreme feeling of generosity and a desire to forgive the world that felt more like drunkenness than reflection. You see, I knew that man. We'd been through life together and now it was clear to me that for whatever it was worth, he was truly suffering the fear of failure. What can I say? I felt sad to see him stepping so insecurely, asking for help, and I confirmed what I'd thought only days before: in spite of everything, Martin was, and would always be, part of my life.

We kept talking; Martin, spicing the conversation up with seduction; I, fully aware of where it was all going, but letting myself be carried by the sensation of connection, that nostalgia one feels when one has history with a man, and maybe by excessive confidence in the dose of Elle I'd taken that morning.

At midnight, he walked me back to Rice Street. At one past twelve, he hugged me good-bye, and at exactly two minutes past midnight I, feeling my heart immune but my knees a little . . . actually a lot, weak from the surprise of having him before me again and the memories of nights in his arms, said:

"Martin?"

"Yes, *negri?*"

"Take me somewhere . . . new."

Result: at three minutes past twelve on the night of December 10 we were on our way to The Suites, a corporate hotel by Town and Country Mall. Sitting in the backseat was that mix of the familiar unknown of ambivalent feelings. Or maybe that was just me.

"I don't know what happened to me. It's as if I'm suddenly able to see clearly," whispered Martin.

And it was then, in that instant, that I suffered a Mother

Teresa attack, everything went to hell and I actually began to think that maybe I hadn't been the only one doing some growing.

"Everything will be fine," I said to him. "You just have to continue believing in yourself without regard for the reality of the moment, just what you know about yourself."

Since when was I wise? Or a psychologist? Ha! Try spectacularly unwise, for in trying to help Martin feel better, I allowed *Gone with the Wind* to become *The Way We Were.*

Memries . . . may be beautiful and yet . . .
What's so painful to remeee-em-ber . . .
We simply choose to for-or-get.

Martin was driving with one hand, the other inside my hair. It's my favorite caress and maybe why when he said "I've been an idiot, Erika," I replied "You and me both," like an imbecile.

"Your self-esteem is critically low, and deep inside you do not believe you deserve to be happy. Rather, you believe you must earn the right to enjoy life."

This is what the book told me later, and it was right. That night, I actually thought that perhaps everything that had happened was the universe's way of guiding me into making the heartbreak pill, and that now that I'd created it, I'd "earned" destiny's returning Martin to me when I least expected it, when pain had softened me and there was no anger or false pride to get in the way of a reconciliation. (Go ahead, throw up. I've done it, too, remembering that night.)

Everything would be the same again, I fantasized. No, it would be better than before. If my pill succeeded, I'd convince

Santi that Martin was the perfect publicist for Elle. After all, he'd told me himself he'd have kept everything "in the family" had Martin and I stayed together.

"In a relationship, you are much more in touch with your dream of how it could be than with the reality of your situation."

Again, please remember, I read this later. Much later.

That night, all I thought was, What dream? Martin was there with me. He'd come back on his own to tell me that he loved me and couldn't live without me. Well, actually, his exact words had been that he was depressed because his business wasn't going well and that he missed our conversations and my advice, but if you add to that his passionate whispers as he made love to me hours later, it's pretty much the same thing, right?

"I don't know how the agency got so out of my hands," said Martin some time later, absentmindedly smoking a cigarette, shaking his head from side to side while I, my evil craving for the past satisfied, listened with my head on his chest, my mind a windstorm that blew in all directions simultaneously.

"All I need is a new client," he said. "Just one with a product visible enough to put us at the center of Miami's public relations map once again.

"I'm sure you'll sign one," I said, marveling about his articulating a desire for the very thing I was thinking, while suppressing the strangely sudden, intense desire to tell him that if he and his associates had concentrated more on their work and on their firm, instead of on being unfaithful, they wouldn't have these problems. "In fact, I know you will," I said instead, kissing him to distract me from the voice inside my head whispering softly that being in his arms again just didn't feel the same and wondering if this new ambivalence toward Martin was the pill or just me.

When he dropped me off in front of my apartment, the sun was up and ready for a new day. We'd never talked about what the next step would be because Martin knew, I was sure, that I'd never consent to being his lover after having been his wife.

Still, once inside, I erased the fact that the sex had not been anywhere near as blissful as I'd remembered, and I also erased my new immature and insecure image of Martin, blaming it on the problems he was going through.

Sure, a part of me tried to tell me that you can't rebuild a relationship on a bed of broken trust. But I just threw her out the window before remembering the only part of the book that I'd read prior to that night: *"You are not attracted to men who are kind, stable, reliable, and interested in you. You find such 'nice' men boring."*

More asleep than awake, I remembered Pedro Juan, the declaration of love he'd been about to make and thought how easy it would've been to fall in love with him, had this been another time in my life.

But I didn't know Pedro Juan. Not really. And Martin had been my life. If I had the opportunity to save a marriage that I'd been happy in for so long, how could I throw it away for something I wasn't sure of—be that Pedro Juan, *Juan de los Parlotes,* or this new me who even I didn't understand.

You see, to put the possibility of fresh, new, easygoing love before the drama offered by the chance to last-minute rescue my marriage from the coals, I would've had to agree with the fact that love can be simple and natural, without being any less passionate.

I would also have had to be determined to listen to the little neurotransmitter's voice inside my head telling me that my pill worked better than I thought because, despite the strong instinct toward the "better-known evil" something in me had changed.

But I wasn't. If anything powered the dreams I had that morning, it was the cerebral instinct to get back what had been taken, to feel rewarded, to be reinstated. It was not the magical tremors caused by the dark, passionately idealistic gaze of a man capable of warming my soul with a single breath.

Because in spite of all I'd learned during those months without Martin, my image of love was still that of a rip-the-house-from-its-foundation tornado, whirling wild, crazy and unsettling. And once again, as I'd done my whole life, when that love called, I, like many another good idiot possessing the stupid organ we call vagina, responded.

{twenty-three}

We'd only been "reconciled" a week.

Even then, when I was only saying it to myself, I'd say it like that, using mental quotation marks, because it's hard to feel something's real when you haven't told anyone about it, and I couldn't tell anyone because there was nothing to tell.

I still wasn't sure about what I'd done and wanted time to think it through before being forced to hear the endless litany of unsolicited advice, warnings, and criticism I'd surely get from my family and friends.

On the other hand, I thought a marriage was something worth saving. Especially if it was with a man you'd loved so much that you might still love him if it weren't for the weeks and weeks of antilove chemicals in your system. After all, if true love could be killed so easily, what would anyone need a pill for?

Meanwhile, Martin still hadn't said a word about the status

of our relationship; he just talked endlessly and compulsively about the business problems tormenting him.

Like that night, for example, when he called to tell me every detail of the horrible day he'd had. He complained so much that I was actually relieved when he said he was tired and wanted to go to sleep early, but would pick me up the following night to take me to a Lenny Kravitz concert.

After six straight nights with him, I was shocked to feel so happy at the prospect of having the night all to myself. I realized how accustomed I'd become to being the sole event planner of my days.

I decided to use the time to practice my speech presenting Elle to NuevoMed Pharmaceuticals' board of directors, scheduled for the following week. As usual, when I thought of my pill, I thought of Pedro Juan. I guess it was because he'd been there, in one way or another, as I created it; all the time believing I could do it.

So I called him with the excuse of getting his feedback, hoping for the chance to say I was sorry for the way I'd acted the night Martin returned.

"Pedro Juan?"

"Yep."

"It's me, Erika," I said, thinking he hadn't recognized my voice. "You busy?"

"Yep."

"You're mad at me."

"Nope."

"For some reason, I don't believe you."

"Maybe you're not listening."

"Meaning?"

"That everything in life has a 'because.' That the good and bad that happens to us are just sides of the same fucking garbage can. That what's really yours, no one can take away and what comes, or doesn't, is probably for the best. That—"

"All right, okay, I get it. No need to get annoying."

"Right you are."

And he hung up.

"Attorney Consuelo?"

"Hold on, I'm with a client."

"Oh, sorry. I can call later."

"No, no. Go ahead."

"I wanted to know if, by any chance, you'd talked to Pedro Juan. Maybe he has . . . Has he . . . said anything?" I asked doing a bad job of trying to find out how much my neighbor knew of what'd transpired between Martin and me the last six days.

Whenever we all gathered at Papi's house, I noticed they'd often sit on the balcony having these long confession-session-like conversations while the rest of us talked or watched TV in the living room, and though it would've been hard to say who'd been confessing to whom, it was still a pretty safe bet that they'd become good friends.

"He thinks he's in love with you."

"He told you this?" I asked.

"No, but I deciphered it. You do know I'm a spiritual lawyer, don't you?" she asked in a snippy tone.

"Then, as a spiritual lawyer, you know I'm not responsible for what another person chooses to feel."

"No, that's his problem. Men are not exempt from falling in love with the wrong women."

"Hey!"

"No, no, no . . . I think it's a good thing you're not considering a rebound relationship with him."

"Who says I'm not?"

"It's obvious. You're in love with playing the role of the main suffering character in your own soap opera, and until that changes, there's no room for a real leading man in your life. Let me explain what I mean . . ."

"Won't your client on the other line be upset?" I said, starting to really want to hang up.

"What client?"

"You said you had a client on the other line."

"Oh, that client, yes, well, no, that was just part of my weekly visualization to attract more business."

I should've known.

"Why don't you put an ad in the newspaper, like the one you have on the Internet?"

"You think I'm a common lawyer putting her image anywhere? No! A spiritual lawyer should know how to attract the right clients using visualization and the power of positive thinking. Now listen, and don't worry, I'm not going to charge you for this: *'It's automatic, it's unconscious. With no particular effort, you create theater of the every day. You are the entertainer-center stage, and worthy of the spotlight. Things are always happening to you. Every "sortie" is a saga.'* "

"Where'd you get that bunch of baloney?"

"From Judith Sills. It's all in her book *Excess Baggage.* Listen to this other—

"You know, I think I hear someone at the door. Yeah . . . there's definitely someone at the door. Absolutely."

"But—"

"Ciao!" I said before screaming "Cooooming!" to no one in particular. If she could have imaginary clients, why couldn't I have an imaginary visitor when I needed one? Besides, I really wasn't in the mood for hallucinating conversations. And who was she calling dramatic? I wasn't dramatic. Not in the least.

"He thinks he's in love with you," the words did a visual fade into my head and I quickly faded them the hell out, hard. I had a presentation to finish, a speech to give, and no time to waste.

It was very late by the time I reached my final lines recommending Quintero, Silva y Echegoyén to the board. I knew both NuevoMed and Elle were going to need a first-class public relations campaign, and though still unsure that going back to Martin was the right thing for me to do, I had absolutely no doubt that he was the perfect man for Elle.

With that thought, I went to sleep never imagining the ton of cement that would crush me the following evening. As Papi's fond of saying, what was left of me wouldn't have been enough for even one of those very small, thin, and rather stylized cigars or *tabaquitos.*

"What's with the whispering?" I asked the two old men I have for parents, as I ate my white rice and *vaca frita* dinner on the little kitchen table overlooking Papi's aromatic herbs garden.

"You tell her."

"You're the father."

"And you're the gossip."

"Someone better talk fast," I mock-sang.

"Finish eating. After you eat . . ." said Papi, sprinkling blue plant food on his Cuban Oregano, his mint, and his Martha Stewart–worthy bright pink tomatoes.

"Now would be better," I said, getting up to find some Tupperware in which to take home what was left on my plate, so I could leave quickly. I love Lenny Kravitz and wanted to be fabulous and on time for the concert.

"All right," said Benji.

"All right then, tell me already. You're killing me here."

"We know you're back with Martin."

"Oh" was all I could say, so caught off guard I needed more than a few seconds to recover from the surprise. "Well, okay. It's true. Kind of. And to be honest, it's a relief for me that you two know because I was a little embarrassed to tell you after all that's happened."

"We've known for two weeks," said Benji.

"Two weeks? How could you have known for two weeks? Martin and I hadn't so much as spoken on the phone two weeks ago," I said because no one's that good a gossip-sleuth. Not even Benji.

"Okay, listen. Two weeks ago today I overheard a 'boy's club' conversation by mistake. Fernando and Hector were convincing Martin to do whatever he had to do to get the NuevoMed account," said Benji looking away with tight lips.

What?

No.

Uh-uh.

No.

"Since I'd missed the first part of the conversation," Benji continued. "I asked Milagros—you know she's Fernando's secretary now, right? 'Cause his wife found out he was sleeping with

Laura and made him fire her? But anyway, I asked her to tell me what was going on. She's my friend now 'cause I give her really good blowouts on that black-blond mop of hair every once in a while—"

"How'd Martin know about the pill? It's the only thing that could possibly make him think I'd have any influence over something like that," I interrupted him.

"Some woman who apparently works with you. I think she's the one who's related somehow to that other—"

"Lizandra? How in hell did she find out? I never said a word to Martin."

"Well," continued Benji, who's very detailed in his sleuthing. "It looks like she went to complain to your boss about your 'suspicious activities' and the idiot, trying to defend you, told her the whole thing and asked her not to say anything, but then—"

"Of course," I whispered. "That's why he wouldn't stop talking about how much he needed one big client . . . he knew. He knew he wasn't getting the account, and he knew the moment news about new drug research got out, NuevoMed would be worth double what it is now—in billing, press, and prestige," the words just spilled out of me, on a roll. "Not only that, he knew that the value of the account would only increase every year that we got closer to FDA approval. That's why he didn't get married. He knew . . . he knew everything . . . and he manipulated it to—"

I had to stop talking; the pain was so searing. It was unlike anything I knew, deep and reverberating like a shot to the face.

"I'm so sorry, *mi'ja,"* said Papi. "We should've told you as soon as Benji heard but we never thought he'd actually try to—"

"We thought it was better to leave well enough alone, but then Pedro Juan went crying to Attorney Consuelo and she wanted to set up an intervention, so Lola called asking what to do—"

I wasn't listening; I could only remember his words that night at the hotel: "Let's start over, *negrita.* You make me happy and I need you if I'm ever going to be myself again."

I swear I didn't imagine it. He said it.

"Maybe there's a mistake."

"I'm sorry, baby," said Benji. "But it's their loss and they're going to feel it even more now because I've just mailed in my resignation letter so screw that and screw him!"

"Oye, you could've at least told me before doing it," Papi said to him.

"Why? I wasn't going to listen to you," Benji said.

And with that they were off and running, leaving me to sink back into my thoughts, their voices just a vague background noise.

When you're very young, you don't consider the possibility of not being happy. Of course you will be. The only reason you're not happy now is because your parents make your life impossible, your mother decided to die of cancer, or because your father was born gay and it takes you awhile to get used to your new "stepmother." Of course you'll be very happy once you're on your own. Or when you finish college and find a decent job. Or when you meet the man of your dreams, get pregnant, and have children.

Then between your thirties and forties, you suddenly run out of excuses. You've either been on your own for some time or are still living with your parents. You've graduated or you've given up. You found your prince charming, married him, and, subsequently, divorced him, or you're living with him, but still wonder where your real prince is. You already earn a decent salary or you know you'll never make enough. You're already a piano teacher instead of a pianist; a radio disc jockey instead of an actress; a nurse instead of a doctor; a journalist instead of a novelist; a stockbroker instead of a millionaire. Your children are already in school and you notice it's not true that you have more time for yourself. Or they've left for college and instead of great relief you have to go to a psychiatrist for antidepressants. Now what?

Well, now you walk around with tiny head incisions, glass-ceiling bruises like those from your heart's recent divorce-induced microdermabrasion. Or you spend your settlement money Botoxing your butt and laser-whitening your teeth so you'll have a nice smile, if not much to smile about. Or you take pills meant for panic attacks and hate yourself for being so stupid to betray yourself. And for what? For marriage? For an institution that means nothing without the authentic human instinct of love to support it?

At some point, I cried. It was a sad cry, wailed low into my arm, saliva spilling from my open mouth and onto my lap. I couldn't help it. I felt emotionally raped and as humiliated as the most abused woman at the shelter. I thought about how ready I'd been to forgive and forget, wanting to help him, unable to harm him with so much as a little indifference despite what he'd done.

Then everything just stopped.

I remember Papi and Benji opening up the sofa bed and tucking me in as best they could. I cooperated, as sure of wanting to sleep as I was that it would be awhile before I'd want to wake up.

{twenty-four}

The good news was my heartbreak pill worked. The bad news? My heartbreak pill worked.

For a few days after finding out about Martin's attempt at influence-peddling, I'd hear the phone ring late at night or his fists on my door, and not know how I'd ever find the strength to answer, and not just because I didn't want to talk to him but because even something as simple as walking or opening a door felt like a huge effort.

The worst part of it? This time it wasn't about love. None of that "you are a sack full of day-old shit but I love you anyway." No, this was worse. I was shocked that he'd been capable of using me without the slightest scruple. I felt like a thing someone has auctioned off on eBay for a reserve-less penny.

Was he so clueless that he thought I'd never find out? In a town like Miami? Please. Not even I could create a pill for the size of the immunity complex Martin suffered from. Unfortunately, I also didn't have one against the heartrending emptiness of knowing I'd ever loved someone like him.

I spent the rest of the week ignoring his halfhearted messages asking me for a chance to explain, concentrating instead on the following week's presentation before the board of directors. Finally, a few days before my speech, I decided to purge my rage and called him.

His answering machine answered and out came everything I hadn't been able to say out loud in a week. I told it how I felt. I told it how much of a mucus-filled insect I thought its owner was and how tempted I was to place an ad in the newspaper to warn the city of the cancerous plague his presence on earth represented. Half an hour later, I had him on the phone.

"What's your problem?" asked the Martin from the divorce. The real one.

"My problem is that you're such a huge piece of shit that you have to lie to someone so she'll sleep with you in hopes she'll get you a job."

"You wanted to be with me as much as I wanted to be with you."

"But I wouldn't have, if you'd told me the truth."

"This had nothing to do with the NuevoMed account, Erika. It was a coincidence, a set of circumstances that happened to coincide, an unfortunate conjuncture, that's all."

"Is that what it's called now? A conjuncture? Tell me, did the conjuncture make you do it? Did it put a gun to your head so you'd lie to me?"

"I didn't lie to you, Erika. I am not married yet, and in any case, what did you want me to tell you? It's not like you're some innocent virgin."

His words made me feel all the horror of what had happened.

"You're right. I'm not some young, impressionable virgin. Therefore, I should've guessed that a man I'd been married to for almost a decade would have no problems using me to get a miserly public relations account," I said, tasting the violence that rose up to my mouth like bile.

"And if I didn't, it's because I never—*never*—imagined you capable of such a thing. But I do now, so don't you ever, in however much is left of your miserable pathetic life, come near me again, do you hear me?"

His pause was that of someone weighing his options.

"Understood," he said finally.

I hung up, leaning against the wall, letting myself slide down it until I hit the floor, feeling enough rage for three sumo wrestlers, each with many more pounds than I. Only now I was angry at myself. This time, I'd been the evil one. I was the one who'd let myself down.

"Erikaaaaa!"

It was Lola, always coming to my rescue like a fairy godmother.

"How do you feel? I knocked three times and had to holler before you heard me," she asked as soon as I opened the door for her.

"Better than I thought. Who told you?"

"Benji called, asked me to come by and check on you."

"I told him not to worry, that I was fine," I said, feeling bad that I'd made everyone worry about me since the divorce, and remembering what Attorney Consuelo had accused me of the day I called her about Pedro Juan. "Lola, do you think I'm melodramatic?"

"Yes."

"Well, at least give it some thought."

"Okay. Yes."

"Lola . . ."

"Well, you *are* dramatic. But that doesn't mean what Martin did isn't a horrible thing."

"You know, Lola? The good news is there's no drama. Sure, I'm angry at myself for being such a jackass, but even while with him, I had doubts. It wasn't the same or, rather, I wasn't the same. And now I'm sure. I don't love him anymore. Probably haven't for a while."

"About time. God, those stairs," she said, rubbing her ankles. "But I'm glad to hear that, because if that's the case, my friend, then the worst is over. Martin is done, dead, and buried."

I considered my friend's words and though I wanted to agree wholeheartedly, something inside me resisted. So I just stayed silent, and continued straight through to the kitchen to prepare us something to eat.

"Uh-oh," I said, opening the fridge.

"What?"

"Nothing to eat," I answered, showing her the ice rink that had opened for business inside my fridge. "We'll have to order some of that greasy Chinese food."

"I have a better idea," she said, grabbing the phone and dialing God knows where. "It'll be quick."

I left her talking and went downstairs again to check my mailbox. There was a letter from Darien and I sat on the stairs to read it.

December 19, 2007

Hey Croquetica,

By the time you read this letter I'll be in Milan. (Why wouldn't you talk to me on the phone before I left?)

You've probably forgotten me already and here I am, thinking about you all the time: the way you laugh, your dark brown sense of humor, your devilishly bad habit of mentioning other men (your ex-husband, your neighbor, etc.) constantly in conversation. (Did I ever mention I'm the jealous type?) Your mouth, your eyes, your summer-poppy hair, and your perfect little Venus de Milo breasts, which I'll be taking a train to Paris after New Year's to see for myself.

Try to remember me, will you? Dream about me once in a while, and if you feel a tug, it will be me calling you with my mind (not to mention other things).

I'm an old man, Erika. An old man trapped in this body. Maybe I came to find you and miscalculated time, overslept, and reincarnated too late or something. I miss you like a damn fool. And it hurts to see so many beautiful things when you're not here to see them with me. But even that I cherish because I know that if I'm missing you, it's because you're still inside of me.

My grandmother always said that you can't lose what you really loved and what I feel for you couldn't be more real, so . . .

I'm sending back your breath, your smell, and your kisses and I send myself with them. Spread me around as needed.

I love you,
Darien

I recalled his words about the dignity of suffering because we love another. For the first time I clearly saw the difference between that pain and the pain over someone who never loved you or loved you but was wrong for you, or loved you for a while but then stopped and forgot to warn you. He'd been on to something, Darien had, and I sat there, ordering my thoughts; some as lucid and practical as concrete and others so light they threatened to float away before I'd had a chance to articulate them.

"Casola's pizza delivery for Isabel Figueredo," called someone from the gate.

It was Pedro Juan.

"I'm sorry, I don't think I know that person, however, there is a homeless former porn actress in my apartment who goes by the name of Lola, if you'd like to come in," I said, trying to induce a smile. "Oh, and it's from Casola's! I must say, sir, you've brought my favorite pizza in all of Miami," I said, taking one of the boxes off his hands, suddenly excited to have the chance to make peace.

"You owe me fifteen dollars and eighty-six cents," he said without cracking a smile.

"Well, you'll have to follow me upstairs because I don't have any cash with me and without cash there's no tip," I followed his lead, making mental note of how my heartbeat had accelerated the minute I saw him.

"Well, I could go up, but I . . . I don't know if I'm welcome."

I looked into his eyes and smiled as wide as I could before answering.

"A good pizza, at the right time, is always welcome."

Two hours later, after a few yawns and three mentions of my need to wake up early the next day, Pedro Juan finally caught on that Lola and I were waiting for him to leave so we could engage in some heart-to-heart girl talk.

I walked him to the door where he pulled me to him, kissing me squarely on the mouth. His lips giving me a light hit of electricity, as if I'd been kissed by a firefly.

"Dinner tomorrow?"

"Sure, I know . . . we need to talk, and—"

"See you tomorrow, *bebé,*" he interrupted and pulled one of my curls tenderly.

As soon as I heard his door close, I opened two cold beers and sat on the balcony with Lola.

"Soooo? How do you feel?" said Lola teasingly.

"You mean, besides angry at you for interfering?"

"But you *were* happy to see him, weren't you?"

"I was." I smiled. "Thank you."

"And Martin?"

"He's . . . a little bit of everything, you know? I love him a little and I hate him a little. I hate him and I hate me for deceiving myself so much, for all that lost time. But I love him because there were good times, and those times were what life was made for. Life with him was good, for a while." I said, looking at the sky as if the words I needed to explain all this to Lola were written there.

"Erika?"

"What?" I said turning to see her crying. "What is it?"

"Nothing. I'm just so proud of you, that's all. You've grown up so much, *Tía.*"

"Oh, stop it," I said to keep from crying myself.

That night, before going to bed, I read Darien's letter again and it inspired me to write one.

December 26, 2007,

Dear Martin:

I write you this letter to leave behind that sad set of events people call "divorce" and recover the memories of happier times I call "marriage."

At first, when you left, surprise or maybe pain didn't let me understand. I thought everything was your fault for not loving me, or mine, for not loving myself. I saw my grief as a terrible black hole, a repulsive deformity that I had to hide, cure, or compensate for in one way or another. I spent months trying to do exactly that and you've already heard about the results.

Then, when you "came back," and after, when I found out what you'd done, I was so hurt I thought I'd never be able to forgive. But I am and I think I have. When I make my presentation in defense of Elle, successful or not, pill or no pill, I will recommend your work to Nuevo-Med's board of directors, knowing I'll be recommending the best publicist in Miami.

It's strange but now I know that the "bad love" I tried to kill was nothing other than a lens that I had to clean in order to get a better view of myself.

Before, for me, love was you. I was wrong. I now believe . . . I want to think . . . that maybe if you'd found another way to obtain what you think vital to your happiness, you'd have acted differently.

I send you warm skies and stars on your bedroom ceiling. I wish you a life full of the most passionate peace you can possibly feel and hope you'll be intensely happy with someone who makes you love life in the mornings and pray for long life in the evenings.

Wish me luck and thanks for the lessons, darling.

Erika

{twenty-five}

On the sixteenth floor of the Delano Hotel in Miami Beach, there was no gray. The world there was blue or white with the possibility of turquoise, ultramarine, indigo, sapphire, cobalt, cerulean, even lapis lazuli, but no gray.

Downstairs, on the crowded sidewalk, where Seventeenth Street and Collins Avenue intersected, two elderly women sporting identical curly cotton heads of hair looked up through their bifocals, pointing excitedly to the building façade's crown: an iconic pleated fan, all cement and plaster, set in delicate white relief, which, despite being a replica of the Art Deco era, had eluded the cliché and now wrapped itself glamorously around the floor-to-ceiling windows of the top-floor conference room where I stood.

The women wore white sneakers, khaki shorts, and matching pastel T-shirts. I assumed they were tourists. They stood entranced, marveling at the grand hotel, and I imagined how much more impressed they'd be when they saw the one-hundred-and-fifty-foot-long rectangular pool and the lobby, with its fifteen-foot ceilings and translucent white curtains that separated each space and its function: the bar from the restaurant, the concierge from the front desk, the gift shop from the elevators—every one of them sprinkled with the best and most eccentric of mid-century modern design: chairs by Charles and Ray Eames, Tom Dixon, and Antonio Gaudí coexisting with African benches, traditional Chippendale, and one Salvador Dalí armchair with high heels instead of legs.

I guess you could say that this place was a two-dimensional surrealist's dream, no borders between interior and exterior, formal and casual, dry and wet, the white of a rising ocean wave and the deceptively similar fluffy white of the quickly moving clouds above. Everything here reflecting opposite perspectives of life: before today, and now; the most important moment of my career as a chemist, as a scientist, and as a human being.

Inside the videoconferencing room, the differences were even more striking. Here, citified-tropical chic modernism transformed into modish-corporate torture chamber style. The long glass and metal conference table was sprinkled with dozens of white votive candles lit inside translucent Alice blue glass tumblers dispersed around the table to illuminate the room. Twenty ergonomic chrome and baby blue leather chairs were there as much to contrast the white walls as to accommodate the behinds of the members of NuevoMed Pharmaceutical Corporation's board of directors.

Ten members, each richer than the last, and all still ambitious enough to show up for a fortuitous business meeting on a Friday afternoon, instead of drinking piña coladas naked on some Caribbean island like decent millionaires. I stood, glued to the window, listening to Santi greet this person and that one, pretending to go through my notes to avoid being intimidated by the dark black coats and Hermès ties I'd surely see as soon as the commonplace courtesies came to an end.

I had dressed in loosely fitted, high-waisted black pants, narrow black suspenders, and a starched white shirt with wide cuffs I secured with tiny steel, pearl, and diamond cuff links.

So you can see how I almost gasped when I turned to greet them before taking my place near the front of the room and found each member of the board, complete strangers to me until then, wearing jeans, shorts, and rubber flip-flops, the only tie in the room was the one strangling Santi's neck.

I made mental inventory: there were three white men in their sixties, one of them red-haired; two Latinos in their forties; a very tall, bald black man wearing the thickest glasses I'd ever seen; and a youngish mulatto with honey-blond braids and gorgeous green eyes. Women, there were only two: a black woman in her fifties, who looked just like Oprah except for her no-apologies afro, and a milky-white woman, tall and very thin, with big blue eyes, jet black hair, and a lively smile. All of them looked like the decent millionaires I'd thought they weren't, and the worst of it was it didn't make them any less intimidating.

I greeted them briefly, feeling myself sweat before their inquisitive, almost invasive, attention; noticing how their lips drew cordial, relaxed, slightly curious smiles even as their eyelids darted speedily from side to side like small skepticism-powered calculators.

"You want to make money and plenty of it. I get it," began Santi, his face serious, eyes lost somewhere in an almost absent-minded manner, as he smoothed his thick mustache with his fingers before continuing. "But money won't just continue to grow on the proverbial cash-flow tree unless we feed it the fertilizer of innovation. The heart of science is discovery. Without it, we're mere drug dispensers," he said, smiling now at every one of the executives sitting around the table.

"Well, I don't want to talk for the rest," interrupted the red-haired guy in his sixties. "But my accountant tells me we've been doing quite well lately with the 'dispensing' of Varitex, and it was about time, too."

"Yes, thanks for the compliment, Miguel," Santi replied, without losing his composure. "That *is* what you pay me for, isn't it? But why stop there? Why not leverage the distribution and marketing infrastructure we've created and use it to sell two products instead of one? Especially if one of them can help cement the reputation of 'small in size but fearless in scope' we've earned by being creative, effective, and more than a little deranged when it comes to our marketing strategy."

"I get here five minutes late and you're already insulting my kids?"

Everyone turned toward a woman of about seventy, thin, stick-straight, and dressed in a simple jersey wraparound dress with a light geometric pattern that reminded me of my mother's favorite dress when I was a little girl. It was her only expensive dress, crossed at the front, tied with a waistband, designed, I later learned, by Diane von Furstenberg. Her gray hair was styled into a loose chignon and she smiled with a kind serenity that made me like her instantly.

"About time you got here, missy," said Santi.

"Now, now, Santi . . . remember I'm still your boss," she said smiling, embracing him affectionately before sitting at the head of the table.

I knew then that this was Norma Silva, the legendary president of the board and the person responsible for our existence as a company. A woman ahead of her time, still as beautiful and liberal as in her youth, born to farmers, orphaned in childhood, who graduated from night school an economist and became famous, in addition to rich, by convincing a select group of investors to create small companies with which to experiment, turning many of them, then miserable millionaires, into superbillionaires with her experiments.

Now that she was here, the energy of the room adjusted immediately. The millionaires put their cell phones aside, drank the last of their drinks, and straightened in their chairs.

"As I was saying," Santi continued. "Without creation, we're dead. We'll not only lose our corporate identity but our reason for being, which will eventually make all of you, well, a little less rich."

Santi made a benign pause, not that anyone laughed.

"This afternoon," he continued bravely, "I want to offer you the chance to create. Right now. This is the time for the high vision that will bring enormous dividends later."

"How much later?" asked the blue-eyed woman.

"Some, the necessary amount, but not too much," replied Santi. "Because as soon as the pharmaceutical world hears about 'Elle, the first-ever heartbreak pill, brought to you by NuevoMed Pharmaceutical Corporation, creators of the very successful Varitex,' the game will be *over.* And we'll be ahead by a lot more than twenty points."

As Santi transformed into the Wizard of Oz before my eyes,

the board members looked entranced, as if hypnotized by him, the sky became the tone of gray I'd thought impossible and big drops of rain began to rush down noisily, casting a watery film on the room's glass walls, which, in turn, made all the millionaires in the room settle further into their seats knowing that, with Miami weather being what it is, they wouldn't be going anywhere for some time.

"Of course, we'll need the approval of the Food and Drug Administration," Santi continued, walking from one extreme of the room to the other as if he wanted to make them dizzy. "But think about this: everyone—doctors, well-meaning parents, and even the media—tell consumers in this country, constantly that they need love, that it's vital to their health, to life. That they should be able to live happily ever after with someone, and that if they can't, they're codependent, they're from Mars or unable to function in Venus, they're women who love too much or men with no clue what women want, or they just don't understand the 'rules' of the game, to allude to only some of the bestselling self-help titles and movies of the last couple of decades. What this tells us is that there's a need for relief out there."

For a few seconds, only the sound of furious rain interrupted the silence. Santi turned sideways to wink at me with the eye they couldn't see, making a long pause to make sure all eyes were on him before continuing. He then turned to them with a killer combination of sincere idealism and creative urgency. "Seven years ago I hired a brilliant scientist; first in her master's class at Emory University in Atlanta. Later, as part of our research team, first in her Ph.D. class at the University of Miami, and for a while now, head of our research department. But back then, when she was very, very young, she told me with great pride that the only reason she was accepting the inappropriate salary I was offering was because her father lived in Miami and her heart was here with him. That same heart has led her to create Elle, the first-ever pill against heartbreak. Discovery accomplished," Santi added, looking directly at Norma Silva. "But we need your vision in order to offer it to the world. Please welcome Dr. Erika Luna."

At that moment, I loved Santi for believing. But I hated him for giving me the opportunity to fail, possibly taking him down with me.

"Imagine having a small switch, somewhere in an unobtrusive part of your anatomy," I began. "Let's say . . . on your ankle, like a tattoo. And imagine that with a flick of this switch, lever, or pull, you could control the most uncontrollable part of your body: your heart."

I stood.

"The good news is you do. It's your brain," I said, walking over to the computerized projector installed for my presentation. "So, problem solved, right?" I continued, trying to imitate Santi's showmanship despite the strangely weak, high-pitched voice coming out of my throat and the sight of him loosening his tie nervously at my lack of assuredness.

"Not exactly," I continued, trying not to let the stone-faced expressions in the room get to me. "Our brains function in a delicate chemical balance. When this balance is altered beyond its capacity to tolerate the resulting emotion, we are left in a state of temporary emotional impotence. We call this 'heartbreak.' It can happen to anyone," I swallowed, beginning to feel bothered by the apparent presence of Coca-Cola instead of blood in the veins of my audience.

"What would be the practical application of this drug?" asked Norma Silva, startling me; with her authoritarian demeanor, forcing me to look at her directly for the first time since she'd arrived. In spite of her tone, her smile was energizing, protective, and understanding and I understood she'd only asked the question to help me realize I had an ally. I remembered my mother in her smile, and I went back to the moment in which my "heart" broke for the first time, watching her die, unable to do anything against the invisible enemy taking her away from me. I closed my eyes and took a long, deep breath.

"Doctor Luna?" The tall black man with glasses asked after a few seconds. "Are you feeling well?"

"Perfectly, thank you," I replied, opening my eyes and returning Norma's smile with a strong one of my own.

Then, I walked resolutely to the basket full of tropical fruit doubling as a table centerpiece and grabbed a mango. I pounded it against the table like a gavel.

"Ladies and gentlemen, this is the brain. The size of a mango and weighing about three pounds. When it doesn't function, we don't function. Sure, some of us are stronger than others, but sooner or later, a broken heart will result in weaker health, in shorter life. Now, we have discovered how to avoid this."

"What makes you so sure of that connection?" asked Business Oprah, her first sign of interest.

"Because there're thousands of lost opportunities in the area of prevention that have been recorded and continue to be recorded, as you will see in your binders," I replied, distributing them. "From suicide, homicide, and abuse to the indexes of depression, crime, addiction, and alcoholism."

"But isn't the heart—or the brain, as you say—capable of

curing itself given time?" asked the mulatto, who'd tied his braids atop his head, put on a pair of pink-lensed Gucci aviator eyeglasses, and was a sight to behold.

"Excellent question. Yes, yes, it is. But that's where the practical applications Ms. Silva was talking about come in. During that time, when you're suffering, you don't function. You don't eat, you don't sleep, and you send your kids to school in wrinkled clothes after forgetting to brush their hair. If you're lucky, you just call in sick for a while and your boss understands," I said, looking at Santi. "If you're not, you drive your car about a dozen times over the body of the man or woman who broke your heart, go to jail and lose the custody of the kids whose hair you forgot to brush. It all depends on how strong you are and what other circumstances led up to that moment in your life. Most people suffer, grow from it, and continue. The rest know that something is at least a little wrong . . . sometimes very wrong. They're afraid of their reactions; they hate themselves for not being able to control the effects of heartbreak, of loss, or longing, when all they really need is a little help. A temporary remedy to help then rebalance their brain's computer until the brain's natural 'switch' kicks in. And, yes: time, friends, art, work, and our survival instinct will do the rest."

"Dr. Luna, I'm sorry. This is all fascinating," said Don Miguel, he of the red hair, "but I can't help feeling I've been trapped inside a very expensive science fiction movie."

I looked at the others and made my tally: Oprah, Norma, and Mulatto cheered me on. Red Hair and Blue-Eyes were skeptical at best, and the rest teetered between possibility and rejection.

"Give us a clinical example. None of this bad love, heartache, affective allergy, or whatever. Give us something we can put our money on," said one of the men in his forties who looked a lot like Emiliano Zapata, the Mexican revolutionary hero; just chubby and without the riding saddle. I understood what he wanted. He wanted the whole mango. He wanted me to include the peel. I decided to give it to him.

"If you look at the graph that details the last five recognized studies published on this topic, the end of a relationship has negative effects on men as well as on women. Heart patients suffering from bad marriages are at three times the risk of suffering a heart attack than those suffering from other stresses like money or work problems."

I waited.

Silence.

"If you continue, you'll see the majority of people who commit suicide don't have a medical record of mental illness or psychiatric treatment. What many of them do have in common is loss, heartache, divorce . . . in other words, heartbreak. Even—"

"I'm sorry, Doctor Luna," Red interrupted me again, glancing through the three hundred pages of information, graphs, and chemical formulas supported by historical and anecdotal evidence Santi and I had prepared as if they were *Vogue's* gigantic annual fashion edition. "Your arguments are certainly compelling . . . in a dramatic, theatrical manner, but I have to be honest with you . . . and I don't know about you guys," he said, looking at the others. "But there's something missing here. I'm sorry, Doctor," he continued, closing the binder I'd handed him with a loud thud. "Too much fantasy and not enough science for my pocket."

What? Had he just called my work theatrical? Had he just been a condescending asshole and treated the presentation I'd worked so hard on as he would a comic book? Oh. No. He didn't!

"On the contrary," I assured him. "In chemistry, fantasy is usually the missing element of most failed experiments. In fact, I remember a college boyfriend, a very talented poet, who'd crawl through self-constructed worlds to ask me why I wasted my energy on the sterile search for drug combinations to discover what already existed, maintain the status quo. You see, for him, drugs were only useful if they helped you to fly in your sleep, propelled you headfirst into the sky."

Santi was in shock. He looked at me between terrorized and livid, willing me to return to script with his eyes.

Those sitting at the table looked just as surprised, if not as uncomfortable. Some, like Norma, had a lively expression on their faces, as if they'd remembered something, maybe their dreams, their successful intuitions or the feeling of conspiratorial premonition that precedes magical possibility.

"And my poet was right. What he didn't know, and apparently neither do you . . . Don Miguel, is it? . . . is that chemists do fantasize. Discovery always begins with hope, intuition, white magic, some fantasy, and a little bit of madness. We have these . . . feelings we call hypotheses. They smell like my mother's balcony in Puerto Rico, a crazy mix of the sweet and the salty floating on wet wood. You know, it drives me absolutely crazy that everyone assumes we're these boring people, that scientists are technical and prone to logic above all, that we only work to prove or discredit concepts instead of to create tangible realities. That we float in data and are strangers to attacks of illogical behavior and unexplainable feelings. I don't understand it but I *can* tell you it's a damn lie!"

There. Just how I liked it. Every one of them openmouthed and ready for more.

"What *is* true," I continued, "is that the history of chemistry is full of colorful characters and imaginative personalities and, what's more, we wouldn't be able to discover a single thing without tempering the logical with the fantasy you so easily dismiss, Don Miguel."

I smiled at him, and I meant it, for in trying to convince him, I'd managed to finally, really, convince myself. I realized I no longer cared whether anyone believed in me or not. I believed in me, and that was enough.

"But you *are* right about something. I'm not looking to cure heartbreak from a practical place . . . secure and small like a wallet, maybe. I'm looking to cure it from a place that understands love's incredible power to destroy human beings and transform them into hurricane disaster areas. By creating a remedy to paralyze harmful emotions, we will help people use their body's natural healing tools while sidestepping the unnecessary suffering we should all be able to avoid."

Norma and Santi were smiling and I no longer had a doubt: I was in heaven and curing love was possible.

"You have all the data you could need before you," I said, returning to script while picking up the files that were left over. "I only hope you'll give me the opportunity to show you that we can create more health, more life, more happiness . . . by making this company the undisputed leader in organic drug innovation. Thank you all."

And I felt it. That click that tells you that you've connected with something or someone. I thought of Pedro Juan and felt butterflies flying around inside my chest, so strong was my need to share all this with him.

As I took my seat, the questions began to come at Santi with frenetic speed. What about marketing, the budget, how many phases of clinical studies were necessary? Finally, Norma thanked us, effectively bringing the meeting to an end and promising a vote and an answer in the next two weeks.

"Before we leave, I want to give Miguel a very special thank you for playing our bad boy this afternoon," she said. "It's our well-meaning method to use doubt, skepticism, and even a little irony to see what the scientists we hope to support are made of, and get a feel for their level of commitment to their own proposal. You'll soon see that the road to the corner drugstore is long and tough, and that a good dose of fiery passion against obstacles is not only good, but vital. Isn't that right, Miguel?"

Astonished at how flawlessly he'd managed to fool us, Santi and I turned toward Don Miguel, mouths open.

And do you know what that shameless man did?

He winked at us.

{epilogue}

"Its absolutely true that time cures everything. But the best thing is that you can decide how long you want to suffer. The faster you realize that every relationship, good or bad, is a gift, the faster you can forgive yourself and the other person. And the faster you forgive the other, the faster you will begin to love and live again."

—Erika Anastasia Luna Morales

That was my most valuable lesson. And if I ever write a book, I'll write it just like that. That's what my pill was: the decision to stop suffering. To love myself more than I loved a man. To live doing my best to be happy.

And that's how it all ended. It's been almost a year since the day I thought the world was coming to an end with a divorce-shaped bomb and began running like a lizard announcing the equivalent of the Apocalypse to the world.

I haven't seen Martin again, even though we live in the same city and only minutes from each other, but I know he finally did marry Marisol and I hope, more for her than for him, that it goes well.

I never sent the letter. What for? Instead, I lost five pounds, seriously decorated my apartment, and hired a research team to help me take Elle to market.

Benji is close to getting his license as a massage therapist and he and Papi are thinking of moving to Key West soon.

Lola and Carlos have been living together for months and I've never seen that *Gallega* happier. (Sorry Lola. I know you're not from Galicia, but from Madrid, and that there is a difference, *joder!*)

Attorney Consuelo? She moved to Paris, is studying French, and exploring the catacombs. She frequently sends me photos over the Internet in which she's in boots and flannel shirts, but always with her happy lunatic mouth smiling wide.

And then there's Pedro Juan. My plan was to take it slow. I mean, there was no doubt I was crazy about the man, but that's exactly why I wanted to be sure before going forward. Sure that I cared about him for what he was and not because he was available or willing to love me. Sure that I, and not a "conjuncture of circumstances," was choosing him. And that's where we were: no commitment, no promises . . . no sex.

We'd often dine together in his apartment or in mine, and usually this is how the evening plays out: I'd buy the candles, the flowers, and rent the movie. He'd buy the food and the wine and we'd hit the wee hours of dawn talking, flirting, tempting the devil a bit.

After some three weeks of this, things began to shift and our routine began to, invariably, end up like so:

"Hey, behave yourself, come on," I'd whisper when his hand

would begin to draw surreptitious circles on the skin over my waist, back, or hips.

"But I'm not doing anything."

"You are and you shouldn't be. How're you ever going to know if I love you for yourself or if I'm just trying to use you for your body?" I'd reply, wrist to forehead.

"Oh, no," he'd laugh. "No, no, no, please, don't let that hold you back. Use me with confidence. Forget all that and use! Please."

"No, I can't. What will the townspeople say? What about society?" I'd answer in mock dramatics.

"I'm going to say this again: you have a charming way of killing the natural impulses of my gender," he'd say then, sighing resignedly, as he caressed my chin while making it obvious he'd prefer to focus his caressing elsewhere.

"It's better this way," I'd say, hugging him playfully, tickling him with my nails, and making him laugh, convincing him to wait one more night, or several.

Until on one of those nights, we decided to watch *The Piano:* a story of love and sex between a deaf woman married to a man she doesn't love, her exotic neighbor, and a piano. In the movie, the husband sells the wife's piano to the neighbor, but the neighbor sells it back to the woman, key by key, in exchange for her kisses, caresses, and, finally, the most sensuous intercourse I'd ever seen. This, of course, gave Pedro Juan ideas.

"Let's see . . . What do I have that you'd want to buy?" he said, smiling his bad boy smile and kissing the hair covering my neck.

"Hmmm . . . I really don't know. Let me think," I said, playing innocent. "Nope, nothing," I said after a few seconds.

"Now how can that be?" he asked, letting his hand slide from my armpit to the curve of my butt, his voice creating delicious warmth inside my left ear.

I was seconds away from the first words of my usual "not yet" and "let's wait" when he pressed me against him urgently, letting me feel the tenseness in his body, and said,

"I love you, Erika."

"You say that because you don't really know me," I said, more out of nervousness and the habit of holding back than because I really believed we should continue to wait.

He looked at me reprovingly, as if he could literally see me going back to the days of bad love and couldn't believe it. But he replied calmly,

"I'm not a study subject to whom you can tell what he feels. I love you . . . crazy or sane, fat or skinny, ugly or beautiful, illogical, passionate, sexy and sometimes, frankly unbearable, but, essential to me. I love you."

I don't know . . . maybe it was all those weekends watching him at the shelter, or the desire that spending time with him always provoked, or maybe it just was and there was no good reason to think Why not? Why not love fearlessly for once? After all, am I not the one saying the cure for heartbreak is just around the corner?

But I thought it. And I felt it. And I recognized with the certitude of my brain/heart that I'd been feeling it for a while.

Watching him wait for my answer that night, I knew I was afraid of losing myself in someone before having had the chance to be lost inside myself for a while. But I was a lot more afraid of letting something amazing pass me by.

"You never let me finish, *carajo!* What I meant was if you

love me now, when you hardly know me, just wait until you really get to know me. I'm telling you, you'll go absolutely bonkers. What am I saying? You'll be lovesick as a puppy, crazy-hopping mad, blind, deaf, and mute like the tale of the monkeys. I'm telling you they'll have to pick you up from the floor with a vacuum, that's how in love you're going to be, mister."

They were the last coherent words I pronounced that night, apart from the "Oh, yes," "Don't stop," "More," and others I'm too embarrassed to write here.

Morning surprised us on the couch, the TV full of black and white dots set to music that meant programming was over for the night. My head was on his chest, a slight clarity seeped in through the windows and the coolness of light rain entered through the balcony.

"Keep sleeping, *bebé,*" he said, kissing me on the lips, his hand in my hair. "There's a lot of time left till morning."

And I slept, without a happy ending in the style of fairy tales, but with my heart/brain full of real-life possibilities.

{acknowledgments}

I want to thank everyone at Atria Books: my editor, Johanna Castillo, for her keen eye and brilliant mind; Amy Tannenbaum for her conscientious and respectful editing; and Judith Curr for her fairness and vision, which is present in every phone call . . . in every email . . . in every idea.

To Celeste Frazer Delgado, to whom I owe the title of *The Heartbreak Pill,* for capturing what this novel would ultimately turn out to be. Helen Fisher, for providing inspiration and order to the topic of love.

Marcela Landres, Barbara Rodríguez, Nereida García-Ferraz, Migdalia Figueroa, Diana Maldonado, Berta Castaner, and Daniel Valdés for eagerly reading early drafts, asking smart questions, and sustaining my own faith with theirs.